GHOST STORIES OF SASKATCHEWAN **3**

Jo-Anne Christensen

GHOST STORIES OF SASKATCHEWAN 3

DUNDURN PRESS
TORONTO

Editor: Allison Hirst
Designer: Courtney Horner
Printer: Webcom

Library and Archives Canada Cataloguing in Publication

Christensen, Jo-Anne
    Ghost stories of Saskatchewan 3 / by Jo-Anne Christensen.

Includes bibliographical references.
ISBN 978-1-55488-428-5

    1. Ghosts--Saskatchewan. 2. Tales--Saskatchewan.
I. Title. II. Title: Ghost stories of Saskatchewan three.

BF1472.C3C573 2009   398.2'09712405   C2009-902992-8

2   3   4   5   13   12   11

Conseil des Arts
du Canada

Canada Council
for the Arts

ONTARIO ARTS COUNCIL
CONSEIL DES ARTS DE L'ONTARIO

We acknowledge the support of **The Canada Council for the Arts** and the **Ontario Arts Council** for our publishing program. We also acknowledge the financial support of the **Government of Canada** through the **Book Publishing Industry Development Program** and **The Association for the Export of Canadian Books**, and the **Government of Ontario** through the **Ontario Book Publishers Tax Credit program**, and the **Ontario Media Development Corporation**.

Care has been taken to trace the ownership of copyright material used in this book. The author and the publisher welcome any information enabling them to rectify any references or credits in subsequent editions.

J. Kirk Howard, President

Printed and bound in Canada.   www.dundurn.com
Printed on recycled paper.

Dundurn Press
3 Church Street, Suite 500
Toronto, Ontario, Canada
M5E 1M2

Gazelle Book Services Limited
White Cross Mills
High Town, Lancaster, England
LA1 4XS

Dundurn Press
2250 Military Road
Tonawanda, NY
U.S.A. 14150

MIX
Paper from
responsible sources
FSC
www.fsc.org   FSC® C004071

For my lovely friend Karen Ritchie —
who always reminds me of how much fun this is

Contents

Acknowledgements

This book could not have been born without the support and help of many people. I hope that I've remembered to say thank you along the way. Even if I have, I would like to take a moment to publicly acknowledge some of you now.

First of all, my sincere thanks to all of the people who took the time to share their stories with me. Without your contributions, there would have been no book. It's that simple. So please know that you have my gratitude.

Next, to the six paranormal investigation groups that are profiled herein, thank you sincerely for your time. You have my admiration for the work you do and my appreciation for all you shared with me.

W. Ritchie Benedict, of Calgary, as always, you were an invaluable resource. It is a pleasure to work with someone who has such a vast knowledge and genuine passion for this field of work.

Vilda and Frank Poole, and their granddaughter Alison, your efforts on my behalf were extraordinary. Saying thank you doesn't seem like enough, but I'll say it anyway. I am in your debt.

To my bud Leslie — in my eyes you represent everything that is fabulous … and, yes, a little spooky, about Saskatchewan. I love you and your whole gang of weirdos.

Others who have really gone above and beyond for me, and deserve mention here are: Jan Drummond, Jacquie Mallory, Margaret Strawford, Kathy Morrell, Therese Lefebvre Prince, Miles Vanghel, and the Zaporozen family.

Finally, a big thank you to my friends and family. Love you always, and couldn't do it without you.

Introduction

This is my kind of place.

That's what I keep thinking. It's the weekend before Halloween, 2008, and I'm at the first ever Paranormal Symposium, presented by the Calling Lakes Paranormal Investigators, in Fort Qu'Appelle. There are presentations on past-life regression, dream interpretation, shamanism, and ghost hunting. Tables set up throughout the hall are filled with information on meditation, energy healing, crystals, and a variety of spiritual traditions. I see that if I want to duck behind a discreet screen and consult with one of the psychics, I'd best book a time now, because their appointment books are filling up. If only I wasn't so tired from the previous night's ghost tour, I could take in more of this.

This is my kind of place.

Meaning not only the symposium, but Saskatchewan. I've always loved this province. I love the clean-swept, wide-open space and huge expanse of sky. I love the prairie pride and the endlessly generous people. I love the stillness of the tiny towns and the creative buzz of the cities. And I love the ghost stories. Now, it seems that other people are loving the ghost stories — and all other things mystical and unexplainable — as well.

My first book, *Ghost Stories of Saskatchewan,* hit the shelves in 1995. I followed up with a second collection in 2000. I then let the subject rest, thinking that I had likely exhausted the province of its spiritual lore. Not that there weren't more ghost stories — there are *always* more ghost stories — but I figured that I had run out of people who were willing to share them. But the times are always a-changing, as they say, and in the last decade, Saskatchewan has taken a turn for the ghostly.

Search the Internet for "Saskatchewan ghosts" and you'll be rewarded with thousands of hits. Those who prefer a low-tech approach can explore this province's supernatural history while touring on foot, trolley, or bus. The truly curious can join any one of a number of provincial ghost-hunting organizations who are not unlike the pros you see on television. It is possible to share your story online or read about the experiences of others there. People are more interested in the paranormal than ever. They're talking more openly about it and getting more educated. In researching this book, I found that the average person was likely to show me photos with orbs (those little balls of light thought to be spiritual energy) or boot up their laptop to play an interesting EVP (electronic voice phenomena — literally, a ghostly voice caught on tape). Everyone is giving more thought to collecting concrete evidence, as well as defining and categorizing spiritual activity. Ten years ago, not many people could explain the difference between an intelligent haunting (where the ghost is aware of its surroundings and can interact with others) and a residual haunting (more of an energetic impression of a single event, or an environmental "tape recording"). Today, most who have any interest in the subject at all can make that distinction. With so many knowledgeable people on the hunt, can proof of the afterlife be that far away?

Tough to say. Ghosts are elusive creatures, and I can't help but think that they won't be "outed" until it suits them. In the meantime, we can wait, and watch, and share our information and stories.

If you have a ghost story that you would like to share with me, I'd love to hear from you. You can email the details to *saskatchewanghosts@hotmail.com* or write to me care of this publisher. I realize now that I will never be finished writing about what haunts this province, and I look forward to writing book number four.

Jo-Anne Christensen
February 27, 2009

Ghost Hunting on the Prairies:
Saskatchewan Ghost-Hunters Society

Case File Quick Facts

Name: Saskatchewan Ghost-Hunters Society

Date Founded: July, 2008

Website: *www.saskghost-hunterssociety.ca*

Mission: To use a scientific, evidence-based approach in helping people
understand and deal with paranormal phenomena.

Founder and Lead Investigator: Miles Vanghel
Favourite Saskatchewan Haunt: The McDaniel's Ghost Light — a
    largely forgotten story from south-central Saskatchewan. (Read on
    for more details!)

Q & A with Founder and Lead Investigator Miles Vanghel

The Saskatchewan Ghost-Hunters Society is a unique, technology- and
evidence-based group that operates out of Saskatoon. Their approach is
purely scientific, and their hope is to eventually collect a body of irrefutable
evidence regarding the existence of ghosts. In the meantime, they provide
confidential, free-of-charge support to people who are struggling to
deal with confusing and sometimes terrifying situations. Miles Vanghel
generously shared information about the society, and about an interest in
ghostly phenomena that has consumed him for more than half of his life.

Q: How long have you been investigating, as a group?

A: We got the website up and going at the beginning of October (2008),
     and we actually got the official team together last July. I've been
     investigating on my own, over the years, but it was getting a little bit
     hectic for me. I wanted to share this with others, and get a like-minded
     group of people together. It definitely helps on an investigation —
     having different eyes, different perspectives, different ideas.

Q: And when did your own interest begin?

A: It all stems back to when we moved from the family farm, into
     Saskatoon. I was about the age of ten. We moved into an older house,
     built *circa* 1912. It had a very creepy atmosphere about it. In this
     home, we actually saw apparitions. Dark shadows moving around in
     the night. Doors would open and close on their own. We'd hear the
     sound of heavy boots going up the stairs at night. What really caught

my attention was, one night, I saw the apparition of a woman walk into my room. She walked to the edge of my bed and vaporized, right in front of my eyes. So that was what really caught me ... because now it had invaded my personal space.

Q: How did that interest progress?

A: Well, we were always taught [to] believe what you see, but don't believe *everything* you see. So it really got me questioning, did I really see what [I thought] I had seen? As I got older, I started studying a little bit more to find out whether science was taking this seriously. Were there actual investigation groups that were out doing this? I saw that there were, and that they were using tape recorders; they were using video cameras; they were using technical ways of trying to capture phenomena. Or ... trying to dismiss claims of it. And I think that's where it really evolved, for me.

Q: So you prefer to take a skeptical approach?

A: A healthy dose of skepticism is always good. Not everything is a paranormal event. For example, as a trades guy, I go into a lot of places where plumbing and electrical can cause some funny reactions in homes. They can throw a person off. On one investigation I was recently on, there was supposed to be a tap that turned on all by itself. But, in reality, the valve stem had just worn out. As the water pressure underneath the hot water side of the tap would build, it would actually open the valve stem itself, and open the tap up. So we could easily dismiss that claim.

Q: What are some of the other explanations you've found to explain seemingly paranormal phenomena?

A: Often, what I've found in places is an unusually high EMF, electromagnetic field. And some people have a higher sensitivity than others to this EMF. Simply, what it can be is your typical circuit box. The panel box in your home with your breakers. What it does is actually emit an electromagnetic field — sometimes in very high doses, which is very unhealthy over time. It can cause skin irritations, nausea; it can actually cause hallucinations in people who have a heightened sensitivity to it. [Another concern] is unshielded electrical wires. If there are enough of them running through a particular area, it creates a "panic box" or "fear box" syndrome, where EMF is showering the entire area. People with a heightened sensitivity will all of a sudden feel that there's something watching them. The hair will stand up on the back of their neck; the hair will stand up on their arms. They will get that really creeped-out feeling in this particular room. But if you take an EMF detector into that area, you'll find outstanding numbers. And they're consistently high. With a paranormal event, it's more like an anomalous spike that disappears very quickly, and you can't find it again.

We find this quite commonly in older buildings. The EMF can be just off the scale. But that's easy to determine, knowing that the electrical wire in these old buildings has been retro-fitted so many times. I will actually catch myself, looking back and saying, "Gee, I've got the feeling I'm being stared at." But I've got my EMF detector here, showing the reason why.

Q: Have you ever worked with a psychic?

A: We don't use psychics or mediums in any way, shape, or form. We don't consider [their findings] to be credible evidence. Simply put, it's not something that you can bring to a hard-core, mainline skeptic [and convince them]. There's always doubt. And, when there's doubt, you don't have proof. Not solid proof, anyway.

The human mind is a very inventive machine — it's always creating. [Any form of] witness testimony can become a story very quickly. It changes drastically, from one minute to the next. What I tell my investigators, with any type of investigation, is to write down their information within ten minutes of an event occurring. We do that simply because, after ten minutes, the mind starts to embellish.

It starts to create different scenarios around what happened. But if you're writing it down within the first ten minutes, then your logical mind is still keeping track of it.

Q: Could you see yourself using a psychic in other ways — perhaps to give you direction in an investigation?

A: I can't really see it in the foreseeable future for us, as a group. But if we were to do that, what we would do is use them like our equipment. Credible ones — they do have a sensitivity to particular energies. So, if we could use them just like an EMF detector, I could possibly see that. But we would [approach it with] great scrutiny.

Q: What equipment do you use to investigate?

A: We use a wide range of equipment in evidence collection. We use EMF detectors, a DVR surveillance system with night vision cameras, digital

Courtesy of the Saskatchewan Ghost-Hunters Society.

A case of equipment typically used on investigations.

thermometers, motion sensors, digital voice recorders for EVP work, night vision torches, video cameras — both hard drive and Hi-8 — digital cameras, 35 mm cameras, two-way radios for communication, and laptop computers for audio EVP evidence review. Within the last two months here, we've introduced K-2 meters into the mix. A K-2 meter has a small light display that shows ranges of EMF, from very low to very high. And what we actually use that for is a spirit communication tool. We use it in conjunction with our audio recorders. We'll set the meter down, and it'll be completely flat. No light flicker. But we'll have a series of questions, generally "yes" or "no" questions, and as soon as we start asking them, the lights begin to flicker.

Q: How do you talk to a spirit?

A: We'll start out by introducing ourselves. If there's an entity there, or a spirit, we like them to feel comfortable with us, and we want to let them know that we're not in any way, shape, or form trying to harm them or scare them. The way we look at it — if a presence is there — we must remember that these were once living, breathing people. So we go in very respectfully. After we introduce ourselves, we'll ask a question. Say, "Is there anyone here in the room who would like to speak with us? If so, what you can do is walk in front of our K-2 meter, wave your hand in front of it, and make those little lights flicker." And we've found that, in a room where we've done a base EMF reading — where there's been no EMF, or very, very minute levels — that this light will begin to flicker, once for yes, twice for no. And what we do is put it on video, so we can actually catch this anomalous, stray EMF actually answering questions on the light display.

Q: Are there certain criteria that must be met before you'll take on an investigation? How can a potential client convince you to take their case?

A: We like to give people the benefit of the doubt. But when we begin questioning, what we do is try to test the client. We want to see if the stories change, or things get added in. We try to look at it very objectively. We prefer to get a collaboration of witnesses that have seen or experienced different phenomena. There have been a series of attention-seekers ... but sometimes, someone you may think is a "crazy" is actually a very distraught person. They may just be extremely upset about what's happening in their business or their home. So you've got to be careful with the questioning. It's such very, very thin ice to tread on.

So, we [do our interviews], and then we make our judgments. We sit around and we discuss whether or not it's worth investigating. We take everything into consideration and make a decision.

Q: **Do your clients want to see evidence, or do they want you to disprove the existence of anything paranormal in their home so they can relax?**

A: It's actually a mix of both. What we'll find is that people are just looking at their own personal well-being or the family's personal well-being. It's a sanity check. That's what it breaks down to. They feel that they're going crazy, or they're losing control. They want validation in either form — that there is something there, or that there isn't. It tends to comfort people to find that we didn't catch anything on an investigation. They relax. But, if you catch something that they don't want to hear, you've got to be very careful. You've still got to let them know the evidence, but you've got to be very gentle while you do it.

Q: **Is your primary mission to find an answer regarding the existence of ghosts — or to help people who are living with them?**

A: Primarily, we're there to help people. [But] my own personal experiences when I was a child left me with more questions than answers. And it still remains that way. In this lifetime, I doubt that I'll ever get to a solid conclusion. Then again — you never know.

Q: **How accurate are the ghost-hunting shows that you see on television?**

A: I think, with all the cutting and the editing, what is kind of left out is the reality that you have a monotonous amount of time when nothing actually happens. They piece the most exciting parts of the investigation together. And what people tend to forget [while watching these shows] is that there's a lot of work that goes into this. There's a great amount of effort. It takes a lot of technical skill to focus on what you're trying to achieve. But it can be very monotonous. Simply, the way I explain it to people is, think of it as working security in the middle of nowhere. You're sitting, staring at thin air. There have been a couple of investigators-in-training who have not come back because they couldn't stand the boredom.

Q: **How many members do you have?**

A: Currently, we have four investigators, including myself, and two new investigators-in-training.

Q: **Do you like to have investigators trained in different specialties?**

A: I want everybody to have a general working knowledge of all the equipment because there may come a point in time where I can't make a particular investigation. I know my equipment top to bottom. But if I'm not there, and [the other investigators] don't know how to operate something, it really defeats the purpose. So I feel that everybody should have a comfortable working knowledge of [all of] the equipment.

Q: **Do you have a favourite case, or a favourite Saskatchewan ghost story?**

A: I do have a favourite — it is a long-forgotten ghost story of Saskatchewan. If you lived between Davidson, the town I was born in, and Imperial, you would have heard the story of the McDaniel's Ghost Light. My grandfather and my grandmother both had told me that they had seen it a few times. My father had also seen it. My older cousins tried to scare me [with stories of it], but it didn't work. I have always, as far back as I can remember, followed ghost stories.

Apparently, in 1910, a young woman who had diabetes had a craving for sugar, and ate the entire contents of the sugar bowl. She went into a coma and died in the house. She was buried on the property until her parents left the homestead a few years later. [At that time] they removed her remains from the property and had her buried in the Imperial town cemetery.

The house sat empty from that time, and fell into disrepair. Over the years, many people from all over the area told of a strange glowing light that would move from the house to the barn every night at 9:00 p.m. A few minutes later, the light would return to the house. The legend was that the light was the young woman doing her nightly chores. During the 1960s or 1970s — I'm not sure of the date — the barn was moved from the property and the light stopped.

I dug deeper into the story and found out the woman's name was Belle McDaniel. I never forgot about the story, [but] waited until I was older to venture out to the old house.

(When Miles turned 18, he went out to the McDaniel's farm to investigate the haunting. At this point, he had begun his search for life after death and was viewing the story from a more skeptical viewpoint.)

During my investigation of the house, I said out loud, "Hello, Belle." After about two minutes, I heard a response in my ear — *hello.* It was a female voice. I had no women with me; only my brothers and one of my cousins. I could feel a sadness and loneliness in the house and I have personally been haunted by Belle ever since.

Q: What is your ultimate dream for your organization?

A: Simply to help people. We want to help them with what's happening in their homes. I've had my experiences, so I know where they're coming from. And I can sympathize. Our other focus is to be seen in credible circles. We would really like to see serious scientists take a look at this and go, "Okay, maybe you do have something …" That would be a dream.

Q: How close do you think we are to that day?

A: That is a very tough one to say. We may never see it in our lifetime. Then again, we may see it in five years. In two years. But I highly doubt it. Until we get a great body of evidence, and we get some of these TV psychics off the air … it's a difficult, uphill battle.

Courtesy of the Saskatchewan Ghost-Hunters Society.

Saskatchewan Ghost-Hunters Society (left to right): Chad Segouin, research investigator, Sean Brower, tech crew/investigator, Frank Paul, tech manager/investigator, Jenifer "Mom" Vanghel, investigator, and Miles Vanghel, founder and lead investigator. Not present for the photo was Gloria Paul, case manager.

The more we can network and develop a good solid network here in the province, that will definitely move us in leaps and bounds. That's beginning to happen; we've connected with Chris Oxtoby, of Prairie Specters (page 183). It's gradually building for us.

Q: It sounds as though it's going to take a lot of work.

A: It's a job — but it's a job that I love doing. It's been my greatest fascination, and I'm happy to be doing it.

1
Public Phantoms

.

St. Henry's Cemetery

Jan is frowning at the screen of her laptop, trying to find a particular EVP that she has pulled from a videotape shot out at St. Henry's Cemetery, in the district of Kronsberg. She sets up the clip with a brief explanation as she searches.

"The question that we've just asked is, 'Do you mind that we're here?' And the answer — it's like a whisper, but if you put on the headphones, you can hear it really clearly." She finds the clip, which is looped to play repeatedly, and hands over the headphones. It is a whisper. A ghostly whisper; two distinct words.

We mind.

Jan's mother, Marj, shakes her head disapprovingly. "They do not want us there," she says.

Jan's daughter, Nikki, sides with her grandmother. "I just don't want to go out there anymore," she says. She turns to Jan and speaks directly. "You shouldn't go either, because you'll go crazy if you keep going out there."

Marj agrees. "Something's going to happen to you," she warns her daughter.

Jan nods. She understands her family's concern. But after a moment she shrugs it off and looks up with a mischievous smile.

"I know," she says. "But I always seem to be drawn out there...."

Jan, Nikki, and Marj are a multi-generational amateur ghost-hunting team that have spent much of their time investigating one particular haunted location: St. Henry's Cemetery in the district of Kronsberg, near Dysart. They've been familiar with the burial ground for many years. It was less than two kilometres from the house that Jan grew up in.

"The house that we lived in was renovated by my mom and dad," said Jan. "It used to be the old Kronsberg school. So, when we were kids, we used to bike out to the cemetery. We'd play there. Just looking for entertainment, you know? But … we'd always end up scared … and we'd pedal our [butts] home, as fast as we could go."

Whatever frightened Jan at the cemetery seemed to have a very long reach. Even at home, in the supposed safety of her bedroom, she could feel its force.

"The window in my bedroom used to face the cemetery," said Jan. "And there were so many nights I would be scared. I'd have to block my window to just be able to sleep, because I could almost feel that they were watching me. Maybe it was a little kid thing, maybe I was being silly, but that's how I felt all the time."

As she got older, and began to talk to Marj about her feelings, she learned that she wasn't the only member of the family to have negative feelings about St. Henry's.

"My dad was from that district," said Jan. "Born and raised there. But he made mom swear, when they first got married, that 'If I pass away before you do, do *not* bury me in that graveyard.' His mother isn't buried there, his father isn't buried there. My dad's brother … he didn't want anything to do with that area. My mom's dad didn't even like going out there."

There was no logical explanation for the family's distaste. On the surface, St. Henry's appeared no different from any other rural cemetery. There had once been a church on site. Many of the original settlers were buried in the graveyard and nothing about this little pocket of prairie *appeared* out of the ordinary. But something obviously was. For, as

Jan nurtured a growing fascination with St. Henry's, she found others dealing with an increased aversion to it.

"Even my brothers, said Jan. "When my brothers come home, I try to talk them into going back out there, for old time's sake … and they refuse. My one brother, he just [recently admitted] that if he has to drive by there, he *speeds* by. Literally just floors it." Jan shook her head. "But, when you drive up to it, you can feel it," she said. "From about a quarter-mile out, you start to feel it."

It's the pull of St. Henry's that Jan mentions so often. *I seem to be drawn out there.…*

Jan began ghost hunting several years ago, at first on her own, then with Marj and Nikki. Occasionally, the three women join forces with the Calling Lakes Paranormal Investigators (page 57). But whether they were on their own or with CLPI, their main investigative focus for a long time has been the cemetery at Kronsberg. For ghost hunters looking for evidence of the paranormal, it was a rewarding place to go. St. Henry's appeared to be saturated with apparitions, orbs, and ghostly sounds and smells. Investigators felt deeply affected by the energy of the place, experiencing anxiety, personality changes, sudden physical illness, and the magnetism that Jan frequently speaks of. They would come away with evidence of paranormal phenomena in photos, recordings, and videos. And the stories … There are so many stories about St. Henry's that it's difficult to know where to begin.

So we'll start with one particular night, when a full moon hung in the sky, and Jan decided to go out to the cemetery at midnight. Not long before, Jan, Marj, and Nikki had discovered that there was an unconsecrated portion of the cemetery — an area where they had always sensed a concentration of strange energy and activity. Jan thought that it might be interesting to leave a tape recorder running in that part of the graveyard, at the witching hour. So she drove out there, alone.

"When I got there, it was about eleven-thirty at night," said Jan. "I pulled into the approach and I was just getting my stuff ready when [I realized that] I forgot a flashlight. So I pulled out my cell phone, so at least I'd be talking to somebody as I was doing it."

Having a friend keep her company on the phone made Jan feel a little better, but she could still feel her anxiety increase as she drew closer to the unconsecrated ground. She knew from experience that she would feel *something* as she crossed into that area.

"When you walk through the cemetery part, you feel fine," she said, "but as soon as you get to that borderline, where the fence used to be, you just feel it. Your skin prickles."

Jan walked up to the point where the cemetery divided. She continued to talk on the phone as she set up her equipment. She could feel her nervousness growing.

"I was scared," she said. "I told my friend, 'I really don't like this — stay on the phone with me.' And she was saying, 'Okay — just be real quick.'"

Jan stepped across the line. At that moment, a deep, breathy sound came through the phone.

"I just froze," said Jan. "I said to my friend, 'Tell me you did that; you made that sigh.' She said, 'I thought *you* did.' So I ran, dropped the tape recorder, and I was out of there. I begged her to come with me when I had to go back to get it an hour later."

When Jan did collect the tape recorder, she found that it had been worth the frightening experience of dropping it off. She had forty-five minutes worth of tape filled with noises that were utterly unexplainable.

"All the way through," said Jan, "you can hear noises, like banging wood, metal. You can hear footsteps. You can hear a little boy talking."

Marj and Nikki had studied the recording, as well, and shared their observations.

"At one point you can hear hammering," said Nikki. "There's heavy breathing, a heartbeat — I definitely heard a heartbeat."

"You can hear chanting," added Jan. "There's singing going on. And then there's so many sections where — I hate to say this; I hate to label it like this — but there's almost that demonic sound. A whole bunch of voices."

Could any of this be ambient noise from the surrounding area? Marj shook her head.

"We lived there for twenty-five years," she said. "We know the area. There are only farmers living there. There's nothing around this grave site, and the closest farm is a mile and a half away."

Could it be traffic on the roads bordering the cemetery? All three women laugh at the likelihood of there being that much action in this deserted rural area at midnight. Even so, Jan has put some thought into ruling it out.

"There are only two roads by the cemetery, and I took both of them," she said. "You can hear my vehicle on the tape. And you can tell, compared to mine, that those other sounds are definitely *not* vehicles."

And there was one other strange event that night. The phone call that Jan made to her friend, from the cemetery....

"That phone call did not register [in my call history]," said Jan. "I was on the phone for a good three-quarters of an hour, and it didn't show up." What's more, Marj tried to call Jan's cell while Jan was on the phone, but she didn't get a busy signal. The phone just rang endlessly. It was as if, at that moment, Jan didn't exist.

A number of orbs — including one spectacular example in the upper-left-hand corner — captured at St. Henry's Cemetery.

The Calling Lakes Paranormal Investigators have visited St. Henry's Cemetery close to twenty times. It's one of the most paranormally active sites they've ever been to. Investigator Amy Drummond has spent a lot of time speculating about the reason for this.

"I think they just picked the worst possible place to put a cemetery," said Amy. "I don't know why, but the ground is just 'wrong' up there. It could be some kind of power spot. I'm not sure. It might be some freak thing that we haven't discovered, yet. But ... if you're buried there, you do not rest. You come back."

And, according to Amy, you come back in a dramatic fashion. Amy is considered by the group to be highly intuitive, which means that she sometimes sees things that other people do not. She describes most of what she sees at St. Henry's in visual, theatrical terms.

"There are people actually climbing out of their graves, like straight out of a bad horror movie," she said. "You'll see black figures running from tombstone to tombstone. Beyond the point where the cemetery divides, [another investigator] and I could see this weird mist on the ground. It had a funny colour to it — it almost had a glow. And, under the mist, we could see people crawling around, very quickly, almost like in high-speed, fast-forward motion. Nobody else could see this fog. But we could. And we were walking around in it. Then this psychic who we'd brought with us said, 'You guys, I have a really horrible feeling about you being over there. You've crossed the border. That's the unconsecrated area — please come back.'"

There's another apparition at St. Henry's — an ominous, dark figure that has been seen by numerous people, on numerous occasions.

"We call it the guardian, or the watcher of the cemetery," said Amy. "If we go out there when things are really active, it will watch us."

Jan, Nikki, and Marj have noticed that the guardian shows up only if they open the cemetery gates.

"But it won't come into the cemetery," said Jan. It's either outside, where our vehicle is, or it's over the trees, by the unconsecrated area. It's like it can't come in." Jan describes the guardian as being an immense, hooded, winged creature. She's seen it swooping over the trees, and lurking around the perimeter of the cemetery. And she believes she's captured it in a photograph.

Jan is scrolling through photo files on her laptop now, looking for one image in particular. She finds it, and brings it up to full-screen size.

"Take a look at this," she says. "Can you see a figure?"

It's a picture of St. Henry's Cemetery taken at night. The flash bounces off tombstones, rendering them ghostly white. The background is night sky. But there does seem to be a black, saturated area … A vaguely human shape in the darkness.

Jan smiles. "That's it," she says. "That's where we saw the guardian."

Not all of the experiences at St. Henry's Cemetery have seemed sinister, however. A number of investigators, on different occasions, have encountered beautiful, concentrated pockets of scent, such as rose or lavender. And both Nikki and the CLPI members reported meeting the sweet spirit of a little boy.

"He wanted to leave with us," said Jan Drummond of the Calling Lakes group. "May (a psychic assisting in the investigation) had to walk him back into the graveyard and tell him that he had to stay, that this was his resting place, et cetera. It was sad."

When Nikki met the ghost of the little boy, she had her mother snap a picture of the two of them together.

"What we got," she said, "is a picture of me with my arm out and there's an orb right beside me."

Orbs are plentiful at St. Henry's. Almost all photographs taken in the cemetery show layer upon layer of the mysterious lights; there are different sizes, different densities, and different patterns visible within the spheres. Again, the remote rural location makes it seem unlikely that there is any ambient light or reflection that might be causing the effect.

"There's not so much as a street light out there," said Marj.

Floral aromas, charming phantom children, and dazzling lights aside, all who venture out to St. Henry's have a healthy respect for the risks to which they may be exposing themselves. The CLPI have felt threatened — particularly on one occasion when massive, menacing, black shadows followed them out of the cemetery and began to crawl around on their vehicles. Jan, Nikki, and Marj have all experienced severe physical symptoms on site, including weakness, chest pain, and dizziness. They do whatever they can to protect themselves prior to an investigation, but these things can still happen. Worse, the spectres at St. Henry's have, on at least two occasions, followed the women home.

"We took one ghost back to Mom's place," said Jan.

Marj nodded. "It just about drove me nuts," she said. "It was in my bedroom … and it would shake my bed every night. Two, three o'clock in the morning, it would wake me up."

Another time, Jan brought something into her own home. Whatever it was, it was fond of opening and closing doors and could drain all the warmth from a room in a matter of seconds. It also infuriated Nikki by whipping open the shower curtain while she was in the shower. She had the bathroom door locked at the time, so it had to have been the ghost that was responsible. Ultimately, however, Nikki blamed Jan, accusing her of being irresponsible and increasingly secretive about her visits to St. Henry's.

"I have dreams about bad things happening to her out there," said Nikki, "the kind of dreams that seem completely real. And when she goes out there, I can tell … and, sometimes, I don't want to go near her after."

Jan shook her head. "I protect myself," she said, "but I guess I don't do a good enough job of it."

"No, you don't," agreed Nikki. She knows that Jan is unwanted there. And it worries her.

We mind.…

One of the reasons that all investigators are particularly cautious regarding St. Henry's is that they aren't sure what type of force they are dealing with. They all agree that it is highly unusual for a cemetery to be haunted, let alone *that* haunted. But everyone seems to have their own

Courtesy of Jan Zaporozen.

There are no lights near this deserted, rural cemetery — except for the unexplainable, glowing spheres that float above the graves.

theory as to why that is.

Nikki, who is highly sensitive, believes that the cemetery is the location of a doorway between worlds. "I feel there's a portal there," she said. "Some of the EVPs we have, it sounds like there's constant traffic. But nobody goes down that road unless they're going to their farm.

"And most cemeteries," she continued, "[are] the worst place to ghost-hunt, because there isn't going to be anything there, unless there's something that's feeding it. That's why I'm thinking that there has to be a portal of some sort. It all kind of connects."

Amy, of the CLPI, doesn't fully agree. "A portal, to me, is a place where anything can come through," she said. "And I don't necessarily think that's the case with St. Henry's. But there are things out there ... things that have never been human. They're barren. They should never have put a cemetery there."

Inhuman entities, mass haunting, a sinister guardian ... and *still* Jan is drawn there.

"I start sensing it, whenever I come home now," she says. "I start feeling the pull for it when I hit Dysart. Dysart is six miles from the cemetery, and it's already pulling me...."

It is impossible to overestimate the dark attraction of St. Henry's Cemetery in Kronsberg.

Hopkins Dining Parlour

The lunch rush is over at Hopkins Dining Parlour in Moose Jaw, and the staff supervisor, Brenda Wilson, is taking a moment to tell a story. It's about a couple from Regina who ran a karaoke business.

"They had come out to see us on a Monday, when we don't open 'til four," says Brenda. "And they took a picture of the building. Then they came back the following Sunday to show us the picture."

In the photo, through one of the windows, the image of a woman and a cocker spaniel dog could be seen. The figures were clear, but transparent. And the picture was taken when the restaurant was locked and empty.

"I've had other people say the same thing," says Brenda. "That if you drive by here late at night, you can see a woman in the window. So now, I don't look in the windows when I leave."

Brenda won't look back at the windows because she's the first to admit that she's afraid of ghosts. Given that, it's remarkable that she's remained employed at Hopkins for over twenty years.

"When I started, in about '85," she says, "I was told there was a ghost. I didn't know if it was a joke, or what."

She knows now that it was not. And many others know it, as well. For Hopkins is known not only as a designated heritage property and a fine restaurant, but as one of the most famously haunted locations in Canada.

This beautiful three-storey mansion in downtown Moose Jaw was originally the private residence of Edward and Minnie Hopkins. It was built in 1905, the same year that Saskatchewan became a province. Edward lived in the home until his death in 1935. Minnie stayed on until she died a few years later. The house then passed into the hands of the Hopkins's daughter, who lived in one part of it, but converted the other rooms into rental suites. In 1978, the Pierce family purchased the house and restored it, turning it into Hopkins Dining Parlour. The restaurant has enjoyed great success over the years, and is famous for its good food and Victorian atmosphere. And since a 2003 episode of the television series *Creepy Canada*, which prominently featured Hopkins, it has become equally famous for its ghosts.

Hopkins's owner, Glady Pierce, never shied away from the restaurant's haunted reputation. In fact, she chose to embrace it. The *Creepy Canada* episode plays frequently on a television set in the lounge, and staff members are welcome to share their ghost stories with customers. Tours of the home are spiced up with as many paranormal facts as historical ones, and if people who come by are as interested in the spirits as the chicken wings, that's all right with Glady. And it's good that she's happy to confirm the strange stories because, with the amount of supernatural activity going on at Hopkins, the haunting would be pretty difficult to deny.

Members of the staff have seen roasting pans fly across the kitchen, watched a balloon "walk" up the central staircase, and gaped at a hanging candle holder as it swung wildly and mysteriously to and fro. After the restaurant was closed for the night, they've heard glasses tinkling and chairs scraping across the floor. They've witnessed misty white apparitions that vanish upon being noticed, and a blue streak of light, the size of a small child, bolting up the stairs. People have had their shoulders tapped, their necks rubbed, and their baked potato trays sent flying from the table. They've listened to spoons banging on the pipes and watched centrepiece candles flare to life on their own. The ghosts in Hopkins are extremely active. It's little wonder that the employees have trouble shaking off the creepy feelings.

One example of that is Brenda Wilson describing how she and another employee are simply unable to stand at the bar with their backs to the open room.

"He knows he'll get tapped on the shoulder, and I absolutely *know* that someone's going to grab me," she said. "And then there's the staring thing. I've been in the kitchen when I just *know* that something's staring at me. And I'm sure that it's going to touch me."

Photo by the author.

The historic Hopkins Dining Parlour in Moose Jaw.

Other parts of the restaurant that give Brenda the chills are the basement, which she avoids at all cost, and the ladies' room on the main floor.

"That bathroom's a bad place for me," Brenda said. "Not all of the time, but often. I'll be sitting there, and I'll get this strong feeling that [something is] going to grab me over the top of the stall, or underneath the stall. It's creepy."

It's no surprise that the basement and the ladies' washroom, in particular, feel uncomfortable for Brenda. Those two locations have been the scenes of many spooky happenings in Hopkins. In the basement, members of the staff have heard the sound of a machine rolling money for the VLTs, when no one was in the office. A new employee — who had been told nothing of the ghost stories — was in the basement putting away stock when he was confronted by a white, faceless apparition. The employee likely went as pale as the spectre, which turned and drifted up the stairs. Still other staff members have seen the image of a woman in the basement, or felt a strong, invisible force pushing them up the stairs. Brenda, herself, has seen someone duck behind a door in an area of the basement that she knew to be empty.

"I do not come down here unless I have to," she said firmly.

The main floor ladies' washroom was one of the areas featured on *Creepy Canada* — and for very good reason. It's an extremely active zone. Customers and staff alike have all walked in to find that the taps had turned themselves on — a phenomenon that sometimes starts right in front of people. And many who walk into the washroom find that it is not as empty as it seems at first glance.

"One lady was sitting there, when she heard someone come in and walk across the floor," said Brenda. "So she said to her, 'God, it's cold in here.' But this other person never answered her. And when the customer came out of the stall, she could see that there was no one else in the bathroom."

Photo by the author.

Some say that the original lady of the house, Minnie Hopkins, never left her lovely Victorian home.

Another staff member — who maintains that she doesn't believe in ghosts — had an experience in that ladies' room that even she had difficulty explaining away. She went into the washroom one evening, just in time to see the tail end of a skirt swirling around the corner into one stall. The employee was about to use the other toilet when she turned and saw that the door to the first stall was wide open and there was no one else in the bathroom.

Brenda has had more than one creepy encounter in that washroom.

"I came in one Friday and sat in the stall," she said. "I heard someone put paper in the garbage; heard the lid go 'ting.' I looked down and saw their shadow on the floor. And I thought, *that's strange, why didn't I see that person?* The door never opened, never closed, and there was nobody in the other stall." On another occasion, in about 1993, Brenda was alone in the bathroom, washing her hands, when she suddenly felt a presence standing behind her. She looked up at the mirror and saw …

"Minnie. Well, we call her that," said Brenda. "Everyone has always called her that." Still, Brenda Wilson isn't convinced that Hopkins is haunted by the ghost of Minnie Hopkins, the original lady of the house. She has good reason to think otherwise. On the main floor dining room, above the fireplace, there is a photograph of the Hopkins family. "That's why I say I *know* it wasn't Mrs. Hopkins I saw that day," said Brenda. "Because [the woman I saw] had a round face, and that isn't Mrs. Hopkins. But, you know, there were a lot of school teachers that lived here when this was apartments." Brenda believes that, because the house was a revenue property for so many years, there are many possible identities for the female ghost.

Not to mention the male spirit.

Though "Minnie" is Hopkins's most famous apparition, another spectre, a man, made himself known a few years ago. This ghost managed to introduce himself through a third party.

"We had a guy come in once. He was selling stuff for the gift shop," said Brenda. "He was a sales rep, here to see Glady. And, while he was waiting, he said, 'Oh, by the way, you have a ghost here.'" This was hardly news to Brenda, so she simply offered the man a seat and continued to take care of her lunch customers. After Glady Pierce met with the man, however, she called Brenda over. And Brenda found that the sales rep did indeed have something new to report. He hadn't sensed the presence of the female apparition that everyone was familiar with. He had seen a man with an eye patch. "He said 'Don't worry about him — he's the silent type. He lives in the northwest corner of the restaurant,'" said Brenda. "And we had stories — quite a few stories, actually — from that exact corner, upstairs."

It wasn't long before the male apparition was roaming throughout the entire restaurant — and being seen by several members of the Hopkins's staff. The bartender frequently saw a man out of the corner of her eye, and would turn to greet him, only to find no one there. One of the waiters saw the ghostly man often. On one occasion he saw him walk from the front door to the hostess stand, which was just out of sight. The waiter, certain that he had just seen a customer enter the restaurant, went running up to the front. But, of course, he found nobody there. Brenda recalled the story of a woman on the cleaning staff who once encountered the male ghost in an otherwise empty restaurant — and was so convinced that he was a real person, she spoke to him.

"She was working right at the top of the stairs," said Brenda. "She happened to look down, and saw a man walking [across the main floor]. She thought it was Rick, our boss, who has since passed away. She looked down and said 'Hi Rick, I'm up here vacuuming.' And the man looked up at her." At that point, the woman realized that the man wasn't her boss, and that he was wearing a rather odd, old-fashioned outfit. "So she came downstairs," said Brenda, "and he wasn't here, of course."

Not to be outdone, the female ghost has remained as active as ever. One time, Brenda and a couple of servers were closing up the restaurant for the night. They had finished cashing out, and had turned out all the lights, when they noticed a single candle burning on one of the tables. They turned to investigate, when, suddenly …

"The lights at the front of the restaurant came on," said Brenda, "as well as all the light fixtures on this wall. And [one server] saw the ghost standing in between the tables, up there. So she screamed, and they both ran."

But "Minnie" never limited herself to late-night appearances. One morning, before any of the regular staff had arrived, the cook was in the service stairwell at the back of the building. As she climbed the stairs, she could see part of a woman — just the tail end of a skirt and a shoe —

rounding the corner on the landing just one flight above her. There was, of course, no one else in the building at the time.

The female spirit has even appeared in front of children. Brenda recalled one little boy, no more than two years of age, whom she found pointing at an empty space, saying "Ghost, ghost!"

"I asked his dad what he was talking about," said Brenda. "The dad said, 'I don't know. He doesn't talk, but he just said he saw a ghost.' I wasn't surprised. [Later on], he told us the ghost's name was Violet."

When Glady's granddaughter was about four years old, she came to visit the restaurant one day. Brenda saw her sitting at a table, shivering, and went over to ask her what was the matter. The little girl told her that a ghost had just gone by.

"I said, 'Like Casper?'" recalled Brenda. "She said 'No, a lady ghost.' Kids do see it."

Kids see the ghosts, staff see the ghosts, customers see the ghosts — and not everyone who sees them likes them. Brenda told the story of one young woman who came to Hopkins to have lunch with her mother and her aunt. Brenda knew the two older women, and stopped by the table to talk with them. As she chatted, she noticed that the girl was extremely quiet and barely touched her food. Two days later, Brenda learned what had happened.

"I guess this lady appeared, wearing a white dress with a yellow apron. She was darker-skinned. And the lady was leaning against the buffet, staring at the [three women] and smiling. And the girl was

One of Hopkins's spectres once laid out silverware in the shape of a cross on this stairway.

thinking that something was wrong with this woman. And then she realized that nobody else was acknowledging she was there. So she got scared, and she left. And she's never come back again."

Another young woman who was upset by an apparition in Hopkins was the friend of a server. The server had been setting up tables one evening, after the restaurant closed. She had moved from the third floor down to the second and was about to go back up to the third when she stopped cold. The silverware that she had just set out on the tables had been moved to the stairs — and was elaborately laid out in the shape of a cross. When the server came back to the restaurant the next day, she was accompanied by a friend who claimed to be psychic. Brenda remembered that day.

"[The two girls] went upstairs to look around. When they came back down, the friend was really, really upset. She claimed there was a lady sitting at one table, and the lady had long white hair and a scar on her face. She was really upset."

But, perhaps, not as upset as one couple from Regina who used to be regulars at Hopkins.

"They used to come here once a month," said Brenda. "They were regulars. Then, one time, they brought a friend with them. And the friend went into a trance type of thing. It just horrified her ... and they never came back after that time."

Even Brenda — as accustomed as she is to the ghostly activity — occasionally wearies of it. Recently, after several days of strangely malfunctioning electronics and telephones, a customer commented that there was "a lot of activity" in the restaurant.

Brenda thought she was commenting on the number of diners, and replied, "I know, we're pretty busy."

The woman shook her head and clarified that she had meant *spiritual* activity. As she spoke, she gestured toward the stereo system in the lounge, which had been doing strange, unexplainable things for days.

"I just said, 'I don't want to talk about it,'" said Brenda. "It had been a long week, with things playing that weren't supposed to be playing, and seeing people that weren't supposed to be there. So we didn't talk anymore after that."

She may have spent more than two decades working with the lively ghosts at Hopkins haunted Dining Parlour, but even Brenda Wilson has her limits.

Victoria Hospital

Prince Albert native Vilda Poole is what you could call a "ghost-story aficionado." She loves to tell mysterious tales and spends many hours reading ghost stories to local school children. One of the best stories that she knows, however, was told to *her* by her daughter, who is a nurse at Victoria Hospital.

"My daughter came home one morning, after a night shift," said Vilda, "and she said, 'Mom, you won't believe what happened, last night.'" She then proceeded to tell one of the most intriguing ghost stories that her mother had ever heard.

To fully appreciate the story requires a little knowledge about the layout of the hospital. There is a main entrance which can't be accessed after a certain hour at night. Instead, people have to go around to the emergency doors. Not far from the emergency entrance is a commissionaire's desk with a bank of security monitors. The commissionaire on duty is able to monitor several areas of the hospital from this one command post, and — if he leans over and looks down the hallway — he can see the information desk by the main doors from where he sits. According to Vilda, this is where the story took place.

"The commissionaire was checking his monitors," said Vilda, "and he was surprised to see a man at the information desk. Now, this was after the main doors were locked for the night. So he was wondering how this fellow got in, you see."

The commissionaire looked down the hallway toward the main foyer, perhaps intending to wave the man over. But what he saw confused him. There was no one standing there. When he looked back at his monitor, however, he could still see the image of the man, waiting patiently at the desk.

"Now, this was hard for him to believe," said Vilda, "so he called a number of nurses over to take a look. Every one of them saw what he saw. Man on the monitor, but nobody actually standing at the desk."

The group continued to watch in amazement as the figure on the monitor began to move around. Some gasped in shock when they watched him clearly walk *through* the desk and sit down in an office chair on the other side. Someone — perhaps a member of the cleaning staff — walked into the area at that point. That person moved the chair, causing the ghost to stand up and walk through the desk once more.

"Then, get this," said Vilda, "that person, whoever it was, came back around the desk and walked right through the ghost! And everybody saw it on the security monitor."

After Vilda had listened to the entire, seemingly impossible, story, she asked her daughter one question.

"I said to her, 'Did you have any deaths in the hospital last night?' And she said that one patient up in the psych ward had committed suicide. Now, I know that patients in psych care are sometimes allowed to wear their own clothing, so I asked her for a description of the patient and what he was wearing. She said, 'Short brown hair, blue shirt, brown pants, about thirty-five years old.' So, then I said to her, 'What did the man on the security monitor look like?'"

Not surprisingly, Vilda's daughter told her that the ghost had short brown hair, a blue shirt, and brown pants. He appeared to be about thirty-five years old.

"Of course, they record everything that those cameras see," said Vilda. "A while later, I went in and asked if I could see that tape for myself. They played it for me, and it was incredible!"

Incredible enough to become a well-known story. In the years since, there have been at least a half-dozen occasions when Vilda was approached after one of her school appearances, and told the same story by some child who had heard it from his or her parents.

Walter Hlewka, another Prince Albert resident, was also familiar with the ghost caught on camera. After working at the hospital for more than thirty years, he was familiar with many incidents that were both routine and unexplainable.

"Our resident ghost liked to ride the passenger elevator," Walter said. "Several times a week this elevator — no matter where it was located — would start up all on its own between the hours of 4:00 and 5:00 a.m." This haunting ride would always end when the empty elevator stopped on the fifth floor.

Walter also reported that the night staff on the pediatric ward regularly heard strange sounds coming from what he described as their "equipment room." They never were able to find a reasonable explanation for the noise.

And the pediatric staff were not the only ones dealing with spooky acoustics. At night, the nurses in ICU would sometimes hear the distinctive clicking of high-heeled shoes walking the length of the empty, tiled hallway. That could be unnerving, but it was much better than the events of one particular evening, when the night staff spent hours trying to locate the source of some periodic bursts of spectral screaming and crying.

Vilda Poole offered a theory regarding these stories. "Hospitals see so much living and dying and drama," she said. "They're very emotional places. It makes sense that they end up haunted."

Whether it makes sense or not, it appears to be a fact. Victoria Hospital in Prince Albert has its share of spirits.

Holy Family Hospital

Prince Albert's Holy Family Hospital closed its doors in 1997, but didn't face the wrecking ball until eleven years later. In that time, there were many whispered stories about the derelict building that had, in its active years, seen so much life and death. People who trespassed on the property, wanting to explore the dark and silent institution, often reported eerie and unexplained noises. The sounds of ponderous footsteps, of something heavy being dragged along the floor, of mysterious bells; all were heard within the corpse of the old hospital. Then, in 2008, the demolition began — and the ghosts *really* started to show themselves.

"I remember when they tore one of the walls off," said one Prince Albert woman. "They left it sitting like that, open, for a long time. You could look in and see all the things that were left behind — curtains, blinds, equipment. It wasn't hard to imagine people walking through those rooms. Or spirits."

It was said that some of the workers assigned to demolish the old building did more than imagine spirits. They actually encountered them. One man who was instructed to tear down an archway reportedly refused to do so after he saw the shimmering apparition of a little girl standing beneath it. Workers on the demolition site were not alone in witnessing the ghosts of the hospital, however. There was one particular spectre — the ghostly, white figure of woman rocking a tiny baby — that was potentially seen by countless people around the world. It happened when the *Prince Albert Daily Herald* unknowingly posted a video of the apparition on the Internet.

It was May 8, 2008. Demolition of the hospital had started only a week before. On its website, the *Herald* posted a ninety-second video clip of a piece of heavy equipment tearing out one of the building's walls. Most of the viewer comments posted were about personal memories of the hospital, or the music chosen to accompany the video (generally deemed not reverent enough). Before long, though, someone had written, "if u look closely when the camera zooms in you can see something moving in the window."

And that's when the message board lit up:

"That is some cool footage …"

"THERE ARE SPIRITS IN THAT BUILDING …"

"I [saw] that in the window, too, and got chills …"

"It gave me goosebumps …"

There were skeptics, as well; viewers who blamed the image on dangling construction debris and overactive imaginations. But most of the comments were from people who were convinced that they had just witnessed video footage of a genuine ghost. One person who posted a comment seemed not to be surprised that a lost soul or two might be wandering around the skeletal remains of the building.

"You wouldn't believe what is in that hospital," this person wrote. "I worked there for years and experienced some freaky stuff on nights."

There probably are many former staff members of the hospital who could tell a strange story or two. But now, thanks to the Internet, many others were able to witness one of the ghostly figures that haunted Holy Family Hospital until its very last days.

The Assiniboia Club

One of Regina's landmark historical buildings — a Queen Anne Revival-style structure situated at 1925 Victoria Avenue — was, for many decades, home to the city's historic Assiniboia Club. The Assiniboia was a private club, and membership was only available to those who were powerful, privileged, and male. There were restricted and modest rooms where female guests of members were allowed to visit — but they had to be accessed through a separate LADIES ONLY entrance, situated around the side of the building. There are sordid stories, however, of prostitutes being smuggled into the upstairs bedrooms for the private enjoyment of club members. And the rumours get even more serious with regard to one particular lady of the evening. She was said to have become quite possessive of one of her clients, a certain club member, who turned to his associates for help. Not long after, this "lady" is said

Photo by the author.

Regina's historic Assiniboia Club is now home to Crave Kitchen and Wine Bar.

to have walked into the club one evening, never to leave. An axe, they say, was the weapon used to finish this poor woman.

Today, you can go through endless spools of microfilm and never find a news story about this brutal murder. That's not to say it never happened, only that it was never a public matter. So many years have passed since the alleged incident, there's now no way of knowing what really happened. Potential witnesses would have by now passed away and any physical evidence would be long gone. However, there are many who say that another kind of evidence was left behind. They're talking about the spirit of the luckless prostitute said to haunt the building where she met her end.

In recent years, as it struggled to remain financially viable, the Assiniboia Club shared quarters with other businesses. Staff and customers of these other operations — primarily restaurants — told many stories of strange things happening in the old building. Billiard balls would regularly drift around on a perfectly balanced table. Lights on the third floor of the building would switch on of their own accord. The security system would register movement on the third floor, as well, when there was no one at all up there. And, on one occasion a server was working alone polishing cutlery when she looked up and saw a vase hovering in the middle of the room. It seemed that anyone who worked in the old Assiniboia Club had a spooky story to tell. But can any of them really be connected to the allegedly murdered prostitute?

Well ... not really.

There is one tale told by a customer who was having dinner at a restaurant in the building several years ago. The man was standing at a sink in the washroom when he looked up at the mirror and was startled by the reflection of a red-headed woman standing directly behind him, peering over his shoulder. The man spun around, only to find that he was completely alone in the room. This would seem to confirm that there is indeed a female apparition on the premises. But whether she is the prostitute in question is impossible to know. One thing is known, however: according to other stories, this female spirit is not alone.

For Halloween 2008, Crave morphed into "Grave" as tombstones mysteriously appeared by the front entrance.

Photo by the author.

A waitress named Dawn was once working in the building at 6:00 a.m., preparing a third floor room for a breakfast function. As she worked, a man walked by and wished her a good morning. Dawn returned the greeting but, after a moment, became concerned. At that early hour there should have been no customers in the building, and she didn't recognize the man as staff. As a precaution, Dawn went downstairs to ask the cook — the only other employee on hand — who the stranger was. The cook informed Dawn that they were the only two people in the building. The doors were all locked and the other morning staff would have to ring the buzzer to be let in. Together, Dawn and the cook searched the premises but, of course, they found no one else there.

There may be nothing to prove that a murder once took place in this stately brick structure, but there does seem to be plenty of evidence of ghosts. What's more, the restaurant currently located in the building — a wine bar called Crave — isn't afraid to play it up. On Halloween of 2008, they turned their small front lawn into a mock cemetery and, with the flick of a single letter, for one spooky night only, *Crave* became *Grave*.

It was a fine touch of irreverence, over the entrance of what was once the most revered of Regina's institutions, the Assiniboia Club.

An Imported Spirit

You own a business.

You know that a resident ghost would give it a little pizzazz.

But your building just isn't haunted.

What to do?

Apparently, it's only a matter of choosing the proper antique fixtures — ones that have a story and, perhaps, a spirit attached to them. Take, for example, the story of Bartleby's/Bart's on Broad, the now-defunct nightclub and eatery profiled by reporter Ashley Martin in the Halloween 2003 edition of the University of Regina's student newspaper, the *Carillon*. Martin interviewed Mike Maroudis, the manager of Bart's, for her article on haunted Regina businesses. Maroudis told many intriguing tales of ghostly activity, as well as an unusual story of how his place of business came to be haunted.

"The bar ... is over a hundred years old," said Maroudis, "and he came with the bar."

Bart's antique bar was shipped to Regina from Butte, Montana, where it was long associated with a historic murder. There was a bullet hole gouged into the wood, said to be from a gunfight between Butch Cassidy and the Sundance Kid and another gunslinger named Kid Letowsky. Letowsky was the loser of this particular battle, and his spirit was said to haunt the bar in which the bullet that killed him was buried. He may have been waiting for an opportunity to avenge his own murder. While he waited, however, he seemed content to amuse himself by playing little tricks on Maroudis and his staff.

Kid Letowsky — or "Buddy," as the staff of Bart's referred to him in his spirit form — liked to move small objects around the room. A server would reach for a glass, only to have it slip just an inch or two beyond her grasp. Items like keys and pens would go missing every day, and turn up later in odd places. Maroudis recalled one incident, in particular, that chilled him.

"When I first took over Bart's," he told the *Carillon*, "my routine was to unplug the jukebox [before] I checked the doors." One night, Maroudis had pulled the plug and gone around to check the side doors when he heard a blast of music. "The jukebox, all of a sudden, went on," he said. "I just ran out the front door."

Mysterious music and moving glassware were enough to convince the staff of Bart's that they were dealing with a ghost. But there was more evidence to come. One evening the spectre appeared as a full apparition to the bartender. There was no one else in the room when it happened, but Mike Maroudis was in his office, where he could see the employee on a security camera. Maroudis may not have witnessed the spook itself, but he did witness the bartender's reaction. According to Maroudis, the man turned as pale as a ghost himself and ran out of the building.

How strange — a bartender with no appreciation of imported spirits.

1800 College Avenue

There is a house on College Avenue in Regina that is nearing the one-century mark. Through the years, this architectural Arts and Crafts-style beauty has been home to at least two Regina families, not to mention a number of businesses. It's also rumoured to be the haunt of at least one ghost.

The McKillop residence, as it is historically known, is currently the location of a business called The Computer Clinic. In an earlier incarnation, when the building was home to Magellan's Global Coffee House, it knew its greatest fame as a local haunt.

For years there were stories of a female figure seen roaming the second floor at times when the house was said to be vacant. But, until Magellan's moved in, this ghost didn't have much else to do. It was the sudden arrival of staff and coffee-loving patrons that truly brought this spirit — in a manner of speaking — to life. Some people would hear a woman's voice singing on the second floor when they knew that there wasn't anyone upstairs. Others reported seeing the image of a woman, ever so briefly, before they locked the doors at night. There were subtle signs of the spirit's presence, including an unusual sensation of warmth and the tantalizing aroma of pancakes. But there were other encounters that were decidedly less subtle, including some that left staff completely unnerved.

According to the Halloween 2003 edition of the University of Regina student newspaper, the *Carillon*, one woman actually left her job after experiencing the clammy sensation of having the ghost walk directly through her. Another employee, a baker, was no doubt shaken one morning when the spirit decided to turn on the automatic mixer. The woman tried to take it in stride but, as she walked across the room to switch it off, the mixer kept advancing to a higher speed. The machine was on its highest setting before the baker was able to pull its plug. A third woman who worked at Magellan's had much calmer encounters with the ghost — but more of them. She witnessed the female apparition on three separate occasions and each time the ghost was wearing a wedding dress. That alone would have captured the woman's attention, but not quite as much as the fact that the ghost was walking nonchalantly past a second-storey window — on the *outside* of the house.

Who this spirit might be, and how she came to be in the house, is anybody's guess. There were a number of stories about deaths that took place at that address, but Trevor Lien, the entrepreneur who lived in the house for three years before opening Magellan's, managed to disprove them all.

So is it, or isn't it haunted? This College Avenue house remains a topic for "spirited" debate.

1800 College Avenue — today, home to The Computer Clinic.

And They Shall Remain Nameless....

The problem with hunting down ghost stories about businesses is that not all business owners think of phantoms as good publicity. Some are more afraid of alienating customers than they are of the shadowy spectres with which they spend their working hours. Therefore, they are reluctant to openly tell their tales. Still, the stories are too good *not* to share — so we'll talk about the ghosts, but remain mum on which places of business they happen to haunt.

The Winning Spirit

There is a casino in Saskatchewan that is located in a building with a long and varied history. It is said that a number of spirits associated with the building's past remain there today. They are not threatening in any way — they just like to go about their ghostly business. Amidst the chaos of slot machines and video lottery terminals, players will sometimes hear disembodied voices. Staff will occasionally feel "something" frigid brush past them. And doors that can't be opened without a key card will mysteriously swing wide, all by themselves. This last bit of spectral mischief has apparently been caught on tape by one of the casino's many security cameras.

Some Guests Never Check Out

If you think it's tough to find a hotel that's haunted, think again. It may be harder to find a hotel that *doesn't* have a phantom or two floating around. There's a lot of living and a lot of drama that happens in hotel rooms and, the fact is, some guests never check out. Sometimes it's because they meet their end there. One hotel, north of Saskatoon, is said to feature an eerie "recording" of a terrible fight in which a man was killed. He was pushed off the hotel roof, and his screams could be heard passing each floor as he fell to his death. The incident was so horrifying that it may have resulted in a residual haunting. Rumour has it that on the eighth day of each month, the man's spectral screams can be heard — starting at the top of the hotel and ending at the ground.

Of course, not all hotels know who their eternal guests are, or how they came to be there. One lovely upscale hotel in Regina has a number of bothersome spirits who behave in an almost poltergeist-like manner. Stories from that establishment range from accounts of inexplicably swinging chandeliers and creepy noises, to tales of full-form apparitions that will vanish right in front of witnesses' eyes. In one suite, a maid was working alone when some cupboard doors suddenly flew open and their contents went sailing across the room. Apparently — for reasons such as this — there are entire floors that staff are reluctant to work on.

Most hotel ghosts are well-mannered, however. A historic hotel in Saskatoon is home to a dignified gentleman who is fond of roaming the halls and drifting up and down the stately staircases. He bothers no one and creates no problems for staff, making this fellow the ideal ghostly guest.

The same could not be said for the spirit who inhabits a small, family-operated motel in the province. There is one particular room so haunted that it is difficult to rent it out to living guests anymore. This spook likes to make up, or mess up the room, depending upon its mood. The maids will check the room after having just cleaned it and find it in a state of total disarray. Bedding will be on the floor in tangled heaps, towels will be strewn all over the bathroom, and small items like soaps will be hidden in any number of unlikely spots. Five minutes later, however, the room is likely to be completely tidy again. Because the owners can never be sure of what state the room will be in, they find it easier to simply not rent it out.

History with Mystery

The older and more historically significant a building is, the more likely it is to have a few resident wraiths. Some seem happy enough to share their one-time home or workplace with the public. Others are less enthusiastic about the parade of visitors in their space. There is a settler's home in the south of the province that has been turned into a small museum and gift shop. The original owner of the home has been dead for nearly one hundred years now, but doesn't seem to realize it. He will occasionally greet visitors on the front porch with an angry expression and a shooing gesture, suggesting that he would rather not have company.

Another historic dwelling — one of the oldest in the province — is now a designated heritage property and home to at least three or four ghosts. Volunteers are now officially discouraged from sharing supernatural stories, but this building's haunted reputation falls into the category of "worst-kept secrets." There is said to be one apparition residing in the basement of the home that is particularly unpleasant to women — tugging on their hair and their purse straps. Spirits in one of the bedrooms are friendlier. They seem to be children; their disembodied laughter can be heard while they play. And someone — no one knows who — is lurking upstairs. There are numerous reports of people on the street looking up to see a face in the second-storey window looking back at them. This happens when it is late at night, and the house is locked up, and all the staff are long gone.

Haunting Health Care

Everyone appreciates efficiency in the healthcare system. But there is a nurse in one Saskatchewan hospital who takes it to the extreme. It might be more accurate to refer to her as a "former nurse," for she's been dead for many years now. Her spirit, however, is still on the job — and working at an admirable pace. Patients have reported seeing her zip by in the halls, moving at a speed that no living healthcare professional could manage. On the rare occasion when she does slow down, she is seen to be wearing an out-of-date uniform and carrying a clipboard.

Cuban Confidential

A woman who owns and operates a small business in Regina's trendy Cathedral Village has reason to believe that she doesn't work alone. One day, when business was slow and there were no customers in the store, she decided to spend some time planning her family's vacation. She was trying to decide between two possible destinations — Cuba and the Dominican Republic — and needed to find some information. She spent some time researching online, but wasn't satisfied with the results. What she really wanted was the opinion of someone who had actually been to those places. So she sat in her empty store, thinking, *Cuba — who do I know who can tell me about Cuba?* At that moment, a radio that had been sitting silent on a shelf blared into full volume. What was being broadcast was the last portion of American president John F. Kennedy's famous speech concerning the Cuban missile crisis. When the speech ended, a cheerful piece of Spanish-flavoured music followed. Then — as suddenly as it had turned on — the radio was off again. The woman was stunned. There was no way to explain what had happened, except to say that some nearby spirit picked up on her thoughts and used the radio to communicate back to her. Unfortunately, the message itself was not as clear. Days later the woman was still wondering where to book her holiday.

Ghost Hunting on the Prairies: Calling Lakes Paranormal Investigators

Calling Lakes Paranormal Investigators

Case File Quick Facts

Name: Calling Lakes Paranormal Investigators

Date Founded: March, 2008 (but the senior members were investigating under a different name back as far as 2003)

Website: *www.darkshadowsweb.com*

Mission: To help people in need of their services, and collect evidence that may eventually lead to a scientific breakthrough regarding paranormal phenomena.

Lead Investigator: Jan Drummond

Favourite Saskatchewan Haunt: Fort San (Saskatchewan's historic tuberculosis sanatorium). The CLPI have investigated what remains of the old San extensively — more details straight ahead!

Q & A With Jan Drummond, Amy Drummond, and John Pawelko

The Calling Lakes Paranormal Investigators is a small investigation team located in Fort Qu'Appelle. In 2008, they organized and hosted Saskatchewan's first paranormal symposium, which brought together more than twenty experts in various aspects of the paranormal. There were presentations, displays, and, for me, a chance to meet with three official members of the CLPI.

Q: How large is your group?

Jan: We have four official members, and then we have guest investigators. The three of us are official members, along with Brett Warner, who is our tech specialist. Diane Ashworth is our guest psychic and investigator. And we've recently asked a psychic medium from Fort Qu'Appelle to come along with us. She isn't with us officially, yet, but I am hopeful that it will work out and that she will want to become a part of our team. She is considered to be a locator; she is very good at locating dead people.

Q: How do you decide who you will allow to come and be a guest investigator with you?

Jan: I'm of the philosophy that if someone's curious and they would like to come and try this, then, why not? I'm very open to bringing somebody because I know how hard it is if you have a huge interest in this, to try to find somebody else who wants to go on an investigation. So, if we're there, if we're doing an investigation, why not bring along other people who are interested? It makes sense.

Q: What's the difference between CLPI and other groups?

Jan: I really don't know too much about the other groups. I'm learning a little more about the SPPRC (page 101), now that we've been talking to them. But I would imagine that we're all out for the same thing. To learn whatever we can, and capture whatever we can. Right now there's no scientific reason why all this paranormal stuff happens. But, we're investigating, and these other groups are investigating, and we're [gathering] all this evidence. And, maybe at some point in time down the road, a scientist will [discover something], and then our work will help that scientist prove [his theory].

Q: So, is your primary goal to gather evidence that might lead to a scientific breakthrough?

Jan: Yes — and to help people. We don't charge anything. If somebody needs our help, I will do my best to help. If you're in a situation where you have something happening in your home, and you're frightened, and you don't understand it — it's pretty hard to live with something like that. If we can go in and alleviate some of those fears, then we're helping somebody, which is important.

Q: What kind of equipment do you use when you investigate?

Amy: Digital video cameras; digital [still] cameras; EMF meters that measure the electromagnetic field; temperature gauges, to see if the temperature drops; digital voice recorders, to see if we can catch anything in the background. We just started taking motion sensors. We've got a tech specialist now. He's a computer whiz. And he's got a program that he'll turn on, on his laptop, and he'll bring up the program and then leave it. Whatever's in the air feeds numbers into the computer, and the computer turns the numbers into words. And from there you can actually have conversations with something that's there.

Q: Do television shows about ghost hunting offer a fairly accurate picture of what an investigation is like?

Amy: I think so. *Most Haunted*, I think, is the most realistic. With *Paranormal State*, they find places that are so badly haunted — and that's great, because people need help with those. But, most of the time, those are impossible to find. In the United States, there are tons of places you can go investigate. They've got so much history down there. But we don't have that up here. So the hauntings that we go to aren't generally really, really awful hauntings.

Q: What are some of the most dramatic investigations that you've done?

Jan: I think the best one we ever had was the Kerrobert Court House. Lots of activity there. Saw lots of stuff. There's such satisfaction in seeing all this stuff, even if you can't record it. The Shaunavon Hotel was interesting. My worst one was Weyburn (page 110).

Amy: The Weyburn Mental Asylum — that was scary. Kerrobert Court House was terrifying. Shaunavon was a good investigation, but it wasn't a really powerful haunting. Fort San had its moments, but we grew up around there, so it wasn't as frightening for us.

Jan: One story that's really cool — it's on our video (*Haunted: The Ghosts of Fort San*, produced by Jan Drummond and Gwen Lowe). This lady's husband was working at the HMCS Qu'Appelle camp, in supply. He had moved ahead of her, but when she joined him, their house wasn't quite ready yet, so they had to live in [one of the buildings in the complex]. So, she was sleeping one night, when she heard the elevator. Heard the elevator doors close. And they had locked their bedroom door, but the door came open and a figure came floating in. It was a nurse in an old-fashioned uniform — a grey dress, with a white bib-front. She came over to the bed and — did it try to smother her?

Amy: Yeah, it did!

Jan: It tried to smother her, and she was trying to push this invisible force off of her. Then the nurse would turn around, float out, and the woman would hear the elevator again. This happened for three nights. And she could never wake her husband up. But, on the third night, the different thing was that after the nurse tried to smother her, she bent down, and patted her hand. Almost as if to say, "It's okay, now — you're out of your misery."

Amy: The other ironic thing is that the elevator that she heard hasn't worked in years.

Jan: The second video that we did (*Paranormal Saskatchewan: Episode 2 — The Ghost Hunters*, produced by the Calling Lakes Paranormal Researchers), we went out and interviewed a lot of the officers and the kids who stayed out there in the summers (with the Western Canadian Sea Cadet Training Program). They'd been out there, some of them, for ten years. And they started to talk about all their experiences. Wow, some of the stuff that went on out there.

Q: How many times have you investigated at Fort San?

Amy: Years. I can't even say how many times; it was years of investigating Fort San.

Q: How much energy is in that place?

Jan: Huge amounts. There's this one room in the basement, in the children's ward, we nicknamed "the mini-morgue," because that's what we think it was used for. They said it was a laundry room, but we think that if a child died — instead of leaving it on the ward where it might frighten the other kids that were sick — they would take it out and put it down in this room. It had a big steel door on it, and I don't know of any laundry room with a big steel door. Anyway, we'd be in this room and have the video camera on, and there'd be orbs coming in and going out, and flying around the room. And other things that we knew weren't orbs, because they had some substance to them. They were fairly large, and kind of odd-shaped, and they'd just go by the camera.

Amy: This is a concrete room — no windows, all walls, no bugs.

Jan: We had it happen so often that we checked to make sure that it wasn't dust. We checked all the things that somebody would use to debunk it. We tried throwing dust in the air ourselves, just to see what effect it would create. But we couldn't re-enact that.

Q: What kind of camera do you need to capture that kind of evidence?

John: I don't think it matters what kind of camera you have. If they want to be caught on camera, they'll be caught on camera. If they don't want to be, they won't. They are superior to what we are. They'll show as much as they want to show.

Q: Have you ever felt threatened by an entity at Fort San?

Amy: We had this one incident where Courtney (a guest investigator) was attacked. We were in the morgue, the lights were off, and we had a video camera set up. Later, on the video, you could see something walk by the camera just before Courtney felt these really cold hands closing around her throat. This thing was really aggressive.

Q: Back to the Kerrobert investigation. Did you find out what it is that haunts the courthouse?

Amy: We never found out what it actually was. It could have been a judge. There was a suicide in the basement.

Jan: Two of them, actually.

Amy: A human skull was kept there, as [evidence in] one of the murder cases.

Jan: I think there was a lot of anger there, a lot of murder cases tried there. A lot of people were sentenced to death there. (To Amy) That thing that you saw come up out of the floor actually did look like a judge.

Amy: That's what scared me. When we go on investigations, we'll sit in a circle and concentrate. We hold hands. Kind of because it brings up the energy a little bit more — but we're scared, so we're holding hands for comfort, too. We were sitting there and [at one point] I looked up. There were three women in front of me. And this thing came up out of the floor [behind them], arms outstretched. Its arms [spanned] all three women. And it came up like this, over top of them, and it didn't stop growing until it was probably a good eight feet tall. I think John saw it, too, and he was watching it. And that scared me, because it would not go away. It was dark, it was hooded, there were no facial features. We assumed it was a judge because of the kind of cloak it was wearing.

Jan: Amy and John have the most experiences, because they are intuitives. I'm not. I'll see the odd thing. I'll get a feeling but I won't actually see as much as they do. I wish I was a little more open, but I'm not. But [in Kerrobert], I was also seeing stuff that was happening. I was seeing little white mists like everyone else was seeing, and orbs flying around the room. And this glow came that just lit up the entire back of the courtroom. [It was coming from] the judge's chambers. All the way down the hall, it was all lit up in this fluorescent-type blue. And I'm thinking, *Okay, that can't be real, it's got to be a reflection.* And everybody's saying, "No, it's not a reflection." I was brushing it off because I couldn't believe that I was seeing it, too.

Amy: And there was the phone call! We had a phone in our room, and it rang in the middle of the night. We didn't answer it. We thought it could be someone playing a prank, or someone calling the office, for some reason. Later, [after the investigation] we walked over to use this phone. And it wasn't plugged in, it wasn't attached to the wall ... nothing. No phone jack, no plug in. So that was really cool.

Q: Do you ever think that you might be in danger?

Amy: Absolutely.
Jan: But we're pretty careful.
Amy: We're very careful to protect ourselves.
Jan: And we try not to provoke things.

Q: What measures do you take?

Jan: We'll picture ourselves in white light. Oftentimes we'll say a prayer before we start. Also, when we're done.
Amy: Depending on what's there, John and I can intuitively force something back. If it's something bad, and it's coming after us, together we can typically force it back.

Q: Do you try to inform yourself about what might be at a location before you go there?

Jan: Yes. We're working on an investigation right now — I can't say where it is, or who it is — but it's possibly demonic. So we're using outside resources to come help us because we've never dealt with a demonic situation before. The demonologist is from SPPRC. He's very knowledgeable. He's been very helpful in telling us what he knows about this stuff: How to go into a place like that. What to do. What not to do. We want to learn everything we can because we don't want to walk in there and cause the family more trouble — or have it come back with us.

Q: Are you going in with the hope that you might be able to clear the house?

Jan: No, we won't be able to clear it. But we'll go in and get evidence because, if it is demonic, it will have to be exorcized. Clergy will have to do that. But we have to have documentation to show the clergy before they'll even go in and do it.

Amy: And if it is just a very, very angry spirit, then we need to bring in an experienced psychic that knows how to [guide it] to the other side. But we have to go in and investigate and get all the proof before we can ask someone to come in and do something.

Q: What about cases where you don't find anything? You have to assume, as investigators, that you're not always going to experience something. Sometimes, your job may be to disprove the rumours.

Jan: Beckavar Church was like that. We went out there and sat in the church for a long time. It was a very, very windy night, so we knew it was the wind that was making most of the racket. John and Amy didn't pick up on anything, and they almost always do. But they didn't sense anything. John thinks it's because they moved the church. The church was originally back about ten or fifteen feet. [But it was moved, for some reason.] John thinks that, because they moved it, whatever was in that haunted space is still in *that* haunted space, but not in the church anymore.

Q: In terms of evidence, do you look for something tangible, or will you count experiences or anecdotal information?

Amy: We only count experiences within the group. To other people, that doesn't matter. They'll say, "I didn't experience it — so prove it."

Jan: We have photos from Fort San that are so full of orbs. They're one on top of the other. Layers, all the way down to the floor. Just covered. We have a full manifestation of a ghost from out there. We have some ectoplasm that we got on video. We have ectoplasm on pictures, too.

Q: What are the different kinds of hauntings?

Jan: Some are conscious and want to be there. They are there for a specific reason and they can come and go at will. That's a spirit. A ghost, although it's an energy of somebody, I think it's more of an imprint than an actual energy. It's actually reliving something over and over and over. It has no choice in what it does. But a spirit has consciousness. It can choose [what it does]. And it can communicate.

Amy: Some are scared to move on for whatever reason.

Jan: Some are afraid to go to hell because they did something bad in this life. And they think God won't accept them. So they're trapped here.

Amy: Or they're scared that a loved one on the other side is going to be upset with them. So those spirits are trapped, but they've trapped themselves.

Jan: Also, when a traumatic event happens, it's like the walls of a building take a picture. It's as if it's imprinted. And then, years later, it starts to re-enact itself. And the more energy there is in an event, the more powerful the imprint will be. Oftentimes, when we walk into a place, they may not necessarily be picking up on a spirit, but they may be picking up on an imprint.

The Calling Lakes Paranormal Investigators (left to right): Brett Warner, tech specialist/investigator; Diane Ashworth, psychic/investigator; Jan Drummond, founder/lead investigator; John Pawelko, investigator; and (front) Amy Drummond, investigator.

Q: Are you able to sum up your philosophy about the paranormal?

Jan: We have a slogan, "To the believer, no proof is necessary; to the skeptic, no proof is possible." That says it all.

2
Haunted Houses

Abernethy

In the summer of 2007, feature-film directors Oxide and Danny Pang released a supernatural thriller called *The Messengers*. The story was set on a sunflower farm in North Dakota but, in fact, the movie was shot in southern Saskatchewan. Shooting took place in the Qu'Appelle Valley, just south of the little town of Abernethy. The Pang brothers probably didn't know it, but they filmed their disturbing haunted house story only a few kilometres from a community that is darkly rich in murderous legends and ghost lore of its own.

Mark Lesperance grew up there. He knows.

"Strange stuff happens in that town all the time," he said.

There are those who say that it always has.

Abernethy is not big in numbers — the last census counted fewer than two hundred residents — but, according to Mark and his friend Amy Drummond of the Calling Lakes Paranormal Investigators (page 57), what the town lacks in population, it makes up for in drama. Mark and Amy have collected stories from the locals for many years.

"I've been told about three or four houses in the area where entire families were killed," said Amy. "These things happened decades ago, so we can't find newspaper stories in the archives or anything. We can't confirm the facts. But my [source] will always say 'I've grown up in this area. I've lived here my whole life and I'll tell you, it's a fact.'"

And, according to many, though there may not be documentation that can confirm these violent events, there is the intangible proof of restless spirits that have been left behind. Abernethy is well known for at least two decrepit, abandoned, and very haunted houses. Mark shared the story of a disturbing experience he had in one of them.

"There's this little house, just outside of Abernethy," he said. "It's been abandoned for about sixty years now. We went out there one time — about eleven o'clock at night. We decided we were going to play Ouija in one of the old rooms."

Mark and his friends didn't do this on a whim. They had actually built their board and planchette according to obscure occult theory, making one piece at a time, working only on full moons. The project had taken them months to complete — so they were understandably disappointed when it didn't seem to work.

"Nothing was happening," said Mark. "We were sitting there, talking. Kept asking, 'Ouija, are there any spirits in the house?' Nothing. Eventually, we asked 'Ouija, do you want to play?' All of a sudden, it went to Yes."

Everyone in the group felt a tingle of excitement combined with the creeping sensation of gooseflesh. It seemed to be working. They appeared to have made contact. They all agreed to take their hands off the planchette to test the powers of the board further.

"We all took our hands off and asked, 'Ouija, is there anything in this house?' It moved again to Yes."

The group was stunned to see the planchette move on its own. But before they could think of another question to ask, something even more dramatic happened.

"All of a sudden," said Mark, "I don't know what happened but the board just flipped up and flew across the room. It slammed into the wall. It was pretty scary. We just ran out of there and left."

That's one haunted Abernethy house, and it makes for a nice warm-up, in terms of storytelling. But there's another house that qualifies as more of a "main event." It also lurks on the outskirts of town, just off the highway between Abernethy and Lemberg. It's a two-storey stone building, a virtual ruin now, which sits in the midst of a copse of trees surrounded by fields. The house is ancient by local standards. No one knows exactly how long it has stood there, but many can confirm that it's been abandoned for at least half a century. Half a century before *that*, however, it was probably a beautiful home.

A beautiful home where — according to folklore — ugly things happened.

It is said that a family lived there in the early 1900s. There was a husband, a wife, and their two young children. There was also a hired hand on the property — a drifter who was young enough and handsome enough to charm the farmer's wife into bed. Their affair went on for some time, but eventually the woman chose to end it. The hired man was livid, and unwilling to accept her rejection. He stormed off the land one day, only to return with a loaded rifle. He kicked in the door of the house and took aim at the farmer, who was sitting at the table with his lunch before him. One shot, and the farmer's throat opened up in a spray of red. His wife screamed and ran from the room. When she was halfway up the stairs, her lover sent a bullet into the base of her spine. Before she rolled all the way back to the bottom, he put another in her skull.

Then there were just the children.

The hired man called their names. He spoke calmly, amiably; he used his voice as if it was any ordinary day and he was talking about ordinary business. The children had heard the shots, however. They had heard their mother scream. And they had locked the door of their upstairs bedroom and pushed a heavy chest in front of it. It would only buy them minutes, but they hoped that might be enough. The bedroom window opened over the roof of the porch, and there was a drainpipe next to it that was easy enough to shimmy down.

The hired man kicked at the door. The frame shook with each blow, and the trunk scraped an inch or so across the floor.

Go now!

The girl dropped out the window and made her way toward the drainpipe. The boy had to wait. He knew the porch roof wouldn't hold them both; it had to be one at a time.

There was another hammering blow to the door. And another.

And then the sound of splintering wood as the boy was pushing himself over the window sill. *Not so fast* someone said, and then he was being grabbed by his trousers and pulled back into the room. A second

Courtesy of the Calling Lakes Paranormal Investigators.

An eerie black mist emerges from the walls of a deserted Abernethy house.

later the rifle roared, and the boy stopped struggling.

The hired man looked around the room. He called the girl's name. Then he stepped over the lifeless body of the boy and peered out the window. He smiled. He could see her in the distance — braids tossing back and forth as she ran across the field. It was a big piece of land she was attempting to cross. There was nothing but fields and more fields. The hired man put his rifle on his shoulder and began to whistle as he walked out of the room.

In the end, he only needed five minutes to overtake her.

"The guy that killed them is actually buried outside of Abernethy cemetery," said Mark. "It's an unmarked grave — just on the edge."

That's the story of the murders said to have taken place in that house. All other stories are about the ghosts who were left behind, and about the strange things that have happened in that haunted, abandoned place. John Pawelko, another member of the Calling Lakes Paranormal Investigators, remembers partying in that old house back in the 1960s.

"The thing about that place," said John, "was that we'd take the furniture and move it around. Then we'd go back later and everything would be back in its original position. There was actually a woman from Abernethy who was looking around the house and took one piece of furniture home with her. It was a dresser." According to John, the woman hauled the dresser back to town, cleaned it up, and filled it with her own things. But the next morning she awoke to find her clothing spilled all over the floor. The dresser was nowhere to be found. "She went back out to the house," said John, "and it was back there. So she dragged all the furniture outside and she burned it."

Many local people had heard the tales of moving furniture. Others had heard eerie noises coming from the house. There were stories of strange lights, and stories of whispering voices. All in all, there was more than enough anecdotal evidence to tempt the Calling Lakes Paranormal Investigators to conduct a formal investigation of the house. It turned out to be one of the most active hauntings they've ever looked into.

The ghosts began to show themselves not long after the group got set up. One investigator was in the attic when he witnessed something happening on the floor below.

"There are holes all over the attic floor," explained Amy. "He was looking down through one of them, and he saw a black shadow walk from one end of a room to the other. So he called down to us, 'Who's in that room? I just saw someone....' But none of us were in there."

At approximately the same time, Amy and John were on the second floor of the house, following another apparition. They both witnessed a man in a black and red checkered shirt moving silently from room to room. Not long after that, Jan Drummond, the group's lead investigator, had an experience of her own on the main floor.

"When we were filming in the house," said Jan, "I heard someone say *baby* really loud. John and this other fellow were the only ones in the room with me, and I asked them, 'Who said *baby*?' They just kind of looked at me. They said, 'Nobody said *baby*. Why would we say *baby*?' But somebody said it, and they said it quite loud. I was the only one that heard it."

Interestingly, the next apparition to be seen *was* a baby — of sorts. One of the investigators was in a downstairs room when she heard an odd scratching sound. She turned around, looking for the source of the noise. What she saw was a human infant, crawling face down on the floor, with all four limbs positioned like reptile legs, sticking out at ninety degrees from its body. The baby-thing skittered across the dusty floor in a stuttering, jerky motion. The sight of it was so disturbing that the investigator felt her stomach churn.

"It scared me so much that I actually walked outside and threw up," she said.

And the night was far from over.

Activity continued throughout the investigation, and much of it was caught by digital cameras. At one point, Amy Drummond detected a black shape following her around the room. She started taking pictures of it.

"What showed up in the pictures is a black shadow leaking out of the walls," said Amy. The photos show the misty apparition growing, shrinking, and moving around the room. In no way could it be mistaken for an actual shadow. Other spirits, or energies, showed up in the form of spectacular coloured orbs.

"At Abernethy, we caught some really unique orbs," said Jan. "We had some big beautiful red orbs. And as they moved upward, they changed from red to pink."

"And coloured orbs are so hard to get," added Amy. "But any abandoned house we go out to in Abernethy — and we've gone to two or three — we get huge bright red orbs."

Usually, orbs will only show up in photographs. But on that night, they were visible to at least one person. John was the last investigator to leave the site. As he pulled onto the highway, he happened to look back at the house.

"There was all kinds of activity going on," he said. "There were lights coming out of the window ... they'd go all around the house ... then go back in the window. One left the house and started moving right toward me. But I was gone! We went home too soon, I think."

Perhaps. Or perhaps the investigators left just in time. Either way, it seems that there is no shortage of paranormal phenomena to investigate in that particular Saskatchewan town. At least, that's Mark Lesperance's opinion.

"Sometimes, just walking down Main Street, the street lights will go out as you walk under them," he said. "Just all of a sudden, *pfft.*" He shook his head and sighed. "And you're wondering, *Should I run?*"

There's probably no need to run — but do keep your eyes open and your camera handy when you're in the town of Abernethy.

John Pawelko and guest investigators leaving a haunted house near Abernethy.

Courtesy of the Calling Lakes Paranormal Investigators.

The Holbein Horror

Josephine Phillip grew up in the small village of Holbein, a short distance west of Prince Albert. For most of her life, she has been sensitive, often able to see spirits, and often able to predict events that she could not possibly have known about. As it is with many people who have such gifts, Josephine has always remembered the exact circumstances of her first encounter with the supernatural.

"I was seven years old," Josephine explained. "I was in the dining room, standing by my mother [while] my father, his sister, and my cousin were sitting at the table playing with a Ouija board. Thinking it was harmless, they were having a good laugh with a glass of wine and a cigarette, all asking ridiculous questions."

The adults may have considered this a harmless pastime, but Josephine would be the first in the family to learn that it was not. As the little girl watched them play, she suddenly felt a cold breeze brush past her face. Instinctively, she knew what had just happened, and she turned to her mother. "Something bad has just entered the house," she said. Josephine remembered her mother's eyes growing very wide for a moment, but she simply told Josephine to leave the room and go to bed. The girl did as she was told, but could hear the adults playing Ouija into the early morning hours.

It would be mere days before the family realized what they had invited into their home.

It would be years before they could banish it.

Two days after the Ouija board incident, Josephine had the first of what would be innumerable strange experiences. She saw a man whom she thought was her father, talking to a woman whom she didn't recognize. The woman was wearing a black dress and had long dark hair. Josephine was curious about the stranger and decided to eavesdrop on the conversation.

"She said she was leaving to go outside to do some work, and he said that he was going to go for a walk," said Josephine. "I remember thinking how strange that was, because my father would rather drive than walk." The following morning, Josephine was still curious about this, so she asked her father about the conversation. "I asked my dad who the lady was … and where he went." Josephine's father gave her an odd look and informed her that no one had come by to visit, and that he certainly had not taken an uncharacteristic walk. When the little girl insisted that she had overheard these things, and had seen a stranger in the house, she was dismissed as having "too active an imagination." Josephine found her father's reaction so discouraging, she vowed never to mention what she had witnessed to anyone else.

That is, until other people started seeing the same thing.

"The old man was seen walking in the driveway, only to disappear in the lilac bushes," said Josephine. "The woman was seen walking on the hill beside the house, but would fade away when she was spotted." Eventually, Josephine realized that she had initially mistaken the male spirit for her father. The two were of a similar build, and Josephine suffered from poor eyesight that kept her from distinguishing between them. Josephine had been the first to see two of the spirits who were destined to haunt her home for as long as the building stood. And they seemed benign enough.

"They were spirits I could handle," said Josephine. "It was the next one that would change my views and bring me to a realization that not all spirits are good."

The next one — the entity that would terrorize Josephine's family for years to come — made itself known within the week.

It was the middle of a dark night that Josephine still recalls as one of the most horrifying encounters of her life. The little girl was pulled from a deep sleep by the sound of raspy breathing and the presence of a bright, hot, orange light that filled her bedroom. Her skin burned and buzzed, as if electricity was coursing through her body, and she was initially paralyzed with fear. Finally, that same terror forced Josephine into action.

"My instinct was to wake someone up," she said. "My sister shared the room with me, and I tried to wake her up." Josephine found that she couldn't rouse her sister, however, even when she resorted to pinching and slapping. So she ran to her parents' room and tried to wake them. Again, despite Josephine's best efforts, her parents didn't stir. She ran to her brother's room and found that he, too, was in an impossibly deep sleep. "Even the family dog wouldn't wake," recalled Josephine. It was a desperate, nightmarish experience and, through it all, the malevolent, scorching presence followed her.

"The light was so bright and hot that I was sweating," said Josephine, "but [the perspiration] would evaporate from the heat almost as soon as it would surface on my skin. I jumped back into my bed and covered my head with my bedspread, but the light was so bright that I could see clearly under the covers." As Josephine lay there, suffocating and terrified, the entity gave her a message.

"It said that it was going to kill my family and it was going to start with me."

Incredibly, in the face of such a monstrous threat, the little girl felt her fear transform into a sense of grim resolution.

"I decided that it wasn't going to kill me, and that I was going to protect my family," said Josephine. She immediately reached for the one weapon that was at her disposal — her small, well-thumbed copy of the New Testament. In the oppressive glow of the searing orange light, she began to read beneath the covers. The relief brought to Josephine by her strong faith was almost immediate. "Coolness washed over my body," she said, "and I fell into a peaceful sleep." The orange light was still pulsing in the room when Josephine awoke several hours later, and the entity would visit her for many consecutive nights. She hadn't managed to banish the demonic presence, but reading from the Bible kept her safe that night.

Unfortunately, there were many, many other nights for Josephine to survive. And the brave seven-year-old was forced to live through them on her own, for it was six months before the evil entity chose to make itself known to the rest of the family.

"My sister was the next one it appeared to," said Josephine. Interestingly, the entity presented itself to Josephine's sister in a slightly altered form. She saw it as a cowboy, with eerily glowing green eyes. Whenever the girl saw him, she experienced the coppery taste of blood in her mouth, and an emotion that could only be described as raw hatred. The entity could also present itself as a very young girl, who was often seen playing with the television set, turning it on and off. Occasionally, in the little girl form, the being would appear standing at the side of Josephine's bed. And it was in this form that the spirit finally convinced Josephine's father of its existence.

"My father didn't believe us until he had an encounter he couldn't dismiss," said Josephine. "The spirit appeared to him as the little girl. Thinking it was my sister, he told it to go to bed. It looked at him and disappeared."

The apparition of the little girl had none of the innocent facade that one would expect to see in such a form. Josephine remembers it having the same glowing green eyes as the cowboy, and a dry laugh that would chill anyone who heard it. And it liked to make noise.

"This spirit liked to play with the dishes," said Josephine. "We would hear them rattle. We would also hear the thudding of cowboy boots that would pace back and forth from the dining room to the living room and back again. There was many a night that we thought it was my brother who, when excited, would run back and forth between rooms." Whenever the family went to scold the little boy, however, they would find him tucked in his bed, fast asleep. There was never any rational explanation for the noises that could be found.

Of course, not everyone believed that. Josephine's family had talked to a number of people about the disturbing things that happened in their home. Almost without exception, they were met with outright disbelief.

"People in [Holbein] believed that we were crazy for saying such things," she recalled. "They said we should stop watching TV." Josephine's mother's family were among the skeptics, but at least one of them — a cousin — eventually changed his mind. "He stayed over one night and heard the dishes rattle and the running in the living room and dining room," said Josephine. She added, "He never stayed over again."

The paranormal activity in the house continued to escalate. One night, the running and stomping noises were so loud that they woke both the girls. Josephine's sister ran to the safety of their parents' bedroom, leaving Josephine alone. The entity must have sensed her vulnerability, for it crept into her bedroom, manifesting in a humanoid form beside the bed.

"I felt it place its hands on me," said Josephine. "[The touch] seemed to go through the bedding and scorch my skin. I remember saying that it was not going to win me over, and to leave my family alone."

But the entity would not be that easily dissuaded. Night after night, it would enter Josephine's room and touch her body. The touching was never hard enough to hurt or leave marks, but it would always wake her. Then, one night, Josephine woke to the familiar feeling of being handled, but the atmosphere was even more sinister than usual.

"I could hear the breathing again, but it was different," said Josephine. "[Instead of the orange light], blackness was all around me. I could feel hands all over me ... then [the creature] said that it was going to take me with it. I remember saying that it wasn't going to take me anywhere, and I physically struggled to get away." No matter how hard she fought, however, Josephine remained trapped by the iron grip of the hands. Finally, she prayed to God for help and was eventually released. Her faith was powerful, even if her body held no more strength than that of any other twelve-year-old girl.

Josephine, at twelve years old, had been battling this evil presence for five years of her young life, and her family realized that it was time to banish the thing once and for all. They decided to have the house blessed.

"We, as a family, prayed against the spirit that lingered," said Josephine. "It was angry when we prayed and did all that it could to distract us, including slapping me and touching the others. It took about three hours of us praying for the noise to settle and the house to finally feel at peace. We used holy water to bless all entryways and we were not bothered by that spirit again."

The unholy entity was finally gone. It is interesting to note, however, that the religious cleansing ritual did nothing to disturb the other two spirits who were so benign in nature. Josephine reports that the woman with the long dark hair and the older gentleman were seen there by many different witnesses until the house was torn down several years ago. These gentle ghosts must have known that since they did no harm, they were welcome to stay. The horrifying presence that attempted to injure Josephine and even steal her away, however, knew that it was being forced to leave. Whatever it was, demon or angry spirit, it did not return after the blessing.

Of course, no one in the family was ever again careless enough to open the door between worlds with a seemingly harmless Ouija board session, either.

Aaron's Apparition

"I lived in a haunted house on 13th Street West, in Prince Albert," said Aaron. "I've seen the (St. Louis) ghost train and a haunted church by Prince Albert, but I have never seen or heard anything scarier than that house."

A bold claim? Perhaps. But anyone who has heard Aaron's story tends to agree with him. This nondescript residence was haunted by a spirit — or spirits — so active, many other ghost stories pale in comparison.

The house in question was a two-storey family home that Aaron shared with his aunt, uncle, and his young cousins. Any house with children tends to be noisy, and this one was exceptionally so. The frightening thing was that the ruckus could rarely be blamed on the kids.

"We would hear kids running around upstairs," said Aaron, "when my cousins were all in the living room, watching TV." If that had been the extent of the ghostly antics, it might have been tolerable. But there was much more. And there was much worse. Frequently, the family would listen to the sounds of children screaming and crying. They would follow the horrific cries and try to determine where they were coming from, but the source of the noise seemed impossible to pinpoint. According to Aaron, "it seemed to be coming from inside the walls." Every time this happened, Aaron's cousins were present and accounted for, so the family knew for certain that it wasn't the children who were making the awful noise.

Aaron's family was not alone in witnessing this particular phenomenon. On several occasions, his aunt and uncle had guests in the house who were made clearly uncomfortable by the distressing sounds. More than once, a visiting friend or family member voiced their concerns, asking if the children were all right. Aaron's aunt and uncle would assure them that all was fine — and then they would point to the living room, where every one of the kids would invariably be contentedly engaged in some quiet activity. From somewhere deep within the walls there would come another spectral scream and the children, who had grown quite accustomed to the noise, would show no signs of even noticing.

The youngsters may have been used to the ghost in their home, but that is not to say that they were unaffected by it. Aaron recalled that house being a tricky place in which to play the usual childhood games.

"My little cousin would be running through the house and he would fall, as if someone pushed him over sideways," Aaron remembered. The assailant was absolutely invisible to Aaron. Whether or not the little boy saw his attacker is another question, entirely. Young children are often able to see things that aren't apparent to adults, and the children showed some awareness of whatever presence roamed through their home. Aaron recalled another of his cousins having an earnest conversation with someone in her bedroom when, as far as the adults could see, "no one was there."

The children weren't the only ones who were targeted by the ghost, however. Everyone in the house experienced unsettling and unexplainable occurrences, ranging from the mundane to the truly disturbing. Lights would flip on and off of their own volition. Strange sounds were heard by all. And on some rare and memorable occasions, things in the house would move. Aaron spoke of one particular time when his aunt left the kitchen to go upstairs to grab a basket of laundry.

"When she came back down," he said, "all the kitchen cupboard doors were open." No more than a minute would have passed, and there was no one else near the kitchen who could have done it.

Another incident that the entire family remembered involved a bible that had sat undisturbed on a shelf in the laundry room for all the years that they had lived in the house.

"All of a sudden, one day, it was moved," Aaron said. "It was turned upside down." Theoretically, anyone might have done that. But the interesting thing was that while the book had been moved, not a speck of the thick dust that covered it had been disturbed. "There were no fingerprints to show that it had been moved by someone," said Aaron.

It's interesting to note that the majority of the spectral shenanigans took place in either the basement or on the second floor of the house. The family felt "watched" by an invisible presence whenever they worked in the laundry room. They felt the same eyes upon them when they were upstairs. Then, one morning that Aaron will never forget, he felt *more* than eyes upon his person.

"I was trying to sleep one morning when someone grabbed my arm and pulled it slowly," he said. Aaron ignored the prankster, pulled his arm back, and tried his best to go back to sleep. Whoever it was, however, wasn't about to let him do that. Aaron felt his arm being pulled a second time, but this time, much more forcefully. Aaron thought it was his uncle, and didn't bother to open his eyes. "I said 'go away,' and I pulled my arm back again," he told me. "But this time, when I pulled my arm, it held on real tight and yanked me just about off the bed."

Aaron opened his eyes and saw the shadowy shape of a person looming over his bed. Terrified, his first instinct was to pull the blankets over his head. A moment later, when he dared to look again, his bedroom was empty.

"No one could have run out of the room that fast," Aaron said. "And if they had, I would have heard them." Aaron was certain that he had just seen the apparition of the ghost that haunted his family.

Today, Aaron no longer recalls the exact address, but every other detail about the house remains firmly rooted in his memory. "I could walk down there and find it," he says, and there is little doubt that he could. With all of the strange experiences that he had there, he will likely never forget the haunted house on 13th Street West.

The Screaming House

There are many historic fieldstone houses dotting Saskatchewan's pristine rural landscape. That's interesting, considering the relative scarcity of stone on the prairies. The fact that the settlers were willing to scour the fields, the coulees, and the creek beds in search of it speaks to their love of stone as a building material, and their high regard for its beauty, durability, and permanence. Indeed, many of these buildings stand today, when their wooden counterparts have long since rotted into the earth.

One fieldstone structure that is of particular interest to ghost-story aficionados is known as "The Screaming House." It sits beside the railroad tracks, just two kilometres east of Indian Head, on the Trans Canada Highway. This small, two-storey house was abandoned long ago. Today, it sits empty and forgotten, serving only as a point of interest to those who might marvel at the colourful split stone, or wonder about the curious fact that the windows on one side of the home have been filled in, their frames packed solidly with more stone and mortar. As it happens, there is a story about those mysterious blocked windows. It goes like this:

Long ago, in the late 1800s, a couple with a young family lived in this little farmhouse. By some accounts, they had two young children, by others, only one child. What is consistent in the story is that one youngster, no more than three or four years of age, was playing outside early one evening as a train approached. The mother heard the wailing of the whistle and the rumble of the massive engine and thought she should check on her little one. She looked out a window in time to witness her child toddling along the tracks just before the train struck him down. Understandably, the woman was devastated. Every time she looked out a window that faced the train tracks, she imagined the horrific accident all over again. Finally, in an attempt to maintain her fragile sanity, the woman's husband filled in both windows that faced the tracks. He reasoned that as long as she was inside her home, his wife would never have to look at the scene of their son's death again.

But, according to legend, the woman never recovered from the shock and could never forget her tragedy — even in death. It is said that even today, if you happen to be in the house at sunset as a train rumbles by, you will hear her anguished screams. Another version of the story says that on gloomy nights you can witness the shadowy spectres of two young children playing near the tracks. Yet another claims that the spiritual energy is so powerful in that location that it is impossible to coax a dog, or any animal, into what remains of the house.

It is common for there to be different versions of this type of ghostly legend. But the real question is not which version of the story is true but, rather, is there any truth to any of them? Is there anything paranormal about

This abandoned fieldstone house near Indian Head is the subject of many ghostly legends.

the so-called "Screaming House," or is this simply a classic case of a folk tale, custom-designed to suit an odd structural detail of the house?

Well — that depends upon whom you ask.

Chris Oxtoby, who writes the blog "Prairie Specters" (see page 183), investigated the house in June of 2008. In the entry he wrote following the visit, he claimed that he "felt nothing," and found nothing more interesting than a small squatter's pad on the second floor. "I wonder," he wrote, "if I returned in the evening, if the farmhouse [would] take on a different feel?"

According to Ed Desfosses, it might. Ed grew up in Sintaluta, a few kilometres down the highway from the Indian Head house. He's known of the place all his life.

"I've heard lots of stories about it," he said. "I've heard they've had psychics in there who've felt the presence of ghosts. They say you can see [the spirits of] the woman's kids." Despite being so familiar with the stories, however, Ed was always reluctant to believe them.

"I've never seen them myself," Ed said. "If I see something … then, okay, I can believe it. If [not], then, okay, it's just talk."

One evening, several years ago, Ed and a few of his friends decided to take a look around the little stone farmhouse and see if there was anything to the "talk." They went into the building with nothing but flashlights and a sense of bravado. They came out with a story to tell.

"There were about five or six of us," Ed remembered. "We went into the house with two flashlights. We walked around the main floor, looked around. The flashlights were fine. We went upstairs, looked around. The flashlights were fine. Then we went down to the basement and suddenly the flashlights quit. *Both* of them."

Luckily, Ed and his friends were carrying lighters. They took them out and used their flames to illuminate the darkness while they fiddled with the flashlights in an attempt to fix them. Nothing seemed to work, however. Eventually, the group gave up. They realized the dangers of stumbling around an ancient basement with nothing but a flickering lighter flame to shed light on the potential dangers. Carefully, they felt their way back up the darkened staircase. Once upstairs, they walked straight outside. The second they did so …

Photo by Andrea Oxtoby.

Beyond the weathered door waits darkness, decay, and, perhaps, a tormented spirit.

"The flashlights came back on," said Ed. The very minute that the group left the house, the lights came back, steady and strong, and at exactly the same moment. "Basically," said Ed, "we didn't go back in. We left."

A creepy coincidence? Or something more? Even a level-headed skeptic like Ed Desfosses seems tempted to say that there is something paranormal going on in this picturesque shell of a home. And there are many who agree. In fact, some theorists believe that the very material the house is made of may have contributed to its haunted status.

Paranormal researchers tend to classify most hauntings as being either intelligent — meaning that the ghost is aware of its surroundings and reacts accordingly — or residual — where an event is replayed over and over, like a recording. Residual hauntings are theoretically created by either the repetition of a mundane action or by a single event of great emotional intensity. The house near Indian Head would seem to fall into the latter category. If the story of the woman witnessing her child's death on the train tracks is indeed true, it is no wonder that her profound shock created an impression that could replay, like a recording, more than a century after the fact. And — according to my correspondence with paranormal writer, researcher, and lecturer W. Ritchie Benedict — the very material that her house was made of might have been the perfect recording device.

"It would largely depend on the physical composition of the object or building, how efficient a storage device it would be," wrote Benedict. He added, "It seems logical that stone buildings that contain traces of quartz or feldspar would be most conducive to such recording."

So, a woman witnesses the grisly death of her child. Her horror is literally recorded in the fieldstone walls of her home. And, for years to come, when certain elements — time of day, approaching train, weather conditions — combine to "push the play button," as it were, a recording of the accident is replayed. It is a theory that has long been applied to European castles, with their man-made mountains of stonework and countless spectres.

"Imagine," Benedict wrote, "if we could develop a device that could "read" sounds and images recorded in old objects and buildings."

His musing brings to mind the age-old saying, "If only walls could talk."

Perhaps — in such cases as "The Screaming House" near Indian Head — they both can, and do.

One of the Family

It is often said that children are more aware of the spirit world than adults. The theory is that young people who have yet to form ideas about what is and is not possible are more open and sensitive. But, in some cases, there may be other factors at work. In this particular story — submitted to a fellow author by a woman I'll identify only as "Patricia" — the children may have been the first to know the ghost because they simply had more in common with him than the adults in the house did.

In 1990, Patricia and her mother moved into a house on Dufferin Avenue, in Moose Jaw. They lived there for three years without noticing much out of the ordinary. There was the occasional strange occurrence — but it was always something that could be easily explained away.

"My bedroom was always really cold, and I didn't like sleeping in it." This was one example that Patricia offered. But it's not unusual for a house to have a room that is poorly insulated or, perhaps, has a blocked heat register. Patricia also mentioned that items placed on top of the TV cabinet in the living room would always end up on the floor. Though that's a little stranger, they might have blamed a drafty window, or the tilt of the floor. At any rate, they never considered the Dufferin Avenue house to be haunted.

In 1993, Patricia and her mother moved to another home — but they stayed connected to the house on Dufferin Avenue. Patricia's sister, brother-in-law, and their two young children moved in. Patricia was a frequent guest as she helped her sister around the house and spent time with her niece and nephew.

The truth was, Patricia spent almost as much time at the house as she had when she lived there. And she could tell that the place was noticeably changed. "When me and my mom left, we left all our furniture with my sister," wrote Patricia, "including the TV cabinet." The cabinet still sat in the living room, still in front of the picture window, and it still seemed to resist having anything set on top of it. The difference, once Patricia's sister's family moved in, was that objects would literally fly off the top of the cabinet, right before their eyes. The bedroom that had once been Patricia's now belonged to the children, and it was still very cold, no matter what the outside temperature was. But other, stranger things had also begun to happen in that room.

"One day, my sister cleaned up the room, picked up all the toys, and put the clothes in the closet," Patricia recalled. The young mother then went to check on her children in the living room. She had gone no more than a few steps when she heard a strange noise come from the bedroom that she had just been in. According to Patricia, "She turned around to see that all the toys and clothes were back on the floor." Had this been a one-time occurrence, it would have been frustrating enough. But, after that, the same thing happened every single time Patricia's sister cleaned that room.

Patricia also remembered how frequently her young niece would sit in the middle of the living room floor and babble for hours on end. If anyone asked her who she was talking to, the answer was always the same. "Paulo," she would say, very clearly. One time the little girl was playing with a teddy bear and having her usual conversation with "Paulo" when, suddenly, she began to cry. Patricia's sister went to her to see what was the matter, and found the child's finger was bleeding. She asked her daughter what happened, and was told, "Paulo bite."

"After that," wrote Patricia, "my sister started paying close attention to what was happening in the house." She kept track of inexplicable events and kept her eyes and ears open, hoping to find some clue as to the ghost's identity. Finally, as she sat up late one night watching television, her attentiveness was rewarded. Patricia's sister caught sight of a shadowy figure in the hallway. It appeared to be a little boy, no more than seven or eight years of age. Knowing this made her feel better. She felt that since she now knew *what* she was dealing with, she could figure out *how* to deal with it.

"Since the ghost was a child, she started treating him like one of her own," wrote Patricia. After cleaning the children's bedroom, she would announce, "If you mess this up again, you're going to go to 'time out.'" Her approach seemed effective, for the bedroom stayed tidy. It wasn't all about discipline, however. When Patricia's sister would tuck her own children into bed at night, she would also tell Paulo that it was time to rest, and call him over to give her hugs and kisses. She would then feel a cold touch to her cheek, and an icy embrace. These may have been unusual routines, but the house remained peaceful and orderly.

Occasionally, Paulo would try to speak to the adults in the house. Patricia once heard her name whispered by a disembodied voice, as did a friend of hers. And if she had any doubts about Paulo's existence, they were swept away one evening when her sister invited the little spirit to give kisses and hugs "to Aunt Patti, too."

"The next thing I knew," remembered Patricia, "I was getting a really cold kiss and hug. It really felt like a kiss on the cheek and a hug, but it was [extremely] cold."

Patricia's sister's family lived in the house for two years before eventually moving to Medicine Hat. When it came time to leave, her sister was extremely upset. She was disappointed that she had never learned who Paulo was, or what had happened to him, and she was devastated that she couldn't take the little spirit with her.

"She now thought of him as her own son," wrote Patricia.

The family hopes that Paulo has since found someone else to play with in the little house on Dufferin Avenue.

Two Houses — Countless Ghosts

It's been a long interview, an interesting one, and the man I'm speaking with has been completely open about his numerous paranormal experiences. Yet, when I ask him whether he would prefer that I use his real name or a pseudonym, I sense instant hesitation.

"Maybe use something else," he suggests. "I used to talk about this stuff a lot. People tend to look at you weird and think you're nuts."

He should know. He's had plenty of ghost stories to talk about over the years. "Daniel," as we will call him, has lived in not one, but two haunted houses in Regina. The first was in Churchill Downs, two blocks west of Winnipeg Street.

"It was a tiny little house," said Daniel, "probably no more than six hundred square feet. You could tell that the original portion of the house had been added on to. The front was extended about six feet. And then there was a dining room put on the back. Behind that, the kitchen was added at some point, and then off to the side of that, a porch was added. And the basement — after the house was built, the basement was dug out by hand."

This jigsaw puzzle of a house had many other curious features as well. There was a pair of cisterns in the basement, along with an old coal furnace. There were a pair of wells in the backyard — one an open pit, and the other covered by a pump. Daniel also remembers there being a chicken coop and a pigpen in the backyard, harkening back to days when the area was perhaps less populated by humans than by livestock. Daniel's parents had researched city records showing that the house dated back to at least 1903 — perhaps earlier — and there was plenty of evidence of that long history. Not only in the odd assortment of fixtures and outbuildings, but in the ghosts.

"When we were kids, I remember a lot of things," said Daniel. "I'd see people in the house that I didn't recognize. I'd see these strange shapes and shadows and see things move and odd things would happen. The house would get really hot, and when somebody checked the thermostat it would be flipped all the way over, as high as it could go. Doors would open and close and lights would turn on and off when nobody touched them. That kind of thing."

"That kind of thing" happened so often that the occurrences became almost routine to Daniel, his younger brother, and his parents. Daniel's friends, however, could never quite get used to it. Living in a haunted house was a bit limiting for a boy who wanted his buddies to come over to play.

"These friends of mine that used to come over, quite often they'd see this fellow walk through the yard or through the house. It was a guy in overalls with a straw hat. One time, a friend came over and we were about to go into the house, when he suddenly just froze. I turned and looked into the dining room and caught a glimpse of this person walking toward the living room — this character in the overalls. At that point, I was pretty scared, too. I said, 'I don't care, we'll go somewhere else for the afternoon.'"

Daniel's father had built a couple of bedrooms in the basement for his sons. On one occasion, Daniel remembers being downstairs in his bedroom playing table hockey with another boy. The bedroom door was open, and Daniel had his back to it. His friend, on the other side of the game table, was facing the door. In the middle of the game, Daniel noticed that his friend had suddenly stopped playing.

"He just froze, and went white as a ghost," remembered Daniel. "I was thinking *What the heck's the matter?* And then he put his arm up and pointed out to the open area of the basement. I kind of turned around and saw this figure for [a couple of seconds] before it disappeared. I remember it seemed to be laughing."

Daniel's friend ran upstairs and out of the house. Daniel followed, and when he caught up to the boy he asked him what he had seen. Daniel's friend described the same figure that Daniel had seen, and the same actions of pointing and laughing. The boys had undoubtedly shared a paranormal experience that put an end to their afternoon of table hockey.

There were also many things that Daniel experienced quite on his own in that house. Some of them were decidedly frightening. He remembers being particularly terrified of one corner of his parents' bedroom. The area felt ominous to him, and he avoided it at all costs. Interestingly, it was in that exact spot that he witnessed a particular apparition on several occasions: a pale woman in a filmy, white dress.

Daniel's parents had experiences of their own, that they spoke of.

"So many little things would happen in the house," Daniel said. "So they got kind of accustomed to it. When little things would happen, they'd say, 'Oh! That damn ghost!'" On one occasion, Daniel's mother was looking for some lost item and growing increasingly frustrated as she searched. She was standing next to a large shelving unit that nearly reached the ceiling when she finally voiced her complaint aloud.

"She was the only one home," said Daniel, "but she said, 'Damn it, can't you just leave things alone?' And she said that at that point, a plant pot at the back all of a sudden lifted up — kind of jumped forward like someone had given it a push — and did a turn in the air as it fell to the ground. It landed right side up and didn't spill a drop of dirt."

Another incident that happened to Daniel's mother must have been even more unsettling.

"My dad used to work on the road a lot," said Daniel. "Kind of a travelling salesman. He would be off working during the week and then he'd come home on weekends. So this would have been a Thursday or Friday night. My mom had locked the door, shut off all the lights, and gotten into bed. Then, after a few minutes, she heard someone unlock the door, heard the door open and close, and — from the bedroom — she could see the kitchen light come on. She thought it was my dad, just getting in a day early. So she got out of bed and went into the kitchen. The light was on, but there was nobody there. She checked the door, and the door was closed and locked. And there was no one around. She told my dad about it when he got home — the next day."

Daniel's parents also spoke frequently about a thumping noise that seemed to come from one particular wall, and for which they could find no rational explanation. Whenever they heard the sound, they would go searching for its source. They'd look in the basement, beneath the location of the noise, and go outside to see if there might be a tree branch or children making the sound. But they never could explain it and eventually decided that it was associated with the haunting. Daniel was always especially curious about that noise — and the wall from which it emanated. He always wondered what they might find behind the plaster.

"Throughout the years, my parents would renovate," said Daniel. "They were always doing that kind of thing — tearing drywall down and renovating. But that's the only wall they never opened up. At the end, I was about fourteen or fifteen, and we were renovating the house again. And I said, 'Let's just open this up and see. What the heck, let's see what's in there.' But they were too scared to do it."

Daniel's parents' hesitation may have been sensible. Previous renovations had revealed a number of items from the house's history, ranging from such innocent things as yellowing, decades-old newspapers to one find that was decidedly less savoury.

"One time, in the living room, we took all the old plaster off the lath so we could drywall over it," Daniel said. "I remember my mom was working away and she called my dad over and said, 'You better see this.' And there were actually bullet holes in the lath. I think there were three holes through the lath, and then one that went into the stud. I grabbed a knife and started digging around, and I dug a .45 calibre slug out of that stud."

Daniel and his family always wondered if there had been a murder in the house, and if at least one of the ghosts was a victim of a bullet that *didn't* end up in the wall. The neighbourhood was rough, so that was a distinct possibility. But there were others, as well. According to one elderly neighbour who had lived across the street for many decades, the house had seen other sad events. This woman claimed that, in the 1940s, a young boy had drowned in one of the cisterns. She also told Daniel's family that their home had long been known as a haunted house and that there had always been strange stories associated with it.

As Daniel and his brother got well into their teenage years, the family must have outgrown the tiny house. They eventually bought another home, but decided to maintain the Churchill Downs place as a revenue property. It seemed like a sensible idea, but they found that keeping tenants in the house was more difficult than they had imagined.

"We had quite a few different ones," said Daniel. "None really long-term. They'd stay a few months usually. And then we got this one family in who started saying that weird things were happening to them in the house. They were the same kinds of things that we had [experienced], but the activity had escalated."

These particular tenants were Native, and turned to their traditional faith to help them.

"They brought in a medicine man to go through the house and do what he does," said Daniel. "And they told us what he found. The story was that there was a boy that was trapped in the house and he couldn't get out for some reason." Daniel and his family were reminded of the elderly neighbour's story of the boy drowning in the cistern. The woman could not have told the tenants about it as she had died several years earlier. The similarity of the neighbour's story and the medicine man's findings seemed to lend credibility to both accounts.

Whatever protective measures the medicine man offered the family, however, were not enough. The ghostly activity continued. The family cat tore around the house as if it was being terrorized by something, the spectral woman in the white dress was seen in the bedroom, and, on one particular night, the husband and wife had an experience that was decidedly sinister in nature. Daniel remembered the story well.

"They said that they were in bed one night and one of them — I think it was the husband — he felt a hand on his leg. It was slowly moving up his leg, like it was patting him. Up his leg and onto his spine. He thought it was his wife. Then, all of a sudden, something grabbed his throat. It was choking him. And he tried to talk, but he couldn't. With one hand, he managed to reach over and kind of swat at his wife. When she woke up and sat up, it stopped."

At that point, the couple decided that it was time to leave. Daniel's father questioned the story, wondering if his tenants had found a creative way to skip out on the rent. He thought otherwise when the people showed up and handed him an envelope.

"They said, 'Here's the rest of this month's rent, and all of next month's rent,'" recalled Daniel. "They told my dad, 'we'll have someone come back to get our stuff. We're not going back in the house.'"

They then told Daniel's father that when the husband had tried to walk out the back door for the final time that morning he found that he couldn't. The door was open wide, but the man felt as though some invisible force was either pushing him or holding him back. Finally, he lunged forward with all the effort he could muster. He got beyond the door frame at that point, but said that he felt as though he had been bitten by a dog as he passed through.

One has to wonder if the house preferred Daniel's family over the parade of renters that followed them. Although the house was always rife with paranormal activity, Daniel could never recall anything of a threatening or aggressive nature. Quite the opposite; his parents felt that whatever force was in the house was protective.

"In 1979," he said, "a week before my parents' wedding, a tornado went through town. It went down our street. It [affected] every single house, but never touched ours. My parents always thought that was weird. They thought the ghost protected the house. The tornado took out the back fence; it [damaged] the house on either side. There was a garage at one end of the block that actually belonged to a house at the *other* end of the block. But not a scratch on our house."

The ghosts may have been protecting Daniel's parents. Or perhaps they were simply preserving their own earthly haunt.

Daniel's second haunted house was also located in Regina, about a half-dozen blocks from the RCMP barracks, near the railroad tracks.

"It was a really old neighbourhood, too," said Daniel. "All those houses were built in the 1910s, 1920s."

Daniel's home was built in 1913. It was the first house that he lived in with his wife.

"It was just a little two-bedroom house," he said, "about 480 square feet. There was no basement, no crawl space even." Daniel and his wife, Kelly, didn't need a lot of room, however. At that time it was just them and their infant daughter. Furthermore, Kelly was attending school out of town and was gone Monday through Friday. On the weekdays it was just Daniel, the baby — and a presence that could not be explained.

"When [Kelly] was gone," said Daniel, "odd things would happen. The bedroom door would come open by itself all the time. I thought maybe it was just the house shifting, but it would drive me nuts. The door would just slowly open. I'd get up and close it, and go back to bed, and a little while later it would do it again. So I would get up and close the door again. I'd make sure it would close and latch. I'd give it a good pull, to make sure it wasn't going to pop open or anything. But a little while later, it would open again."

Daniel was equally frustrated by other mischievous activity in the house.

"We had a photograph done when my daughter was born," he said. "It was quite a big picture. I had that sitting on top of the dresser, at the back. But it would fall off all the time. It would fall in the middle of the night for no reason. Off the dresser, onto the floor."

Daniel might have managed to explain the falling photograph. He might have blamed it on an air current, or a poorly balanced frame. But, one night, he saw with his own eyes that it definitely wasn't anything that innocent.

"[It started out with] the thing happening with the door," he explained. I got up to close the door, and five minutes later it was open again."

Daniel was tired and frustrated and swore at whatever it was that was keeping him awake.

"At that point," he said, "the picture didn't just fall. It actually flew across the room. I didn't sleep for the rest of that night."

To make matters worse, when Daniel would tell Kelly about his strange experiences in the house, she would completely dismiss them.

"She'd say I was crazy," he said. "She never believed in ghosts. And every time she came home, [the phenomena] stopped happening."

Daniel continued to tell Kelly his eerie stories, however, thinking that she would eventually come to believe him. But she was never convinced until one particular night, only a couple of months before they were scheduled to move. Daniel was telling her about the ghostly events of the week, saying that the sooner they were to leave the haunted house, the better. Kelly had finally heard enough stories.

"This house is not haunted!" she said.

Two minutes later, they heard a crash in the kitchen. They ran to investigate, and were stunned by what they discovered.

"There was an empty pickle jar that was washed out, and it had been sitting on the counter," said Daniel. "Well, now this pickle jar was lying in the sink, rolling back and forth, back and forth. We stood there and watched it for a good two minutes, and this thing wouldn't stop rolling. Normally, something that's rolling in the sink would settle down and stop in the middle of the sink at some point. Well, it didn't. It kept rolling and rolling and rolling. Finally, I put my hand on the jar and stopped it. But when I let it go, it started rolling again. Finally, I picked it up and put it back on the counter."

Kelly was finally a believer. Of course, Daniel always *had* been.

Living in two haunted houses will do that to you.

A Welcome Presence

When Arin Ostensoe moved into the little house in Marsden, she already knew it was small. She knew that she would never fit a decent-sized table in the tiny kitchen, and she knew that the staircase leading to the second storey was treacherously steep. She knew that the floors were creaky and that the basement was smaller than the foundation. And she knew that it was haunted.

Her husband, Rick, had bought the place before they were engaged, and had been living there for three years. So Arin had heard the stories. She knew that she would be sharing living quarters not only with Rick, but with a spirit who also called the place home. And she was okay with that.

"Marsden is a small village of about 260 people," said Arin. "Everyone knows everyone else." The advantage of that was that Arin was also quite sure that she knew who the ghost was, and had already decided that it was someone she wouldn't mind sharing her home with. So she moved in, knowing that the odd strange thing was likely to happen.

From the time Rick had taken possession, in 1997, he experienced those things. Small items would regularly disappear, only to reappear in the exact spot where they had gone missing. But the presence wasn't strictly mischievous. It could also be helpful. Occasionally, after a night out, Rick would fall asleep in the living room instead of in bed. On those evenings, the ghost seemed to be looking after him.

"In the morning, he would be in the same place," said Arin, "only he would have a pillow and be tucked in with a blanket."

Despite such thoughtful gestures, not everyone was comfortable with the idea of sharing quarters with a ghost. Rick and Arin have a number of friends who stayed in the house once — and then swore that they would never stay there again. One fellow who actually lived with Rick for a period of time remembered lying in bed, listening to the sounds of footsteps and of cupboard doors opening and closing — when there was no one else awake in the house. Another friend spent a night in the house and was awakened early in the morning by the sounds of running feet and a clear woman's voice. Again, the only other person in the house at the time was Rick, and he was sound asleep. A third friend woke up at the same early hour and told Rick that he had to leave the house.

"He never gave his reasons for wanting to leave," said Arin, "but he also refuses to sleep in this house."

Arin wasn't as easily put off, however. She packed her belongings and moved in with Rick in 2000. As she expected, a number of odd things happened to her there, but she considered them more interesting than frightening.

"We had a bookcase in the upstairs back bedroom," she said, as she recalled one such incident. "It was a revolving one, like in the libraries. We kept our books on one side, and there was nothing on the back rack. The books always faced towards the stairs, so you could see them upon walking up. [Once, when] we had gone away for the weekend, when we came home the bookcase was turned so the empty racks faced the stairs and the books faced the far wall. That happened a couple of times … and it didn't turn very easily, or quietly, for that matter."

The ghost seemed to have a knack for such things. There was a closet door, near the kitchen, that was extremely difficult to open. "You would have to yank on it," said Arin. "It wouldn't just pop open." Still, there were many times when Arin found that the door had simply swung open on its own.

The ghost seemed to be equally fascinated with the exterior doors of the house. Arin remembered one time when she and Rick were awakened at six-thirty in the morning with three loud raps on their front door.

"Rick got up to answer it," said Arin, "grumbling about people showing up so early. When he opened the door, no one was there. Then we realized we hadn't heard the screen door open and shut. It was, and still is, very creaky and loud. We could always hear it open before anyone knocked on the inside wooden door. But we hadn't heard it that time."

When Arin heard a mysterious knocking on the back door one afternoon, it was even *more* obvious that it was the ghost who was visiting.

"The back door leads to a porch," explained Arin. "To get to the porch from the kitchen, there were two doors. The second door can only be unlocked from inside the kitchen." Still, whoever was there was knocking on the inside, wooden door. The second door hadn't been opened, the porch door (another loud, creaky one) hadn't been opened, and Arin had seen no one climb the porch steps, which passed directly in front of the kitchen window. "I was the only one home," said Arin. "I just went back and sat on the couch, wondering if I had heard the knocks or not."

Other times there was no questioning the ghostly activity. Arin would frequently go upstairs to find that all the cupboard doors had been flung wide open. Not only were these doors difficult to open, but there was seldom anyone up on the second floor.

"We mostly used our upstairs as storage, or for when guests stayed over," said Arin. At one point, the couple even put a padlock on the door leading to the second floor, because that was the only way that the door would stay closed. Still, someone would play with the revolving bookcase and the cupboard doors. And, on occasion, ghostly footsteps and the loud groaning of the old floorboards could be heard from the "empty" rooms upstairs.

Arin and Rick always sensed that their ghost "lived" on the second floor of the house. Their dog, Pil, an energetic shepherd-spaniel cross, seemed to agree.

"Every time someone would go upstairs, Pil would follow and go right into the back bedroom," said Arin. "The back bedroom is where the ghost stayed — at least, that's what we always felt." When the door to the stairway was left open, Pil would make countless trips up there every day. "I'm not sure of the reason for his fascination," said Arin. "There wasn't anything of interest up there for a dog." Still, Arin and Rick had to start locking the door to keep their curious pup downstairs.

Interestingly, as much as he loved going upstairs, Pil hated the basement. Arin and Rick tried coaxing him, forcing him, and even carrying him down the stairs, thinking that the dog would eventually get used to the space. But nothing worked.

"If we would open the door and try to coax him down, he would bark, snarl, and show his teeth," said Arin. "When we tried dragging him, he put his paws out and tried his hardest to get away." When Rick finally picked Pil up and carried him down to the basement, the dog spent twenty minutes in a state of extreme agitation, sniffing and frantically searching the room. Arin and Rick simply could not ease their pet's anxiety. "He even bit my husband once," said Arin. "We stopped coaxing him after that. My dog doesn't have a vicious bone in his body."

Pil may not have been vicious, but he was likely sensitive to spirits, as animals often are. Even when his owners went down to the basement, he would seem upset and concerned. According to Arin, he would "keep vigil" at the top of the stairs until whomever was down there came back up. She suspected that the cause of her pet's anxious behaviour might have been a second, separate entity that lived in the basement.

"I always had a weird feeling in the basement, and didn't like to go down there unless it was absolutely necessary," said Arin. Rick, on the other hand, could be content down there for hours, tinkering with things. "It was mostly women who got a 'creepy' feeling in the basement," noted Arin. She said that the presence in the basement seemed more male, and theorized that it may have been the husband of the feminine spirit upstairs. The basement ghost may have simply been protecting its former space. "It definitely used to be a small work area," said Arin. "Maybe he spent his days down here." There was a clear distinction between the feeling that came with the ghost upstairs and the one in the basement, however. It left Arin wondering "if the thing in the basement was a darker entity."

There was an old cistern in the basement, and Arin also wondered if that had anything to do with the strange feeling down there. It had been covered, for years, with a wooden board. "One day," said Arin, "my husband was finally able to open it. As soon as he did, the light went out. I said, 'Great, the bulb just burnt out.' But the moment I said that, the light came back on again. Was it a coincidence? I don't know. But we never had to change the light bulb in the basement for as long as we lived in the house."

If Arin had any doubts that her experiences in the house were caused by something paranormal, they were likely banished on the day that a former occupant of the house dropped by. The woman had come to deliver a wedding gift for Arin and Rick, but ended up staying to share stories about things that had happened to her in the house.

"She said [that] shortly after having her last child, she was sitting on the couch feeding the baby when she felt a hand on her shoulder," said Arin. "She heard a woman's voice say 'She is a very beautiful child.' Another time she was out in her garden when she felt the spirit's presence. Suddenly, she had an urge to go check on her baby. When she came into the house, she found her other children accidentally smothering the baby." The woman reported the ghost helping in less important ways, as well. On one occasion she had put laundry outside on a clothesline to dry. Later that day she went into the bathroom. When she emerged, moments later, she found that her laundry had been brought inside and neatly folded. It sat waiting for her in the kitchen.

Because the spirit was so gentle — and even helpful — Arin and Rick always welcomed her in their home. They knew that she was someone who had loved children, in life, so when Arin became pregnant in 2002, they wondered if the happy event would inspire a flurry of activity. What occurred was not a flurry, so much as a significant event. Two weeks before Halloween that year, Rick woke up at 6:00 a.m. to find their ghost standing in the bedroom looking at him.

"He could see that she was wearing a black dress," said Arin. "It was something like a smock, something old-fashioned and shapeless. She had a crooked nose, and she was looking at him with disappointment. It made him feel like he had let someone down. He felt really horrible. It was the first time he saw her."

And it would be the only time. The moment that Rick shook Arin to wake her up, the apparition vanished. Rick was left with the guilty feeling of having disappointed someone, but he had no idea what he had done. Perhaps the spirit knew that, with a baby on the way, it wouldn't be long before Arin and Rick would have to move to a more spacious home.

Eventually, that's what happened. A couple of years after their son Rocco was born, Arin and Rick moved down the street to a larger, newer home. They had grown so attached to the ghost that shared their little house, however, that they were reluctant to leave her. So they extended an invitation.

"We asked her to come with us when we moved," said Arin, "but I think that house will forever be her home." It would seem that way. After four years in the new house, Arin and Rick have yet to hear a single ghostly rap on the door. Though they still own the revolving book case, it no longer moves on its own. And Pil, their beloved dog, has explored every inch of the home that they live in now, and seems comfortable everywhere he goes. It must be a calmer existence but, still, Arin is sometimes wistful.

"We miss our ghost," she says. "I know we sure wouldn't mind a visit from her. We loved that house so much and would still be living there had it only been larger."

Arin's and Rick's experience is proof that not all things paranormal are unpleasant. To Arin, the resident spirit in that little house in Marsden was a very welcome presence.

Ghost Hunting on the Prairies: Saskatchewan Provincial Paranormal Research Centre

Case File Quick Facts

Name: Saskatchewan Provincial Paranormal Research Centre

Date Founded: October, 2004

Website: *www.spprc.com*

Mission: The SPPRC is dedicated to helping people understand unexplained phenomena and strange happenings within the province of Saskatchewan.

C.E.O.: Michelle Waddell

Favourite Saskatchewan Haunt: Marr Residence, in Saskatoon. "That's the place that intrigues me the most, because I haven't experienced it," says Michelle.

Q & A with Michelle Waddell

Michelle Waddell is the C.E.O. of the Saskatchewan Provincial Paranormal Research Centre, a registered non-profit organization that investigates ghostly phenomena all over the province. She took time out of her hectic schedule one evening to talk about the organization, and her passion for the work that they do.

Q: When did your interest in the paranormal begin?

A: My interest in the paranormal began way back in 1995. I was living with some friends in a house in Saskatoon on Queen Street. It was an old home, built in 1903, and it had a lot of history. It was a huge house, and when I lived there, they had separated it into two separate townhouses. That's where it all began. I was there at night, most often by myself. I would see things out of the corner of my eye; I would see things run past me; I would see dark figures standing behind me in a reflection. We had one of those old TVs with a knob you had to turn, and we didn't have a remote control. But it would frequently change channels on me. It would flick rapidly through every channel. In my friend's bedroom, which was next to mine on the second level, there was a male figure. He was very angry, and he used to pull out all of her drawers and dump them. There were little girls who used to play in the staircase — when I would go up the stairs I used to hear giggling and laughter, and it sounded very childlike. It was always behind me and, when I would turn around to look, you could see something kind of blur behind the banister, as if it was hiding. There was a young girl in my bedroom, too. She used to turn off my stereo at night. I would play my stereo when I would go to sleep, to drown out the noise. You could hear this constant walking, this pacing in the hallway. It sounded like corduroy pants or jeans; somebody walking with really rough jeans. You could hear it continually play, over and over. It would drive me nuts. The night that we moved out, I asked a friend of mine who was a psychic ... to come check out the house. He [discovered] nine entities in the house, and told me about them. While he was telling me, I just sat there nodding my head, because [he was describing] what I had experienced, and what I thought they were. It was pretty intense. But I'm glad, in a sense, that it happened, because it got me to where I am today. I think that if it hadn't happened to me, I'd have a very different opinion on the paranormal and the unexplained. I *believe*.

Q: What did you do after that?

A: I went on this [journey of] self-exploration. I tried to make sense of everything that happened in that house. I started doing a lot of reading to find out what this was all about, so I could convince myself that I wasn't crazy, and it actually was spirits, and that what happened there was concrete.

I got involved with the SPPRC — it's been about two-and-a-half years now. I came across it on the Internet. I was searching around for paranormal groups in the province. Through watching TV shows, I got kind of interested in becoming part of a group like that. (At that time, the SPPRC was operated by its founder, Barb Campbell. Two years later, Campbell chose to leave the group and handed control of it over to Michelle.)

Q: How does the SPPRC differ from other paranormal research organizations?

A: We are the largest group, and we do pride ourselves on that. As of today, we have seventeen full members, about thirteen standard members, and about twenty-two associate members. Standard members are people that can access the website and get an SPPRC email address, but they can't participate in any of the investigations. Associate members, that's basically web membership, where they can access the website.

Q: What kind of reputation are you trying to build?

A: We pride ourselves on [being] very professional when we go places.
We tend to try to be as scientific about it as possible. And our primary
goal is to educate not only ourselves, but the public. I think it's very
important to educate the people who are dealing with this kind of
thing. You can't keep them in the dark … it's very, very important to
have them understand what's going on. Sometimes, I even ask them
to participate in the investigation because we want them to grow
from the experience, as well.

**Q: Does each member of the group have a specific classification or
job description?**

A: When most people come into the group, I tell them to just join as
a "researcher." Even if you have a specific area of interest, through
self-education, you might change your mind. In that first year,
after going through a few investigations, people grow a lot. In the
group, you might find a little niche; you might find that you want
to be a videographer. Or maybe you'll want to study up on some
demonology. You'll find what your passion is.

  Now, I'm a paranormal photographer — but it's not like if we
go out to an investigation, that's all I do. And it's the same with
everybody else. You can use a lot of the other equipment. I always tell
people, it's like a wide-open tickle trunk. When we go somewhere,
we bring out all our toys and we put them all out onto the table and
everybody just grabs a couple of things. Then we get started, trying
to gather some information.

Q: What type of person is best-suited to do this kind of work?

A: I find the people who have experienced something themselves are
the people that come to the group. But there are all kinds. I've had

very intellectual people — professors, and teachers — that have joined the group. And regular people who think that they might have psychic abilities, and they join because they want to work with Barb Powell, our lead psychic ... and try to become a lot stronger. It's all about education, so I'm usually open to that. As long as you have the passion and the willingness to grow ... It's not specifically [suited to] one type of person.

Q: What process do you go through with an average investigation?

A: [First], I have to be sure that the client is of sound mind and body. It's hard, at times, to police the situation. You just have to be a really good listener ... take all the information in, and ask the proper questions to find out if this is a legitimate thing. Most of the times I do a lot of my own research, as well, on the property. When I do the phone consultation, I usually ask the location and the address so I can do a bit of research on my own before I even go out there. [Learn about] the history of it. Maybe there was a battlefield, long ago, or maybe there was a slaughterhouse there. There could have been things that happened on that land that are making the hauntings happen within the home.

When we go in to do our initial investigation, the intent is to gather as much information as we can, so that when we sit back and evaluate it, we can come up with some sort of a conclusion. [Then] we go back for a second consultation with the client. At that time, we present all of our findings to them, and talk about what's going on. Then we leave it up to them. We say, "Here's what we can do." And we let them know.

Q: What are clients usually looking for?

A: Help, validation, explanations. It's a little bit of all of that. We can do a house cleansing. We can just give you some advice, because we're all very knowledgeable about the powers of crystals, and about burning sage in the home. We ask [about] their religious beliefs because [we can design] a kind of procedure that they do on their own to call upon the angels to protect their home — that kind of thing. We can get in touch with some clergy; bring in the church, if that's the route they want to go. But we always let them know if it's something that they need to be concerned about, or maybe just a residual energy that's kind of like a tape recording.

Q: Is it difficult to convince clergy to come out?

A: Well, it takes awhile. [For one investigation] in Regina, we had to call upon the church. There was a demonic entity in the home and we just couldn't get it out. We tried. We went back four times. And we pretty much knew [it was a demon] from the second time that we were there, because it was sexually attacking a woman in the home.

One of the psychics that was with us, she was picking up on a lot of stuff, and she was writing these things down. She couldn't understand what she was writing — it was just channelling through her. And it turned out to be Hebrew. Finally, the demonologist in our group, Josh, said, "This seems demonic, because it's not leaving, and you've done *everything*." We needed someone to come in who had a bit more holy power than we did.

[The client] had to wait a month for the church to come out. In that time, we suggested that she get some crucifixes — just small gold ones — to put underneath her. Because she constantly felt that something was there, [lying under her], or touching the backs of her legs, when she sat down. The crosses helped. Something was still there; it was still in the home. But the crosses got her through.

We went back out there, about a month after the priest had been there, and she looked so much better. She looked really sickly before — pale, with a greyish tone to her skin. But there was colour in her skin afterward, and the house felt so much better, too. It didn't feel so heavy. It felt really sick in there when we first went in.

Q: What brought the demon into the house?

A: It was brought in through the use of a Ouija board. The lady of the house was using one to try to contact her mother. She was using it and storing it in her bedroom, and that's where the entity was concentrated. That was the first time I witnessed levitation — in that bedroom. [The client] was lying on the bed. And she actually, at one point, levitated about a hand's length above the bed. She just floated up, with nothing touching her. And she had stiffened right up. I tried to move her arm, but it was like she was frozen.

Q: Are there any other particularly interesting investigations that you've taken part in?

A: We went to an investigation out of town last October (2008). The house that we went to had been moved from a farm into town. And when it was brought into town, they dug out a basement for the house to sit on. When they dug the basement, they found a well, and they just cemented over it.

One of the children's bedrooms was in that basement, and she was being affected by something that was there. Through a couple of visits there … one of our psychics picked up on a conversation between two spirits. [We] deduced that long ago, before Saskatchewan was even a province, there was a settler's home on that land. [The psychic] kept having visions of a small home, and beside it was a well. And the husband had killed two of [the family's] children by dropping them into the well. And the mother….It was like a recording, and she was walking continually through the basement, over to the well. And he was standing at the well, yelling at her, saying it was all her fault. And she was sobbing. This is what they were picking up.

We shared this whole story with the family. And the girl [that slept in] the basement, she said, "It's okay, now that I know." She was okay with it. She didn't want us to clear it out or try to stop it. And she was the one who phoned us after [seeing the image of the mother] on a video recording she had done in her room.

If it's something like that, where it's not a malevolent spirit, and it's not harming anyone, sometimes people are okay with that. They can accept it.

Q: Are some investigations more challenging than others?

A: Definitely. Just recently, in January (2009), there was a home here in Saskatoon where we had to go out quite a few times. Normally, we do the initial investigation, and then we go back later to share what we've found and maybe do a house cleansing....or a crossing-over of spirits, or whatever. So, normally, it's two visits. But this last one we did was quite extensive. I think we were there five times, and that was four to six hours each night. And that was over the span of one month. We would go there....communicate with the spirits. Everything would feel good, so we would leave. Then [the client] would phone me at three o'clock in the morning, in a panic, four days later.

It took a long time, but we finally [managed to clear the house]. I contacted [the client] this week, to ask how things were, because I hadn't heard from her in a very long time. And she said, "The house feels so calm. It's so clear. It feels like it's my home." She said there's nothing there now. I could tell by the tone of her voice that everything was okay, and that was so satisfying to me.

Q: Is this work rewarding?

A: That's the whole thing with this. Even though it's a lot of work, it doesn't *seem* like a lot of work, because it's a passion. And all you want to do is help. And when you have successes — and all of our cases have been successes — to have the people of the home say that they want to thank you, but they don't feel that thank-you is enough. That's enough, right there.

Q: What are your plans for the SPPRC?

A: My ultimate goal for the group would be at some point — even though, right now, we're a non-profit organization — to operate it as a business. An investigation group that is sustainable on its own, where we could pay our members, and I could get paid for what I do. We've been approached by a TV station here in the city to do a show, and that's something that I would like to do. I just don't know if it would necessarily be good for the group right now. I think that we still have to work on polishing our persona. But it's something I would consider in the future. And maybe a magazine or something like that would be a good endeavour. Something that we could publish quarterly.

Q: Would Saskatchewan be ready for that? Are people's attitudes regarding the paranormal changing?

A: It's become a lot easier in the last couple of years. I find that society is a lot more accepting of this kind of thing now.

3
Haunting History

Weyburn Mental Hospital: Resident Evil and Forgotten Souls

For most of the twentieth century, the town name "Weyburn" was synonymous with the sprawling hospital that existed there. While there was more to Weyburn, the town, than the psychiatric hospital that bore its name, there was no denying that there was a symbiotic relationship at work. According to local resident Margaret Strawford, most of the citizens of the town either worked at the hospital, or had a family member who did. She speaks from personal experience.

"I worked there in '71, '72, and '73," Margaret said. "Then I went back from 1989 to 2005." She went on to name several relatives who were employed at the hospital in one capacity or another, and to share a few of her personal memories. Most were melancholy reflections concerning the closing of the hospital — by then called Souris Valley Regional Care Centre — in 2005. But some went back years earlier, and were decidedly darker in nature.

"I remember, when someone died, having to take the body down to the morgue," said Margaret. "That was a bad feeling — taking a still-warm body and putting it on a cold metal table."

Her memory serves as a stark reminder that death is a part of institutional life, and that many "residents," as they liked to call them at Weyburn, met their end in that hospital. And it was suggested more and more, in the hospital's final years, that those who lived and died there might never have left. Ghost stories abound wherever there is

Courtesy of the Soo Line Historical Museum.

An aerial photograph taken in 1960 shows the enormity of the hospital.

an abandoned, forgotten building. But Weyburn Hospital had a more-ghostly-than-average reputation, which was understandable, given its sad and controversial history.

In 1919, the *Regina Morning Leader* announced that Weyburn would be the site for a new, badly needed mental health facility. By the time construction was completed, in 1921, the Weyburn Mental Hospital (the name would later be changed to Saskatchewan Hospital, and then to the Souris Valley Regional Care Centre) was one of the largest buildings in the British Empire. It was also on the leading edge of mental health care. Unfortunately, that didn't mean much at the time. Mental illness was poorly understood in those days, and treatments consisted of hard work and hydrotherapy, which meant submerging restrained patients into tubs of icy or scalding water, binding them tightly in sheets to close off the blood vessels, then rubbing their bodies vigorously to restore the circulation. Not surprisingly, these methods rarely resulted in any kind of improvement in the patients' conditions, so other treatments were sought out. Over the years, Weyburn Hospital was the scene of many experimental therapies, including electroshock, insulin, and lobotomies.

Dr. Humphrey Osmond: the man who created the term "psychedelic."

The staff — particularly Dr. Humphrey Osmond, who was head of the facility from 1951 to 1961 and is famous for having coined the term "psychedelic" — pioneered experimental psychiatric drug therapy, including the use of hallucinogens such as LSD and mescaline. Many of these methods were used until the facility ceased to operate as a mental hospital in 1971.

By that time, people who held opinions about the hospital generally fell into one of two camps: there were those who felt that Weyburn had offered compassionate assistance to those who could not help themselves, and those who believed that nothing short of atrocities had been committed there. Both sides made a good argument. It was true that staff usually did the best they could, given the knowledge they had at the time, and that Weyburn Hospital provided a home to many who would have otherwise had no place in society. But it was equally true that the facility was often overcrowded and understaffed, that there were horrific stories of cruelty and sexual abuse, and that many of the therapies were primitive and inhumane. There was also the question of whether mental institutions, in general, were designed primarily to help the patients or to serve society by providing a sort of holding facility for misfits of all descriptions.

It is a fact that Weyburn Hospital held patients with a broad spectrum of challenges, and was criticized for drawing no lines of distinction. They routinely housed the mentally ill alongside the mentally challenged, as well as others who had little reason for being in such a place. Depressives, addicts, unwed mothers, orphans — the unwanted members of society — often ended up in Weyburn Mental Hospital for many sad years, if not for the remainder of their lives.

How could there not be ghosts?

In the thirty-year period during which the hospital served as an extended care facility, it became apparent that a strong residual energy from the past existed there. The building was gradually closed down during that time, put to sleep, room by room, wing by wing. Many believed that while the human activity stopped in those areas, spirits continued to roam the silent halls.

When the fourth floor was shut down, hospital staff began to hear voices drifting down the stairwells. And, late at night, if you were on the grounds and happened to glance up at a fourth-floor window, you might have seen the silhouette of a woman who was said to pace endlessly back and forth. Those who walked the hospital corridors said the echoing sound of footsteps would often continue for a very long time after they

Courtesy of the Soo Line Historical Museum.

The deserted northeast wing of the hospital.

had stopped in their tracks. And, in one particular room, there was a ring sitting on the floor that would mysteriously disappear and reappear, from visit to visit. The grounds became legendary with local teenagers during these years. They would come out by the carload, hoping to hear whispering voices or see shadowy figures slinking amongst the trees. There were many who did experience those things. Others were sufficiently spooked by the atmosphere of the place.

Most of the stories came not from thrill-seekers, however, but from more credible sources. They were accounts told by people who worked in the building and others who were associated with it in some way. One such person was Jacquie Mallory, curator of the Soo Line Historical Museum (page 133). As curator, it was Jacquie's job to ensure that any artifacts from the hospital were rescued and preserved. But, for a person who is extremely psychically sensitive, the hospital was not always an easy place to be.

"Three years ago, I was in there right when they closed," said Jacquie. "A friend of mine who was a nurse took me through. And my senses went into absolute overload. There was just so much garbage, and I didn't know where it was coming from. And the pictures I took were just loaded with orbs. That place was humming like a beehive."

Other people reported similar sensations of the hospital being crowded with spirits. One man described "a parade" of invisible people rushing past him as he walked down a seemingly deserted hall. Another person was in a wing all by herself when she heard a clear voice behind her. "There you are!" it said. The woman radioed the crew that she was working with, and was told that every other person on site was in another wing of the building.

None of these stories would surprise Margaret Strawford.

"I felt that there were presences, life forms in the building," she said. "I believe there was something there."

Margaret was not alone in her belief. Many people thought that Weyburn Hospital had to be haunted. There were those who wanted to experience that haunting first-hand; perhaps even prove it. Not surprisingly, a number of paranormal researchers asked to visit the building.

Chris Oxtoby of "Prairie Specters" (page 183) was granted an official tour of the site just before the demolition crews came in. Chris captured the atmosphere of the hospital, which was nothing more than a deserted relic by the time he visited. He described the shock of encountering a flock of trapped pigeons, and wrote about the damage caused by vandals, weather, and decades of neglect. He walked down still hallways that felt, to him, like monuments to the suffering of countless patients. But — aside from a minor sensation of being watched, at one point — he met no ghosts. He was told of another group who had better luck, or worse luck, depending upon how one looks at it:

> Our guide told us of a group that came from the University of Saskatchewan to investigate the hospital, setting up in a large room in the old wing. The group was to have performed a seance and became so frightened by what happened that they left the building right then and there, even though they had use of the hospital for two days. Later it was found out that they had seen "things" flying about the room outside of the seance circle.
>   "Prairie Specters"
>   Monday, September 29, 2008

When the Calling Lakes Paranormal Investigators (page 57) went out to Weyburn, they had a similar experience of being "circled" by some sinister spectre as they worked. But that was not all that happened to them. The group encountered such a massive amount of dark energy at Weyburn that they still, several years later, agreed that it was one of their most frightening investigations. It was bad enough that veteran CLPI investigator John Pawelko classified it as his absolute worst paranormal encounter. "I wouldn't go back there," he said. "I wouldn't. That's the only place I've had a bad experience."

The group chose to work in a large room that they believed had once been a surgical suite. They set up their camera, sat in a circle, and joined hands.

"We were sitting there in the dark," said John, "and all of a sudden we could see this thing walking around. We could just see it above the waist. Dark. Walking. And, all of a sudden, it went the other way."

Amy Drummond, another investigator, was sitting beside John. She saw the dark figure, as well. "It would appear, disappear. Appear, disappear. Appear, disappear," said Amy. "And, then, suddenly … it stopped. It was gone."

At the moment the dark figure vanished, John turned to Amy. That's when he saw it....

"Behind Amy, there was this cow's head. Red eyes. Just awful, horrible-looking thing," said John. His face twisted in disgust as he recalled. "It was trying to stick its tongue in the back of Amy's head."

Amy could feel it.

"I knew that there was something coming at me," she said. "I gasped, and covered my head, and curled up in a ball because I couldn't get out of the way fast enough."

John was able to move fast enough to do something. Despite a bad knee that makes it difficult for him to get up from a sitting position, John was on his feet and had flipped on the light switch within seconds.

"That was the only time we've ever turned on the light," said Amy. "It was that bad. I don't know if that was an attempt at possession … But it was definitely an attack."

So, what exactly was it that the group witnessed at Weyburn?

"Resident evil," said John. "[A manifestation] of all the evil that went on in that room. Lots of horrible stuff went on in that place. Eventually, it took on a life of its own. And, after awhile, the people in the room didn't even realize it was controlling their actions; making them do what they were doing. Evil begets evil. The more evil you do, the stronger it gets, the more you get. It's a continuous cycle."

There are others who might say that Weyburn Mental Hospital was not charged with evil so much as it was with emotion and the weight of history. Margaret Strawford spoke of the staff feeling sentimental in the year before the facility was permanently closed.

"We were on our way out, and we knew it was happening," she said. "The last couple of weeks, people started writing their names on the walls. It was like saying 'Joe Blow was here.'"

Margaret, who had always enjoyed writing, decided to do something a little more significant. She had an idea for a farewell poem, and thought

An interior photograph taken in 2008 shows evidence of the building's decay.

that one of the hospital walls would be the perfect canvas for her work.

"I thought, *what are they going to do — fire me*?" She laughed. So she wrote her poem on a wall. It expressed the feelings of so many, as they left the hospital for the last time:

> The clocks have stopped, the lights are out, the people
> have all gone,
> The hallways now are empty, of folks who called them
> home.
> The Golden Staircase disappeared, the pitted stairwells
> worn,
> The plaster cracked, wood railings chipped, the curtains
> stained
> and torn.
> No curling rink, the workshops gone, the gardens now
> are bare,
> The tunnels dark, the boilers out, no one to even care.
> No more the cries and silent screams to echo in the night,

No more the staff to help the souls and put the wrong
to right.
The silence of the bedrooms, ghostly whispers in the halls,
The stories and the tales they could tell are embedded in
the walls.
The clocks have stopped....
The lights are out....

Those lights were turned out for the last time in the spring of
2005. Remaining patients and staff moved to a new long-term care
facility named Tatagwa View, and the old hospital entered into the final
phase of its existence. In the three years that followed, as the building
crumbled and decayed in a rapid structural decline, it also seemed to
lose whatever spiritual energy might have been left there. In the end,
it was like a psychic battery that had completely drained. Interestingly,
people who didn't even know each other shared this opinion.

Chris Oxtoby's guide told him, "It's empty now. Whatever was here
has left."

By the end of his visit, Chris felt certain that "the tortured minds
who lived and lived on in this place have finally found their peace."

Jacquie Mallory, the museum curator, was one of the last to walk
through the hospital. "There was so little activity," she said. "Hardly
anything anymore." This relieved Jacquie, who had been worried
about where the ghosts would go once the building was demolished.
"I feel so much better," she said, "knowing that there's not much in
there anymore."

Margaret Strawford agreed that the activity in the building decreased
dramatically during the three years that the hospital awaited demolition.

"Before it closed down," she said, "I could feel something. But last
summer (2008), I took a tour of the hospital. It was all gone." Margaret
recalled that the staff used to speculate about exactly where the ghosts
would go once Souris Valley Regional Care Centre shut its doors. "And
the joke," said Margaret, "was 'Maybe they'll go to Tatagwa!'"

And now ... it seems possible that they have.

✝

Margaret Strawford has worked at Tatagwa View, and reported that it was not unusual for her to catch a glimpse of a darting figure in her peripheral vision. Jacquie Mallory knows other members of Tatagwa's staff, and has heard other stories.

"One lady told me a story that happened right after they moved over there," said Jacquie. "It was really late one night. Everybody was sleeping and she was doing meds. All of a sudden, this man in black walked right by her. [He was] wearing black, head to toe. It's not like it would have been a patient, they wear pyjamas. Different people have said there's a lot of activity in there now."

It's possible that some of the spirits have moved over to the new facility. It's also possible that many of them "moved on" to a more final destination once there were no more living people from which to draw energy. Wherever they are, everyone hopes that these souls have now found peace.

There were some residents who spent their entire lives committed to Weyburn Mental Hospital. But to spend an eternity there? That is simply too much to ask.

Ghost Hill, Ituna

When the community of Ituna was first settled, the name Ghost Hill was given to a small rise of land several kilometres west of town. A few years later, no one could remember exactly what had inspired it but, in 1924, that nondescript mound of earth lived up to its name. On September 13 of that year, the *Regina Morning Leader* ran a front page story about the locally famous spectre that had been appearing there throughout the summer:

> For months the "ghost" of a woman has appeared near there. Residents of the town, district, and of adjoining places for miles around are thoroughly intrigued —

and thrilled. Hundreds have seen the mysterious figure both by night and day and the excited is [sic] divided into three categories — believers, half-believers, and scoffers. Ghost-hunting excursions have taken the place of dances, socials, and concerts. Nearly every night, and often during the day, old and young make pilgrimages to watch the spot where the strange visitations occur. Some have camped on the scene for many hours at a stretch. Many have seen the ghost, or something which they are convinced is supernatural. Others have departed, disappointed and skeptical.

According to the article, the spirit began making her appearances in early June of that year. The first to witness the apparition was a twenty-two-year-old man named Nick Finuke, who lived a little more than a kilometre from the hill. He was close by the hill at noon one particular day, when he saw a figure draped in white appear on the summit. The person — who looked to be female — appeared in stark relief against the bright sky. Finuke thought it odd that anyone would be out there alone, and he walked closer to investigate. As he approached, he noticed that the woman appeared to shimmer in the light. Her image seemed unstable, and it grew and shrunk before his eyes. Finuke rubbed his eyes, certain that he was experiencing some sort of optical illusion. The closer he came to the hill, however, the less substantial the woman appeared to be. Finuke finally realized — to his tremendous shock — that he could see through the woman. At that moment, the ghost vanished before his eyes.

Next to witness the wraith were a group of children who attended a school less than a kilometre from Ghost Hill. The youngsters were in the school playground and, from that distance, saw something mysterious appear on top of the hill. They couldn't tell if it was an animal or a human being, only that it had appeared and then disappeared quite unexpectedly. They reported the incident to their teacher, Miss Ethel Clark, who dismissed it as childish imagination. A few weeks later, Miss Clark would change her mind when she witnessed the spirit herself.

Apparitions are usually elusive, and sightings of them are rare. But the spectre of Ghost Hill was quite unusual in that regard. She made regular appearances that summer and was seen by many local people. According to the *Regina Morning Leader*, they even knew when to expect her:

> It was a punctual spirit. Each day, about the noon hour, it would appear for a time and each night at midnight the intangible would again reveal itself for the edification of silent watchers. Children came to watch for the visitation and regarded its presence as almost commonplace, after the initial thrills had worn off. Farmers working at a considerable distance in their fields would observe a white shape wafting across the hill and they knew the ghost was walking. Then, as certainty of the fact that something enigmatic, something mysterious, was going on became established, the excursions and ghost-hunting trips commenced.

By the beginning of July, word had spread that there was something of supernatural interest to be seen at Ghost Hill. Carloads of visitors from Ituna and many surrounding communities began to show up at the hill. Some had a serious scientific or spiritual interest in the apparition, but most came as a lark. Ghost Hill was suddenly a picnic and party destination. The landscape became littered with discarded food and wrappers, and what had been a peaceful, rural setting was disturbed by constant, raucous noise. Farm families who lived in the area must have been incredibly frustrated. It wasn't long before it became obvious that even the ghost disliked the ruckus.

After a while, when revellers were making noise, the spirit would not appear. When automobile headlights were aimed at the hill, she would not show herself. The boisterous ghost hunters had no luck — but those who were stealthy, silent, and patient were often rewarded with a sighting. Those people would wait for a quiet night, then climb to the top of the hill and secret themselves in the bushes there. Many of those amateur investigators reported seeing a white vapour rise from the ground and grow to the height of a woman. The longer they watched, the more realistic and stable the image became — though it always remained semi-transparent. The ghost was consistent in her habits, as well. She always appeared in the same spot, she was always silent, and never approached anyone who saw her. When she showed up at night, it was more likely to be when the moon was full. In the daytime, she favoured hot, windless weather. By September, as the days and nights grew cooler and the spirit grew increasingly elusive, many were wondering if she had, like the birds, gone south for the winter. That didn't stop a reporter from the *Morning Leader* from visiting Ituna to see what all the fuss had been about.

The reporter went looking for the most credible witnesses, and found them in the school teacher, Ethel Clark, and the school's attendance inspector, Fred Manchuk. Both were practical, intelligent people who seemed unlikely to get caught up in the ghost-hunting frenzy — yet, both claimed to have seen the mysterious spirit. Miss Clark witnessed the apparition at midday, but from a distance of about a kilometre. From that far away, the teacher wasn't able to describe the features of the figure that she saw on the hill. What struck her as being abnormal was the way that the white-draped apparition moved. Ethel Clark might not have paid much attention to someone walking along the crest of the hill, but this person seemed to be gliding, or drifting, just above the ground. Fred Manchuk reported seeing something similar. "It seemed like a woman," he said, "going along as smoothly as if she were skating. Yes, there's something funny there."

Wanting to see for himself, the reporter found some local people who were willing to take him to the hill at midnight:

Straining [to see] into the patchy blackness of the poplar grove certainly it seemed as if between the two small poplars where the ghost was reported as having been seen many times, there was a misty shape. It was faint and formless, however, and close inspection invariably failed to get a more definite view.

Having had no luck at night, the reporter went back to the hill the next day, at noon. He conducted a "minute examination" of the area, but did not see the spectre or anything that could have rationally explained the apparition. The only thing of interest that he did find was a mound of earth, made by burrowing animals, which had been fashioned into a mock grave by one of the less reverent ghost hunters.

There were many in Ituna who thought that there was likely a real, unmarked grave somewhere on that hill, containing the physical remains of the restless spirit. Others believed that the hill might have been an aboriginal burial ground. Still others recalled a murder that took place in the district some years earlier, and thought that the soul of the victim was the white wraith who wandered amongst the poplars.Unfortunately, little attention was paid to the unlikely coincidence that an actual ghost had appeared on the very piece of land known as Ghost Hill. It's impossible not to wonder how the knoll came by its name, and whether the spirit that was seen there in the summer of 1924 had showed herself, decades earlier, when the area was first being settled.

Sadly, these questions will likely never be answered. The misty, white apparition of Ghost Hill may have only been active during that one season, for there are no subsequent reports of her appearance to be found. But — to quote the *Regina Morning Leader* — "At any rate, it's decidedly queer."

The Human Wireless

His name was A.B. MacNaughton and, to most of his neighbours, he appeared no different from any other man. He farmed a rolling quarter-section of land in the area of Valeport and was known as a hard worker. He might have lived his entire life in relative obscurity had it not been for a letter he decided to write to the *Regina Morning Leader* in April of 1924. Within two months, the newspaper published an extensive article about MacNaughton, proclaiming him to be The Human Wireless — Able to Lift Veil of the Future. It was a bold statement. But, then, MacNaughton appeared to have an impressive ability.

"Mac," as he was known to all, had been having visions since a very young age. Growing up, he always knew when another student would be punished at school or whether a thunderstorm would spoil a planned outing. As a child, however, his strict parents strongly discouraged his predictions and he learned to keep them to himself. The visions continued to come, growing increasingly more vivid and detailed as he reached adulthood, but Mac would be well into middle age before he again shared them with anyone other than his wife.

The incident that inspired the letter was the crash of an American plane in Alaska. At the exact hour that it occurred, Mac saw the crash in one of his visions. He knew that the pilot, Major F.L. Martin, had survived, along with his companion, a man named Harvey. Perhaps thinking that he could offer information that would aid in the search effort, Mac wrote down every detail of what he had seen and sent his letter off to the *Leader*. That letter was likely dismissed, until a week later, when Martin and Harvey made their way back to civilization and told a story that matched MacNaughton's account in nearly every detail.

Mac had written that he saw the plane flying through a dense fog. Suddenly, there appeared a mountainside, with stunted pine trees and wide expanses of rock. The plane crashed into what he knew was the northwest slope of the mountain, which was in western Alaska. (He enclosed a rough sketch of the Alaskan coastline, with an "X" marking the spot where the wreckage lay.) After about a minute, two men emerged from the left side of the plane and proceeded to examine the craft. The undercarriage was smashed and the right wing was folded back along the side of plane. After taking time to assess the damage, one of the men climbed back into the wreckage and brought out a small package, which he opened. There were sandwiches inside, which the men ate as they discussed how they should proceed.

It is interesting to note that, at one point, Mac actually communicated with the men in his vision. He asked them what had gone wrong, and they replied that the fog had limited their visibility. Mac said that it was a shame, and noted that if they had been flying just a bit higher, or a little to the right, then they would not have hit the mountain.

The fact that MacNaughton reported a vision of a specific plane crashing before the accident was confirmed was astounding enough. What made the story even more fascinating was a letter that Mac received from the pilot of the plane a few weeks later. It read as follows:

My Dear Mr. MacNaughton:

In some respects your vision of our wreck in Alaska was quite accurate and in order that you may be able to judge I will state to you the actual conditions. The mountain into which we flew in the fog was struck as we were travelling southward, but [we crashed] against the northwest side of [this] mountain in western Alaska. The lower right wing was crushed and carried back against the side of the ship. The upper right wing was carried back about halfway between the tail and next to the ship. I must say that it was only a few seconds after the crash that Harvey and I got out. We got out on the right, not on the left side. We did not look underneath as the fuselage of the ship was on the ground, but we did walk around the ship and examine it. It is true the fog was so thick we could not see where we were going, which was responsible for us striking the mountain. Had we been higher up, or further to the right, we would have missed the mountain. The ground was lower to the right than at the point where we hit.

It is perfectly true that after surveying the wrecked plane we took out the sandwiches which we had prepared for use during the flight to Dutch Harbor, and ate them, at the time talking over the proper procedure and about trying to get back to safety.

To have had this vision is really quite wonderful. I wish you could have informed me of this before we had the experiences. It would have given opportunity to prepare for travel through the snows under conditions which exist in the western peninsula of Alaska.

F.L. Martin

It was not long after the arrival of Major Martin's letter that someone from the *Leader* paid MacNaughton a visit. The reporter found a man who looked far more like a weathered farmer than any kind of clairvoyant, but declared him to be "a likeable sort, a good conversationalist, obviously well-read and keenly intelligent." And — whether Mac looked the part of a seer or not — he was able to offer a list of convincing incidents confirming his ability to see distant or future events.

In March of 1923, he reported he was walking from his barn to his house when he was struck by an image of devastation. He could see wrecked houses and uprooted trees; fields of grain that were destroyed and dead livestock scattered like debris. Several months later, Mac read a newspaper article about a disastrous cyclone that had struck Lumsden and recognized another vision come true.

In May of the same year, a neighbour came to tell him of an automobile accident that he had passed several miles down the road. Mac said that he already knew, and described the exact location of the mishap, as well as the occupants of the vehicle.

In the summer of 1923, as American president Warren G. Harding travelled through the west on his "Voyage of Understanding," Mac felt certain that it would become a voyage of tragedy. He had a vision of Harding, in which it seemed that his likeness had been carved in marble. The image was accompanied by a feeling of depression. "I interpreted my feeling as a bad omen for President Harding," said Mac. He was proved correct when Harding died, unexpectedly, on August 2.

In the fall of 1923, as Mac worked to bring in the harvest, he was suddenly confronted with the apparition of a white-haired old woman. She smiled sweetly and directed him, "Tell my boy I am better and am writing to him." The name and location of the woman's son flashed in Mac's mind then, enabling him to do as she asked. When he contacted the man, however, he was told that while the woman's description matched that of his mother, she was extremely ill and much too feeble to write. Five days later, the man received a letter from his mother, whose health was much improved.

These were but a small sampling of MacNaughton's visions and premonitions. All were interesting, but paled in comparison to his inexplicable and detailed knowledge of Major Martin's plane crash, which the *Leader* described as his "most extraordinary feat of clairvoyance." As for an explanation of his abilities, Mac offered these words:

> In all parts of the world, fellow men and women are constantly thinking, scheming, contriving, suffering, experiencing happiness, woe, hunger — all sorts of emotions and sensations. Thought-transference has been proven possible by other than the spoken and the written word. Who knows but that I am just a "receiving set" for these thoughts and sensations that are unconsciously broadcasted by fellow men?

Indeed, the "Human Wireless." The article went on to describe Mac as "a seer in overalls; a prophet in a dilapidated derby; a clairvoyant of the out-of-doors." But — whether he looked the part or not — there is little question that A.B. McNaughton was a man with a genuine gift for seeing what others could not.

Skippy

Countless tales have been told about the bond that exists between a boy and his dog. This might qualify as just one more of those stories — if not for a unique twist suggesting that the bond can survive even after death.

This account was sent by an anonymous reader from Codette, Saskatchewan, to the *News of the North*. They published the letter in the July 1962 edition, under the heading Unexplained. It read as follows:

> Jimmy, my thirteen-year-old nephew, had a dog named Skippy. He was just a mongrel dog picked up at a city pound. The boy and dog became inseparable. Every Thursday night, Jimmy went to a Boy Scout meeting, returning home about 9:00 p.m. Each Thursday night, Skippy would be at the front door promptly at nine o'clock to welcome Jimmy home.
>
> Then Jimmy took ill with polio and died within twenty-four hours. For almost a year after his young

master's passing, Skippy went to the front door at nine
o'clock every Thursday evening, lying on the mat with
his nose at the crack awaiting Jimmy's return.

How does a dog know what day of the week it is?

For that matter, how did Skippy know what time it was? It's just
another of the many strange and unexplained stories that make up
Saskatchewan's history.

The Haunts of Yorkton

To the east, over the roof of the hospital, night was melting
into grey dawn. From the back door floated an apparition —
translucent in a halo of mist. The form took on the shape of a
woman dressed in a floor-length cotton tunic with bib and
apron. A white nurse's cap was pinned on her head.
— Kathy Morrell, *Haunts of Yorkton II*

In 2005, the Yorkton Centennial Committee presented an interactive
ghost walk they called *The Haunts of Yorkton*. DARE TO WALK WHERE
SPIRITS HAUNT beckoned the posters. The people of Yorkton took
that dare. In fact, response to the dramatized history tour was so
enthusiastic, an even more ambitious version of the production,
featuring "a choir of haunts," was mounted in 2006 and 2007. Finally,
in March of 2008, the Yorkton Chamber of Commerce presented
The Haunts of Yorkton with a Community Award of Excellence, in
recognition of its contribution to the city.

People do like their ghost stories....

The truth is that the ghost story motif was a simply a device used to
bring the history of Yorkton to theatrical life. But there was one tale told
in *Haunts of Yorkton* that is considered to be a bona fide local ghost story.
"If a ghost story can be said to be true, it is true," said Kathy Morrell, who
researched, wrote, and produced all three *Haunts of Yorkton* productions.

It is the story of the Kiwanis Kiddies' Playground, which is now closed but once existed across from Queen Victoria Cottage Hospital.

According to Yorkton legend, the playground was haunted by the lonely spirit of a small child. Frequently, people walking past on a calm summer's day would see a single swing swaying back and forth, as if carrying an invisible rider. Neighbours would look out their windows and notice that, while the playground appeared to be deserted, the merry-go-round was spinning — and picking up speed, at each turn. The rusty bolts of the teeter-totter would groan and someone would hear the rhythmic bumps of first one seat hitting the ground, and then the other. Eventually, an explanation for these mysteries evolved. People began to tell the story of a little girl who accidentally died during a routine surgery in the early days of the hospital, and was secretly buried on the land that later became the playground. While it's doubtful that this particular story is true, any Yorkton history buff knows that it's entirely possible that *other* bodies are buried near the hospital....

Photos by Kathy Morrell.

(left) Kevin East, a member of the cast of Haunts of Yorkton II, *told ghost stories associated with the Victoria Cottage Hospital.*

(right) Megan Cottenie, a tour guide for Haunts of Yorkton II, *visits with Gordon Ball, her former chemistry teacher.*

The January 29, 1953 edition of the *Yorkton Enterprise* ran an article headlined Skeleton Find Stirs Old Cemetery Mystery. It reported that city workmen digging sewer trenches had discovered some skeletal human remains. The find set off discussion regarding the lost location of Yorkton's first cemetery. It was believed that there was a specific burial ground, prior to the opening of the Yorkton Cemetery. This theory was confirmed by the earliest cemetery records, indicating that the first burials in the new cemetery were of bodies moved from the old cemetery. Unfortunately, in 1953, no one seemed to remember where that old cemetery was. That is, no one living in Yorkton. But when the article ran, it was read by W.F. Hopkins of Victoria, British Columbia, who wrote to the *Enterprise* with a valuable bit of information.

"I know where the cemetery was," wrote Hopkins. "I remember it distinctly because … I was present when the body of my mother was moved." Hopkins went on to reveal that Yorkton's original cemetery had been "in the sand hill to the west of the Queen Victoria Cottage Hospital."

In other words, near the haunted playground.

Another fascinating fact from Yorkton — the city that may be both literally and figuratively haunted by its history.

The Unexplained Light

In the August 28, 1963 edition of *News of the North*, a woman from North Battleford won a five dollar prize for writing in with her "Example of the Unexplained." She told a story from 1907, concerning her father, who was a homesteader in Saskatchewan's early years.

In those days, the word *neighbour* could refer to someone who lived an hour away if travelling on horseback, or considerably longer if one was walking. The homes of the settlers were built far apart and the distance was made to seem greater by the lack of proper roads. Simply going to visit the next farm over sometimes meant planning a virtual expedition.

This woman's father — we'll call him Joe — started out one evening to visit a friend who lived about seven miles away from his own homestead.

There was no road; there wasn't even a fence line to follow, but he was in high spirits and confident that he knew the way. Joe might have been able to find his friend's home easily enough in the daylight hours, but the sun set as he walked along and he soon found himself in complete darkness. It was a moonless night. Even the stars were shut out by a layer of cloud. There was nothing to light Joe's way and, eventually, he had to admit to himself that he was hopelessly lost.

Joe wandered aimlessly in the darkness for quite some time, hoping that he would eventually stumble upon some landmark, something familiar that would help him find his way. He had nearly resigned himself to the idea of being lost until daybreak, when he saw a tiny pinpoint of light moving in the distance. It appeared to be a lantern, carried by someone. Joe walked toward the light until it finally disappeared. By then, however, he could make out the dim outline of his friend's house. There were no lights in the window, but Joe could see the roof against the sky. He kept his eyes trained on that barely-visible silhouette and kept putting one foot in front of the other. Finally, he arrived.

Joe knocked on the door and called out. The door opened and he was welcomed in by his friend's wife. Joe entered the warm, dark room and felt relief wash over him.

"If I hadn't seen your husband carrying the lantern to the barn I would have been lost for the night," he told the woman.

She reacted with surprise.

"He wasn't carrying a lantern," she replied. "We haven't had a bit of coal oil for the last two weeks!"

Joe and his friend did their best to think of a logical explanation, but the mystery of the helpful light was never solved.

A Fiendish Sacrifice

"Why is Saskatchewan so haunted?"

This is one of the questions that I am frequently asked in interviews. The answer isn't simple. First, it's difficult to objectively say that any particular place is more haunted than another. And even when it seems obvious that a certain area has a higher than usual concentration of paranormal activity, it's impossible to say what causes it. There are theories that certain natural materials or geographical features are conducive to the "transmission" of spooky data. Or that the area in question may be populated by people who are either more open to paranormal experience or more sensitive to it. And, of course, there are locations that have a history of traumatic or dramatic incidents. Moments of intense emotion seem to leave a sort of psychic imprint on a place, resulting in a residual haunting, a spectral "recording" of the event. Certainly, Saskatchewan's history has its share of such moments.

Everyone knows stories of the North-West Rebellion, the Black Tuesday riot in Depression-era Yorkton, or the tornado that devastated Regina in 1912. The history books are filled with information about high-profile events that loom large in the province's rear-view mirror. But,

Photo by Andrea Oxtoby.

every once in awhile, we are reminded of tragedies that took place on a smaller scale, affecting far fewer people but creating heartbreak and devastation for those whose lives were touched. The March 10, 1891 edition of the *Regina Leader-Post* ran a story like that; one that is that horrific in nature, if not huge in scope. The headline read A FIENDISH SACRIFICE, and the lead paragraph described the article as "the story of a deed which rivals in fiendishness those of Massachusetts in witchcraft days."

Saskatchewan's beautiful scenery has witnessed an often violent history.

The story began in June, 1890, when a Native man named Blue Horn went hunting and trapping with an eight-year-old boy who was the eldest son of another man. While checking his traps one day, Blue Horn instructed the boy to return to camp. It was the last time the child was seen alive. When Blue Horn arrived back at camp and discovered that the boy hadn't yet shown up, a massive search party was organized. Everyone in the camp made a great effort to find the boy, but they were unsuccessful. Eventually, they gave up.

The following March, another hunter made a gruesome discovery in those woods where Blue Horn had been trapping. The *Leader-Post* described the scene:

> [It was] the skeleton of the child in a standing position, its arms stretched out and wrists tied to two trees. He did not remove the skeleton, but went to inform the father of the lost boy in order that he might see it and identify it as the remains of his lost son. From circumstances surrounding the affair it is evident the lost boy had been offered as a sacrifice to secure good luck in hunting by Indians.
>
> As it is their custom, the savages had hung about the body bits of cloth and trinkets to propitiate gods.

It's a horrifying story, but not a ghost story. Or is it? Could such an emotionally wrenching event take place and *not* leave behind some psychic scar? It's impossible to say. I only know that when I am asked why a province as quiet as Saskatchewan would have so many restless spirits, stories like this one tend to come to mind.

The Soo Line Historical Museum

It's a typical day, which means that Jacquie Mallory, curator of the Soo Line Historical Museum in Weyburn, is dealing with the antics of a ghost.

"Today, we had to fix something in a showcase," she said. "We have a silver and ivory statue of Eleanor of Aquitaine, and she's wearing a headpiece. It's anchored onto her head, and it's in a sealed showcase, and it's been sitting there, untouched, for a year and a half. But, today, the headpiece was just lying in the showcase, like somebody took it and flung it off her head. So we had to take the time to take that all apart."

A strange event, but not unusual in this particular museum. "Weird things happen," said Jacquie. It's an understatement, if ever there was one.

When Jacquie accepted the position of curator in 2006, she had already worked at the museum for a number of years. So she knew that the place was haunted, and she understood all the particular challenges that came along with that.

"Things go missing on us a lot," she said. "Something could be right there and the next day it's gone. And either it doesn't show up, or it shows up in a really stupid spot." Staff constantly experienced problems with electronics, as well. "From the photocopier and the two computers to the phones and the fax. Even the cameras we use for cataloguing. Something's always wrong with something. It's just so, so frustrating."

Jacquie also knew that when she took over, she would have to put up with what she calls "the shadows" — a number of shifty, elusive entities that lurk in particular areas of the museum and watch the staff. "There are lots of shadows," she said. "We always have somebody standing in our kitchen, and if you look up, you'll see just a glimpse of them, and then they're gone. And there's one that likes to stand in the doorway that goes out of the lobby, into the next area. There's always something standing there."

Another unexplained phenomenon in the museum is ghostly music.

"At the very back [of the museum] there's one man's collection of radios," said Jacquie. "There are probably forty radios in there, archaic radios that don't have batteries in them anymore. And I've had [two different people] tell me that they heard music playing out of that room. And neither person knows the other, because they didn't work here at the same time."

Most staff members have had at least *some* strange experience in the museum, but Jacquie is a highly intuitive person who has always experienced the full magnitude of the spiritual activity there. Missing office supplies, malfunctioning computers, and lurking spectres were the occupational hazards that came with her chosen career. The museum is housed in a 1910 power plant, and could certainly be haunted by the ghosts of men who once worked there. And it's generally accepted that objects, can have spirits attached to them, particularly antique objects. That is where the Soo Line Historical Museum's potential to be haunted goes through the roof.

"We have ... maybe thirty thousand artifacts in this place," said Jacquie. "We're not sure, specifically, what things might be attached to." What Jacquie and her staff are sure of is this: the level of activity changes as different displays are put up.

In November of 2008, the museum presented a military display in the lobby in the weeks leading up to Remembrance Day. As soon as the military artifacts came out of storage, the paranormal activity went through the roof. "Crazy, crazy stuff," said Jacquie. "A lot of dark shapes and unexplained things." When the display was dismantled, everything calmed down. The museum staff was not surprised. They've always noticed that different artifacts instigate different levels of activity. Clothing seems to be a particularly powerful catalyst.

"Certain clothes we put out ... things happen," said Jacquie. "I have seen where we've put certain clothes on a mannequin, and weird stuff starts happening. Activity starts immediately. We have one display ... it's a lawyer's office that we've set up. And in that lawyer's office, we dressed a male mannequin in an old — probably one-hundred-year-old — men's suit, with a cut-away jacket. Put a top hat on him. We had that thing up for probably six or eight months. And it was *awful*."

During the time that clothing was on display in the lawyer's office, Jacquie could feel a presence in that area. On one occasion, as she passed through the museum, she saw a ghostly figure sitting behind the lawyer's desk. She didn't say anything to the staff but, later on, a summer student approached her to say that *he* had seen an apparition in that exact spot. According to Jacquie, that's something that frequently happens.

"We're not all feeding each other the same information," she said, "but, when we start comparing, we find we have the same kind of stories."

And many of those stories come from students who work in the museum during summer months, or on temporary assignment.

"Our summer student — he's very intuitive," said Jacquie. "When he started, when he had to work in the evening, he wouldn't even go [through the room with the lawyer's display] at night to take the sign down from the south-facing door. He would go outside and walk around the side of the building to get the sign when he closed up at night. All because he was so freaked out by that mannequin with the costume." According to Jacquie, there were two other students who refused to go into that area of the museum alone. One — a fellow whom Jacquie described as "a big, strapping boy" — finally agreed to enter the room, as long as he could wear his I-Pod to distract him from the creepy sensation he experienced there.

"Finally," said Jacquie, "I took the darn thing down. And, then, all those feelings went away. The other kids [that came to work] weren't nervous, or scared. It all felt so much better after it was gone."

Some displays are permanent, however, and there is no option of packing them away if the ghosts that are attached to them become too much to bear. One example is the museum's flagship, the Charles Wilson Silver Collection. It is the largest one-man collection of silver known to exist in Canada, and it was bequeathed to the Soo Line Historical Museum by Wilson in 1995. Jacquie and her staff feel quite certain that the spirit of the man came along with his treasured belongings, in order to watch over them.

"We know Charlie's attached to the collection," said Jacquie. "He's in there [with the] private collection, and he stands in the one place where he can view everybody coming in. We have a bed that belonged to him and, every so often, we have to go in and smooth out the bed, because it looks like somebody has been sitting on it. Also, Mr. Wilson used to be a smoker, and we smell cigarette smoke in here quite often. [And, one time] I walked in there and saw a reflection of somebody in the glass of the one showcase, when there was nobody in the room. But I walked in and saw a person standing there ... right beside where he usually stands."

Jacquie trusts her intuition, but was nevertheless pleased to have her feelings corroborated, on one occasion, by someone other than a staff member.

"We had a psychic come in here a while ago ... from Ontario. He was in town visiting. And I didn't say anything about *anything*, but he walked into that room and saw [Charles Wilson] immediately, just standing there. He described him to me, and the description was bang on. And he saw him in the corner where we all feel that he is. Having a psychic say it, that just verified it for us."

Of course, the psychic was only verifying what Jacquie and her staff already knew. They had long been convinced of Charles Wilson's presence in the museum and, what's more, they liked having him there. He was a dignified spirit, and a protective one. It seemed possible that he even kept other, lower entities in line.

"I don't know how to describe it," said Jacquie. "He's the one that we feel the most in here. He seems to be the kingpin. Others are sneakier...."

And, on one rare occasion, more menacing. The other woman who works full-time at the museum once encountered a shadowy figure that seemed threatening to her.

"She said that something followed her from the radio room," said Jacquie. "She was scared, so she went into Charlie's room. And she said she saw a black shadow go right by, but it would not come into Charlie's room. She felt safe going in there."

In terms of otherworldly protection, Charles Wilson is not the only ghost who has shown concern for the well-being of the museum's staff. Another protective spirit appeared in the basement a number of years ago, when Jacquie was first appointed curator. She had just begun combing through the many storage areas, seeing if there were any items that needed to be moved or re-catalogued. While working in the section where the military artifacts were stored, she would often catch a glimpse of a soldier, peeking out at her from beneath the shelving. Jacquie could never see the man's uniform, only his face, which appeared to be either smudged with smoke or covered in mud. After she had seen the apparition a number of times, she discovered that she was not the only person who had. The summer work student confided in Jacquie one day that *he* had encountered a spectral soldier in the basement. His description of the ghost matched Jacquie's exactly, right down to the smears of dirt on the man's face. So there was no doubt that the soldier was there, and it would not be long before the museum staff knew *why* he was there. It was revealed as Jacquie continued her inventory of stored artifacts.

"I was down there one day," she said, "working in the corner where we keep things from World War I and World War II. I picked up one of these [shells] and I heard a clunk inside. And I thought — that's not good, because these things should be empty. There should just be that outside [housing]." When Jacquie picked up another shell and heard the same clunk of interior workings, she became very nervous; nervous enough to phone the fire department. Someone was sent to investigate, and he was equally concerned. One more phone call was made and, before she knew it, Jacquie had military personnel on her doorstep.

"Whoever they were," she said, "they came from Winnipeg and they were dressed in military clothing. They went through all this stuff and they took about eight things. Took them out [to a range] and blew them up." Jacquie was informed that the shells had not been powerful enough to blow up a building, but that they certainly could have caused great personal injury to whoever was handling them when they exploded. "Had they been dropped, they would have blown off a hand, or an eye, or something like that," said Jacquie.

As for the apparition of the soldier … he was never seen again. But Jacquie felt certain of why he had been there.

"He was trying to send us a warning," she said.

Clearly, the majority of the spirits that Jacquie and her staff work amongst are benevolent. As for those who are on the darker, more mischievous side, Jacquie knows how to deal with them. In a nutshell, she tries to never show fear.

"I am a firm believer that if I'm really scared, then whatever is here is going to feed off of that," she says. "So, when things happen, I just go 'Oh! You've *got* to be kidding me!'"

Jacquie's way of handling such things seems to be serving her well. She manages not only to co-exist peacefully with the ghosts but, in many ways, enjoys them.

"It is interesting," she says. "Not everybody gets to go to work … and have these kinds of experiences."

Of course, not everyone would want to. Fortunately, those people don't work at the haunted Soo Line Historical Museum.

Ghost Hunting on the Prairies: Ghost Hunters Research Team

Founding members of the Ghost Hunters Research Team, Wendell Kapay and Dana Hryhoriw.

Case File Quick Facts

Name: Ghost Hunters Research Team

Date Founded: September, 2004

Website: No website, yet — but the group's email address is *frozen-ghost@ hotmail.com*

Mission: To help spirits, and communicate with them. To find proof of the afterlife.

Founding Members: Dana Hryhoriw and Wendell Kapay
Favourite Saskatchewan Haunt: Fort San. Dana and Wendell never got
the chance to investigate the San, but find the stories intriguing.

Q & A with Dana Hryhoriw

Ghost Hunters Research Team is the name of Regina-based duo Dana
Hryhoriw and Wendell Kapay. They've been helping people with their
paranormal problems for more than four years, and handle as many as
thirty investigations each year. Despite this intense schedule, Dana carved
out some time to talk to me about the work that she and her partner do.

Q: Are you and Wendell the sole members of the group?

A: We have two other part-time members who will come and help us
but, most of the time, it's Wendell and I.

Q: How do you manage to take on so many investigations each year?

A: Well, it's pretty hard. Usually, we do a lot of what we call preliminary
investigations. That's what we have time for, and it's usually all people
want, and that's two to three hours. Two to three hours at a client's
house. We do more of those than anything. A lot of people, when it
comes right down to the actual investigation, they tend to want to
back out. They want to know, but they don't want to know.

   The hardest part of the whole thing — even harder than finding
time to do these investigations — is finding time to play back all
the video tape and digital recording. It's hard to find the time and
patience to sit and watch two hours of a dark room.

**Q: What is the difference between a preliminary investigation and a
full investigation?**

A: Preliminary, we'll only spend a limited amount of time, and we'll only bring the basic equipment. We won't actually lug everything over and set it up. We'll go for a lot of EVP recordings and ask [questions] to see if we can get a reaction out of the spirits. Whereas in an actual investigation, usually we'll try to do some research beforehand, like at a library, or interview neighbours and whatnot. And we'll set up our equipment and have an actual home-base set up where we monitor everything from. It usually takes a lot of time to set up a full-blown investigation.

Q: Why do people frequently back out prior to the full investigation?

A: I think it's a matter of "Ooooh! Can I live in here after I know for sure?" And people tend to watch too many movies, and they will tend to stereotype spirits. Wendell and I try to teach people that, yeah, there are malevolent spirits out there, but we look at [spirits] this way: they were somebody's loved one; they lived a life; they had laughter, sadness. We try to show them the good side: That not all spirits are malevolent. They're not going to hurt you.

Q: What criteria must be met in order for you to accept a case?

A: We try to pick people who are not taking heavy prescription medication that can affect their senses. And we try to steer away from mental illness, or from anybody who's a heavy drinker. We get a lot of calls from people who are intoxicated, and we tend not to take those seriously. And, usually, you can judge somebody by the things they say. If they sound disrespectful towards the spirit, or towards us and what we do, we tend to steer clear of those.

Q: What sort of equipment do you use?

A: We use the basics. We have camcorders with night vision. We have wireless cameras with infra-red vision. We use infra-red thermometers — the instant-read ones. We have a parabolic dish, tape recorders, digital voice recorders. We use digital cameras, 35 mm cameras, everyday stuff. None of the fancy stuff you see on TV. We use baby powder....

Q: Baby powder?

A: We track movement with baby powder. We check for fingerprints. As an example, we did an investigation with a small-town Saskatchewan bar — one of the oldest buildings in town. We set up a few glasses on top of baby powder, just to track the slightest little movement — movement that people wouldn't notice. It's quite handy for fingerprints, as well. You can set up some baby powder in a room just by itself, and you may find fingerprints that have no reason for being there.

Q: So low-tech can be effective?

A: Absolutely. A compass is another tool that I like to use. It's never let me down. I use it like an EMF detector. I don't believe in EMF detectors ... I find there's too much interference these days to get a proper reading. But the compass acts like [an EMF detector]. Any time there's a spirit around, the compass tends to kind of have a mind of its own. But if you go in front of a TV, or anything that has electromagnetic force, it won't disrupt the compass. Not too much interferes with it, so it's a pretty good, useful tool that I like to have.

Q: What are your standards of evidence?

A: Usually, for me, EVPs are something very concrete. It's pretty hard to try and explain away an EVP. Photographs, it depends. Orbs are pretty tricky, because you have to watch out for dust. It's a matter of getting your eyes trained to decipher what might be dust and what might be an actual orb. Videotape is always nice — evidence of things moving on their own. Generally, though, I like to go for an EVP. But I also take impressions and feelings into consideration.

Q: How do you feel about the numerous TV shows about ghost hunting?

A: Well, I guess when it comes to those shows, I'm a skeptic. I think a lot of those shows tend to give people the wrong idea. They're in it for ratings, so they'll tend to embellish. And, sometimes, they go over the top. I will admit, though, that some of the shows nowadays are starting to be a bit more [realistic]. We watch *Paranormal State*. That tends to be not too bad. They don't seem afraid to admit if they go to a location and don't get anything. A lot of [other shows], it just seems a little convenient that every place they go, they provoke such intense reactions.

We are not what you see on TV. That's the biggest thing we have trouble with sometimes — trying to justify ourselves to our clients, [because] we're not coming in with big, fancy camera equipment. There is no television crew following us around. But [the clients] expect an entourage..

Q: Can you tell us about one of your most exciting investigations?

A: It was an all-boys foster home we went to. The kids were scared. That's one of the reasons we accepted the call. [Something was] in the basement, and the kids didn't want to stay down there anymore. And I've had that experience as a kid....

We had set up some cameras in one particular room that was always colder than usual, and nobody wanted to sleep in. We had the cameras set up, and the drawers were closed, and everything was nice and neat. I had decided to remain downstairs [in another area] by myself, while the rest of the team was upstairs. I was just asking general questions to see if I could get a reaction. All of a sudden I heard banging and screeching, like wood grinding on wood — that sort of screeching. I [called upstairs] and asked everybody if they heard it. They said that they did. So I asked them to come downstairs. I just stayed at the couch. Once we were all together, we turned on the lights and walked into the room. Now, this was only five minutes ... since we had left the room. And every single drawer was wide open and there was clothing scattered all over the room. It was just amazing. That sent chills down my spine. Usually you tend to get more subtle, kind of shy clues. A spirit kind of saying, "I'm here, but...." This one was kind of wide open ... advertising for all.

Also, in that house, in the other room, you could smooth out the blankets on the beds — freshly made beds — and you'd go back to check thermometers or other equipment in that room and it was as if somebody was just lying on that bed. There would be crinkles in the outline of a body. And you'd smooth it out again, and go back a few minutes later ... and it would be [mussed again]. It was just amazing.

Q: What's the next logical step in a case like that?

A: It all depends on our clients. Most of them just want to know that [they're] not crazy and those things are really happening. The house is haunted. Most of them are okay with that fact [once they understand that] it isn't a violent or malevolent spirit. They're fine with it.

If they want to banish [the ghost], that's not something we do, but we can maybe suggest an alternative for them to try. Most people know, though. We tell our clients right off the bat that if they're looking to banish a spirit, we won't participate in that.

Q: Given that, what is your own purpose when you do this?

A: Our basic reason for being in this type of work is to communicate. That would be the ultimate goal for us — to communicate. Have actual proof — not to show the world, but just for ourselves. And if somebody passed away and had a message for a loved one, that would be a privilege and an honour for us to take that message and share it with a loved one. We're more or less there to help the spirit.

Q: Have you had any personal experiences?

A: When Wendell was a little boy, after his father passed away, there was a rocking chair that his dad always sat in. Wendell said that chair had a specific creak to it when somebody would rock in it. One night, when everyone was asleep, he heard that chair, squeaking as if his dad was rocking in it. That was creepy. And cupboard doors were opening and closing by themselves. And those things had never happened to them before. So he believes that his dad stuck around for a little while after he passed away.

As for me, I've never considered myself sensitive, or psychic, or anything. But I still, to this day, cannot explain [a premonitory] dream I had about my grandfather. (In the November 9, 2008 edition of the *Regina Sun Community News*, Dana told the story of a recurring dream that she had when she was in the eighth grade. She saw herself in school, wearing a particular outfit, when she was called to the office. Once there, she was told that her parents would be picking her up because her grandfather had passed away. Dana was close with her grandfather, and was extremely upset by the dream — and by the fact that it was recurring every night. To ensure that it would never come true, Dana decided that she would simply avoid wearing the clothing that she saw herself wearing in the dream. But one morning, she woke up late. She dressed quickly, without thinking. Later, at school, she was called down to the office. She looked down and realized that she was wearing the outfit from her dream. She cried all the way to the office, where she was informed that her grandfather had died.)

Q: Has doing this work changed your belief system?

A: It kind of helped answer a question, for me. Now I truly believe that when somebody dies, it's not just "lights out." There is something more to death than [the fact that] your heart stops beating. I didn't know what to believe before. There are so many stories. But I definitely believe now that everybody has a soul.

4
Legends and Lore

The Vanishing Coffee Shop

There is a tale told about a mysterious coffee shop that once existed at the bottom of the hill in Flaxcombe. It has all the markings of a particular urban legend that is often told about an inn, or a gas station, or a tavern. This version is made unique by its change of venue and, of course, its Saskatchewan setting.

As there are no actual witnesses to these events (and, in all likelihood, none of this ever happened) I've taken creative licence with several details in the retelling. Therein lies the fun of passing on a legend!

Harold Tilley was not a quitter. Quitting was a habit one couldn't afford when one was in the business of door-to-door sales. But by eight o'clock, Halloween night, 1946, Harold decided that admitting temporary defeat was not the same thing as quitting and, so, he gave in to it. He closed up his sample case of brushes and gadgets and miracle cleaners and put it in the trunk of his Hudson, next to his battered, brown, travelling-salesman suitcase. Then he drove out of town. He was careful not to hit any of the costumed trick-or-treaters wandering the streets with their pillow slips full of candy corn and caramel apples. But, deep in his heart, he cursed them for ruining what would have otherwise been a fine evening of huckstering. Nobody wanted to buy a damn thing when there were little hooligans arriving at the door every five minutes, demanding candy. Most people wouldn't even let him in. One old woman with bad eyesight had thrown a handful of licorice treats into his sample case and closed the door in his face. That was the moment when Harold realized that the day was simply done.

He was travelling west. His route had taken him through all the small towns on Highway 7, from Saskatoon to Kindersley. He knew there were nothing but whistle stops until he got well across the Alberta border. So Harold figured that, if he could accomplish nothing else on this day, he could at least make some miles. He would drive through the night, and wake up in some place with suburbs full of housewives in need of his Dura-shine Floor Wax and labour-saving vegetable choppers. It would be a new day, a new place, and a new quota to meet. He turned on the radio, put his foot on the pedal, and drove.

He'd been on the road for no more than twenty minutes, however, when he realized that he hadn't had dinner. His stomach grumbled complainingly as he thought of the licorice that he'd thrown away in disgust after his last call. He realized that he should have eaten in Kindersley. Should have found a diner; gotten himself a big plate of meatloaf and gravy and chased it with a slice of pie. The thought made Harold's mouth water, and he considered turning around and doubling back. But it was late — too late, probably, for any place to be open. So he pushed the thoughts of food away and drove on with grim determination.

Minutes later, the Hudson's headlights flashed off a battered sign that told Harold he was entering THE VILLAGE OF FLAXCOMBE. He'd been there before, he thought. Lots of nothing and a bit more nothing on top of that. No chance of even grabbing a stale sandwich there. But, as Harold drove down the hill into the dark valley, he saw something that gave him a sliver of hope. It was a business of some kind; it had big windows that were brightly lit and a sign that he couldn't read from the distance he was at. But, as he drew closer, he could make out the words COFFEE SHOP written out in big loopy letters that had been stripped of their paint. And through the windows, Harold could see a long, oval lunch counter bordered with red vinyl stools. His heart soared and his stomach thanked whatever gods saw fit to watch over starving salesmen. His evening may have passed without a sale, but it would not go by without dinner.

At the very bottom of the hill, Harold turned off the highway and onto an acre of dirt and gravel that appeared to be the coffee shop's parking lot. He nosed the Hudson up close to the front door. There were no other cars in the lot and, through the big windows, Harold could see that there were no customers occupying the seats at the counter. That suited him fine. It meant faster service and maybe even a chance to chat up the waitress, if she was attractive.

As Harold walked through the front door of the coffee shop, he noticed two things immediately. One, the waitress who was lingering just behind the saloon doors leading to the kitchen was obviously more of an aging matron than a looker, despite a head of flaming red hair that was clearly of chemical origin. And two, the room was almost unbearably hot. Had it been any other time, Harold would have walked back out and looked for someplace better. But it was late, and he was famished, and this was the middle of nowhere. Stifling or not, homely waitress or not, he needed to put some food in his stomach. He slipped off his overcoat, removed his hat, and took a seat at the counter. There were folded paper menus in a metal holder, and he took one.

"So, what's good tonight?" he said in his cheerful salesman voice.

He got no answer. Harold looked up from his menu and glanced around the restaurant. The waitress wasn't behind the swinging half-doors anymore. She was standing near the far end of the counter now, by an ancient coffee maker. She stared out the window into the dark, moonless night, seemingly oblivious to the fact that she had a customer.

"I'll take some of that coffee, for sure," said Harold. He was used to driving at night, but that didn't mean that he liked it. He knew that a jolt of strong, black coffee would help him along. As for what to go with it — Harold turned back to his menu and weighed the options. There wasn't much variety, but the prices were cheap. He was flipping the menu back and forth, trying to decide between beef stew and johnnycakes with sausage, when his hand bumped into a stained porcelain cup and slopped a bit of dark liquid onto the counter. Harold swore under his breath and pulled a paper napkin out of the holder.

And then he thought *When did she give me that?*

It was the cup of coffee he had asked for, sitting right in front of him. Yet, he hadn't seen the waitress pour it, or walk over. In fact, she was still right in front of the ...

No, she had moved. Harold looked around and found her standing on the customers' side of the counter now, a few feet to his left. She was staring out a different window with the same forlorn expression.

"Excuse me," Harold said.

The woman didn't respond. Harold saw that she wore a nametag, pinned to the lapel of her rumpled uniform — CATHY, it read.

"Excuse me, *Cathy*," he tried again. "Sure could use a little something to eat."

The waitress sighed heavily and stared straight ahead. Harold sighed, as well.

"Okay, I get the picture," he said. "Kitchen's closed. Well, how 'bout a couple of those doughnuts you have in the case?" Harold turned and pointed at a big platter that was half-filled with crumbling pastries and covered with a glass dome. When he turned back to the waitress, she was gone. Harold scanned the restaurant and saw that, somehow, she had already managed to reposition herself by the pastries. Then he set down his faded menu and saw that a chipped plate with two broken doughnuts had been placed in front of him. The waitress wasn't much of a talker, but she could hustle. Harold had to give her that. He resigned himself to a modest and silent supper, and settled down to enjoy it.

At least, he tried to.

The coffee was so bitter and putrid, it had to have been brewed hours earlier. And the doughnuts were stale to the point that, when Harold bit into them, they disintegrated to dust.

"Is this the best you've got?" Harold demanded. But when he looked around the room, he could see that he was talking to the walls. Cathy, the speedy and silent purveyor of horrid food and drink had moved sound-lessly back into the kitchen. Harold could see her standing mannequin-like, just beyond the saloon doors, hidden except for her sturdy shoes, support hose, and the shock of fiery hair. She was ignoring him again. Harold had had enough. Enough bad food, enough rude service, enough stifling heat. He wiped the perspiration from his forehead and stood up.

"Thanks for everything," he called out, in a sarcastic tone. He took a few coins from his pocket and threw them on the counter, not worrying whether the amount was close to being correct. He then picked up his coat and hat and walked out the front door.

The night was cold — verging on wintry — but Harold didn't mind. He drew in deep breaths of fresh country air and didn't put his coat on until he'd first cooled off for a few minutes. As he wondered how anyone could stand to work in that kind of heat, he looked back at the coffee shop. Close as Harold was to the front door, he found that he could no longer see it. Some strange fog had settled in around the building, completely obscuring it from view. Harold could see the eerie glow of light from the windows, but that was all. He shook his head and decided that it was past time to leave Flaxcombe. He got back in the Hudson, pulled out onto the highway, and drove.

Thirty minutes had passed, maybe even more, before Harold tried to stop again. This time he pulled into a gas station that seemed reassuringly lively, despite the lateness of the hour. A cheerful attendant ran out to the pumps and had the Hudson gassed up in record time. When Harold went inside the station to pay, he was met with the most glorious aroma.

"Mmmm, coffee!" he said. He closed his eyes and inhaled deeply.

"Fresh pot," said the attendant. "I can get you a cup, if you like."

Harold indicated that he *would* like, very much, and the man handed him a steaming paper cup. Harold closed his eyes as he took his first sip. It tasted nothing short of spectacular.

"You wouldn't believe the mud I drank at the last place I stopped," he said, and he told the gas station attendant about his awful experience at the Flaxcombe Coffee Shop.

The man listened to his story with a quizzical expression. He shook his head once Harold had finished.

"Couldn't have been Flaxcombe," the man said. "There's nothing there. No coffee shop, that is."

But Harold was certain of it. He remembered seeing his headlights bounce off the rough-looking sign that welcomed visitors to the village.

"No, it *was* Flaxcombe," Harold said.

But the gas station attendant was adamant.

"Used to be a place there," he said. "A sort of diner, at the bottom of the hill. But it burned down, years ago. On this very night, actually, Halloween, 1936. Few people tried building on that spot since then, but nobody has any luck. Been three more fires on that same land in the last ten years."

Harold said nothing, but he was thinking that the man had to be talking about some other place. He was thinking that the coffee shop had been pretty strange, and *very* hot, but it was a real place. He had walked into it. Sat on a stool. Felt the scorching heat of a furnace working overtime. Talked to the waitress …

The gas station attendant interrupted Harold's thoughts.

"That was a sad thing, that fire," he said. "Local woman died in it. Waitress named Cathy."

And Harold dropped his paper cup of coffee as the man finished by saying, "We used to call her 'Red.'"

Although this story has all the earmarks of a well-known urban legend, I was curious as to what seeds had allowed it to grow in the fertile soil of Flaxcombe. I tried to find the source of the story, but had no luck. I asked around to see if it was well-known amongst locals, but had no response. I even inquired as to whether there was any one location in the village that had a history of fires. That still remains to be known. Given the folkloric quality of the story, it's probably an urban legend with little or no basis in fact. But it was just too good not to share.

A Haunting History

Foam Lake is a community of some twelve hundred souls, located between Yorkton and Saskatoon, in south-eastern Saskatchewan. The sign that welcomes visitors proclaims this small town to be THE BEST PLACE IN THE WORLD TO LIVE. Though it is not advertised with the same degree of enthusiasm, this place is also known for a creepy little story that reads like a campfire tale.

This legend is said to take place, not in the town of Foam Lake, but in the beautiful rural landscape that surrounds it. One hundred years ago, there was a family that farmed there — a family with numerous children and more than their share of hard luck. The children were always ill, it seemed. They suffered coughs and fevers and maladies of every description. If there was a "bug" going around, they were all sure to catch it. If one of them cut themselves peeling potatoes or stepped on a nail in the barn, the wound was certain to infect. And there were many wounds to invite infection, as they were the most accident-prone group of children anyone in the area had ever seen. Visits to the doctor were frequent, but no amount of medical treatment or cautionary advice seemed to change a thing.

At some point, the whole thing became suspicious.

This was at least forty years before the psychiatric disorder known as Munchausen by Proxy (a syndrome that causes a caregiver to harm those in their charge) was identified, but people were savvy enough to suspect garden-variety abuse. It was simply difficult to accept that the children from one family could suffer so many ailments and injuries. At some point, it is said, the mother of the household was investigated. Her ability to care for the children was questioned but, ultimately, no neglect could be proved.

After that, things changed in the family. The children were as wanting of medical attention as ever, but trips to the doctor were avoided in order to avoid the attention that they inevitably drew. Similarly, neighbours who offered to help were curtly dismissed and told that they were not welcome on the property. The mother and father drew a figurative veil of privacy around themselves and allowed no one in. But, inside that veil, things carried on as they had before.

The children continued to suffer an inordinate number of bumps and bruises and sniffles and stomach ailments. And there were things that were much worse. Some of the little ones were bedridden for weeks at a time. Others sustained crippling injuries. Inevitably, in such a situation, tragedy struck. One of the youngest children was burned so severely that he died. And, as the years passed, his brothers and sisters all followed him to the grave. Each of them perished in the house, an innocent, young victim of some mysterious disease or horrible accident. The parents lived alone on the farm until their own deaths, many years later.

So, the family is now gone.

But the house is said to remain.

And those who have seen it would say that the building and land were not left unscathed by the terrible events that took place there. That house may have ghosts, or, depending on how you interpret the story, the house may *be* a ghost. It certainly has strange qualities that set it far apart from any other abandoned dwelling.

It is said to stand alone, surrounded by a small grove of trees, in the middle of a windswept prairie field. Such a thing should be easy to spot — after all, *anything* in the middle of a Saskatchewan field is easy to spot — but people say that it is actually quite elusive. If you're searching for this particular house, you may drive or walk around the area in frustration, unable to see it at all. That is, until it is directly in front of you, as big as life and as clear as day. Until that moment, the house seems almost invisible, like it doesn't want to be found. Perhaps because it doesn't welcome visitors.

The interior of the house is even more disconcerting. You may notice a wall that is covered in fading floral paper — then look again, a moment later, to see nothing but exposed lath. You may notice a chair that appears fit

A spectral farm house with a disturbing past haunts an ordinary Saskatchewan field.

Photo by Andrea Oxtoby.

enough to sit in — then see, at second glance, that it is badly splintered and leaning against a wall for support. You may see a window that offers a clear view of the fields beyond — but the next time you look, the glass is cracked and clouded with decades of grime. Nothing is as it appears in this house. It is enough to drive a person mad.

It is almost as if the house itself is hiding in shame. Or perhaps it is trying to maintain the facade of normalcy — or a tradition of secrecy — kept by the parents of the hard-luck family that lived there a century ago.

Prairie Bloody Mary

Anyone who has ever been a teenager at a slumber party or joined in a campfire story-telling session knows some version of the legend called Bloody Mary. Details vary from telling to telling, but the bones of the story is this: a person in a darkened bathroom faces the mirror and chants Bloody Mary in an effort to summon the evil spirit of a long-dead witch who, upon appearing, will then either scratch your eyes out, make you insane, or pull you through the mirror to live with her. This begs the question, why go to such effort to manifest someone who is such an appalling guest? Most people would cite the thrill-a-minute rush of having the pants scared off them with a group of friends. The odd slumber-party-game aficionado may have heard that if you're strong enough to stare the old witch down, she will be forced to give you her powers. But many are just curious to see if the ritual will work. Which, of course, it won't.

Right?

This is, after all, an urban legend and therefore cannot possibly be real. Right?

One Saskatchewan woman claims otherwise.

Amber Morgan (not her real name) was thirteen years old when, in her own words, she "found out that the game Bloody Mary can actually work."

She and another girl were visiting at a third friend's house. In the small southern Saskatchewan town where they lived, they were accustomed to making their own entertainment. On this particular day, the girls decided that entertainment would be a game of Bloody Mary, which they had never before tried. Although it was a sunny afternoon, they had perfect conditions in which to experiment — a dark basement bathroom with no windows and a door that shut out every ray of outside light.

The three girls locked themselves in the little room, held hands, and turned off the light. Immediately, they were plunged into darkness so complete that they couldn't see each other or anything around them. Together, they tried to remember the details of the ritual.

"We were trying to think, *how many times do you say it?*" said Amber. "Was it thirteen? No. Was it a hundred? No. Someone thought it was sixty-six. Finally, we decided that we would just keep saying it until something happened."

And so the girls began chanting, "Bloody Mary, Bloody Mary, Bloody Mary ..." Amber can no longer remember how many times the girls repeated the witch's name, only that eventually, something did begin to change. In the bathroom that was completely without light, the girls suddenly realized that they could see their own dim outlines in the mirror that they faced. There was a slight illumination that was allowing them to see. But the light wasn't leaking around the door. It seemed to be emanating from the floor. And it had an eerie, otherworldly, decidedly emerald cast.

"All of us noticed at the same time that the floor was starting to glow green," said Amber. "Soon, it was so bright that it was reflecting in the mirror. It was starting to light up the bathroom. Eventually, we could see our full reflections in the mirror; each of us could see each other. We were shock-struck. We couldn't move, we were just so surprised that it was working."

The girls may have been shocked by the sickly green fluorescence, but they were genuinely terrified by what happened next. As they stared, transfixed, into the mirror, they saw a looming black figure slowly materialize in the bathtub behind them. At first, it was shadowy and insubstantial but, with each of the girls' chants, it grew larger and denser until it became an unmistakably solid form.

"That did it, of course," said Amber. The spell was broken. One of the girls screamed, threw open the bathroom door, and ran. Sensibly, Amber followed her. They ran through the basement, up the stairs, and into the main floor of the house before they realized that the third girl was not with them. Amber and the other girl were frightened, but also concerned for the safety of their friend. Reluctantly, they crept back down the stairs leading to the basement. Their teenaged imaginations must have been working overtime, wondering what they would find. Their friend, with her eye sockets bloody and raw. Their friend, hopelessly mad and raving. Their friend, peering desperately out from the other side of the mirror.

What they found was their friend, lying in the bathtub in a dead faint.

"She'd been so terrified by what she saw that she never made it out of the bathroom," explained Amber.

Teenagers are resilient, and the girls recovered quickly from the shock of their experience. More than that, they spent countless hours speculating about what had happened and sharing the story with other close friends. Of course, people who hadn't seen the phenomena with their own eyes had a hard time believing that such things could actually happen. Most were happier — and more comfortable — thinking of Bloody Mary as a harmless urban legend.

Amber wasn't content to be mocked, however. Several months later, she was in her own home with two other friends, as well as her brother and a buddy of his. She had heard the phrase, "Yeah, *right*," one too many times, and decided that she had to silence the doubters. In her mind, the only way to do this was to repeat the experiment.

"I'll bet you we can get it to work," she coaxed her friends. "We got it to work last time!"

Somehow, she convinced the others that this was a good idea. The group went into the bathroom, closed the door, shut off the light, held hands, and faced the mirror. They began to chant, "Bloody Mary, Bloody Mary, Bloody Mary, Bloody Mary …"

"We just kept saying it, and saying it," said Amber. "And, again, the room started to get this weird light to it. But I kept checking the mirror for the apparition, and there was no reflection. And I'm thinking, *what's going on?*"

Then, suddenly, Amber realized that they were in a different bathroom, with a different floor plan. This time, there was nothing behind them but a wall. Was it possible? She looked to her right, where the bathtub in her bathroom was located. There, behind the etched-glass shower doors, hovered the menacing black figure.

"Everyone started to freak out," said Amber. "We all ran out of the bathroom and up the stairs."

The girls' hearts were pounding and their hands were shaking. But, somehow, they still had the presence of mind to realize that they had on their hands a golden opportunity to inflict a little torture on the boys, who were a bit younger than they were. Thinking quickly, Amber told her brother, "We're gonna hide! You guys should hide, too!" She then led her girlfriends and her dog into a bedroom closet.

The girls were once again in the dark, but this time trying to stifle giggles. Deciding that it was time to take the game up a notch, all three girls screamed out for help.

"Oh, my god, you guys! She's in here with us!"

Amber could hear the boys panicking and scrambling from their own hiding places. She and her friends were shaking with silent laughter but trying to sound horrified. She might have wondered if the prank would eventually blow up in her face — but she could not have imagined how.

When the boys reached the closet, they tried to open the door to free the girls. What they didn't know was that the girls, inside the closet, were doing their best to brace the door shut. The harder the boys worked, the more frantic they became, and the more entertained the girls were.

Until, oddly, the dog began to whimper.

That stopped Amber cold. Her dog was a serious guard dog; fearless when it came to protecting her. And yet, at that moment, he was cowering against Amber's leg, shrinking away from the opposite side of the closet. Amber looked up … and screamed for real.

There, in the dim light that bled in around the closet doors, Amber could see the threatening black figure. It was every bit as sinister as it had seemed before, and now it was inches away from her. She stopped bracing the door. Suddenly, she was desperate to open it. But, despite the combined efforts of the girls inside the closet and the boys outside, the door wouldn't budge. And that was practically impossible, considering that it was a typically flimsy sliding closet door.

"If you pushed on this door, it would fall over," Amber said. "But, at that moment, we could not move that door."

Fortunately, that moment didn't last forever. The door eventually burst open, and the girls, along with Amber's terrified dog, spilled out into the welcome light of the bedroom.

An hour later, the entire group was huddled at the kitchen table. Sunshine poured in through the windows, creating a safe, cheerful atmosphere that had calmed them down quickly. They had rehashed the frightening events several times and had already begun to doubt their own senses. Everyone had seen the eerie, phosphorescent light; everyone had seen the shadowy, menacing spectre. They had all shared the same experience, but they were no longer unanimous in their belief. It could have been a trick of the light. It might have been a product of their own excited imaginations. Amber was frustrated. She had set out to convince her friends, but seemed to have failed. In one desperate, final bid to make them believe, she called out, "Bloody Mary, if that was you, call us right now!"

As if on cue, the telephone rang. Everyone froze. Finally, Amber picked up the receiver.

"Hello?"

There was a loud click in her ear, followed by dead silence. No dial tone, no static. Silence. Amber hung up the phone with a shaky hand. Her friends stared at the receiver, finally convinced.

Make that "temporarily" convinced. Their conviction dissolved a few minutes later when Amber's mother walked into the house.

"I just tried to call you," she said. "My cell phone was working until you picked up and said 'hello,' and then I hit a dead zone."

"So the phone thing was a coincidence," Amber admitted, later. "But that just happened to finish it off for us."

Many years later, Amber remains certain of what she saw on those occasions.

"It was definitely there," she says. "I saw that black figure. It wasn't my imagination. I mean, I'm imaginative, but not like that."

It's interesting to note that she was never able to reproduce the experience again. And she still has no idea why the ritual worked on the two occasions that it did. She supposes that everyone involved was young and open-minded and, in a very real sense, was inviting and welcoming in unseen forces. But why then, and not the countless other times that Amber and her friends created similar circumstances?

"We tried [playing] Light as a Feather, Stiff as a Board; we tried holding seances; we used a Ouija board — none of that stuff ever worked for us. But Bloody Mary worked *twice*. Both times, in broad daylight. Two different groups of people. Two different houses, so it wasn't like the house was haunted, or anything. And months apart. The first time was May, and the second was September. To this day, I don't get it."

That's probably a good thing. For if the legend is true — if it really *is* possible to summon such a powerful and malefic force — then one must hope at least that it is not that easily done. With luck, there is an extra element — one accidentally and unwittingly stumbled upon by Amber and her friends on those two isolated occasions — without which the ritual won't work. Because to have the ability to call up such powerful and dark forces with what is essentially a game; with a simple ritual that is known to children the world over....

Now, *that's* terrifying.

The Secret of the House

It was a weathered, abandoned shell of a house, standing sentinel at the edge of a field where two dusty back roads converged. There were a hundred like it across the flat Saskatchewan prairie — hollow spectres leaning from wind and rot, scoured clean of any paint, furnishings, or fixtures that might have once made them welcoming. This one was not unusual as far as the eye could see. But there are things that the eye can't see. Important things, sometimes.

They were a fairly young group of boys who decided to visit the house that evening — no more than sixteen or seventeen years of age. Certainly old enough to drive, but too young to walk into the local bar and order a drink. They lived in that twilight age between childhood and adulthood, and the world offered few places for them to feel independent, away from their parents' watchful eyes. And so they ended up at the house, which offered a sturdy enough floor and roof and a chance to behave as they liked.

There were three of them in all. We'll call them Danny, Mitch, and Shane. Their real names have been lost over many tellings of the tale, but no matter. It was never their names that made the tale worth telling. It is their experience that you will remember.

It was summer when it happened, during one of those endless stretches of heat that makes everyone long for evening and the bit of relief that comes with the setting sun. The boys all worked with their fathers during the day, tending the family farms. But evenings were their own, and the three of them —friends since elementary school — had made a plan to meet at the old house, which was as close to an equal drive from their three homes as they could get. Danny could usually talk his older sister into bootlegging a case of beer for them, and they were all looking forward to having a couple of cold drinks and a bit of time to "shoot the bull" and relax.

It was late when they met up. The sun was melting into the horizon and the faint chirping of night creatures could be heard in the surrounding field. Mitch had a cooler filled with ice and a battery-operated radio. Shane got out of his battered pickup truck carrying bags of potato chips. Each of them brought a folding lawn chair. They had all the makings of a party, including a location where they wouldn't be bothered.

The house was shrouded with years of dust and debris, but that didn't bother the boys. They settled into the largest room, put the beer on ice, turned up the music, and kicked back.

Soon, the sun had set completely. It was then that they realized they should have brought a light.

"We're lucky the moon is full," said Mitch. He was right. The moon was fat and round and the night was clear. Silvery light poured through the windows, so the boys had a clear, if eerie view of their surroundings. They talked, and laughed, and passed the time. Nobody missed the light.

Until midnight.

They were sure of the time, because it had just been announced on the radio station they were listening to. The moon, making its path across the sky, was no longer shining directly into the room — the boys had become dim shadows to one another. The atmosphere, which had been lively and light, suddenly seemed sinister. And it was then that they heard the noise.

"What was that?" said Shane. He was the first to jump from his lawn chair.

Before the others could respond, it came again.

"Are you doing that? Are you?" Mitch demanded. He was now on his feet, as well. He spun around nervously, examining every corner of the dark room. His shoe caught the corner of the cooler and sent it skidding across the floor planks.

Danny didn't jump, but held his hand up in a gesture to quiet his friends. He cocked his head, waiting for the sound. Within seconds, it came: a human cry — almost a scream — that rang with utter agony. Somehow, it seemed to be coming from inside the room and beyond it at the same time. Danny's blood turned cold, but he remained calm.

"Listen," said Danny. "Let's see if we can figure out what direction it's coming from."

Shane and Mitch had other ideas.

"Forget it! I'm outta here!" said Mitch. He grabbed his radio in one hand and his cooler in the other and bolted out of the house. Shane followed. Both boys abandoned their lawn chairs and Danny. But he wasn't far behind them. He was braver than his friends, but not so brave that he wanted to stay in an abandoned house in the dark listening to spectral screams. He was in his car, spitting gravel with his rear tires, mere seconds after the other two. He was at least two kilometres down the moonlit dirt road before his heart rate began to slow to anything resembling normal.

He was in his bed, with the covers pulled tight around him, before the ghostly echo of the scream began to fade from his ears.

Of course, the next day, they all felt foolish.

They met up at the convenience store late in the afternoon and bought frozen treats to relieve the heat. Outside, they sat at a picnic table in the vacant lot beside the old store and found that they could barely look one another in the eye.

"Was it maybe a bird of some kind?" Shane finally asked.

Mitch shook his head.

"Not at night," he said. "Bats, maybe. I could see that. They make some freaky screeching noises sometimes."

Danny ate his ice cream in silence. He didn't offer an opinion until, finally, his friends asked for one.

"I don't know what it was," he said, as he crumpled his wrapper and made a perfect two-point throw into a nearby trash can. "But I can tell you that the only way we'll ever know is if we go back tonight."

The other boys gaped at Danny in disbelief.

"Forget it," said Shane.

"No way," echoed Mitch.

"But doesn't it *bother* you?" asked Danny. "Aren't you going to wonder about it years from now?"

"Not likely," said Shane. His eyes told a different story, but his fear surpassed his curiosity. He shook his head at Danny's foolishness, got up from the worn, old picnic table, and walked away.

Mitch stood up as well. He looked at Danny with a furrowed brow.

"You aren't really going back there, are you?" he asked.

Danny nodded.

"Tonight," he said. "At midnight."

When Mitch shook his head in disbelief, Danny simply shrugged.

"I gotta know," was his simple explanation.

At 11:45 that night, Danny pulled his rusty old car slowly onto the soft dirt shoulder at the crossroads. He experienced a strong, sudden urge to flee but fought it down because, as he had told his friend, he simply had to know. Had to know if it had been his imagination, or the beer. Had to know if it would happen again. Had to know what could make that kind of unholy noise out in the middle of the clean, wholesome prairie.

It was another clear night, and the moon was missing only a hair's-width of fullness, so the house and the path leading to it were well-lit. Still, Danny switched on the flashlight that he had this time remembered to bring. He was prepared with other supplies, as well, including his father's hunting knife, which hung from his belt in a leather sheath. He touched that often, for courage. When he reached the doorway of the derelict house, he unsnapped the top flap of the sheath. Just in case he might need the knife quickly. Just in case.

The main room of the house was just as the boys had left it. The lawn chairs that they had jumped from remained overturned. The powerful beam of the flashlight illuminated trails in the thick dust and debris that carpeted the floor — more evidence of the previous night's party. Everything looked the same. As the minute hand on Danny's watch crept closer to twelve, he wondered if everything would *be* the same. He gripped his flashlight with one hand and wrapped his other hand around the coldly reassuring handle of the knife.

Suddenly, he was pitched into darkness.

Ice-cold shock flooded Danny's body. In the panicky moment that it took his eyes to adjust, he wondered if he'd been struck blind. Soon, though, his pupils dilated enough to let him see dim shapes in the watery moonlight. His heart still pounded, his breath still came in ragged gasps, but he realized that his flashlight had simply stopped working. Odd, considering he'd just put new batteries in, but still — what else could it be? Danny let go of the knife handle and used both hands to unscrew the bottom of the battery case. Sometimes they just needed a little jiggling to fix the contacts....

That was when he heard it.

It began low, a guttural moan that quickly rose, moving up the vocal scale until it reached a keening crescendo. The scream pierced Danny's head; he dropped the useless flashlight and clapped his hands over his ears for protection. It was worse, far worse than it had been the night before. But it was, in many ways, the same. The cry rang with the same agony and it seemed, again, to somehow be coming from within the room and just beyond it at the same time. As the tortured sound faded, Danny took his hands away from his ears and listened as carefully as he could. Then he thrust one shaking hand into the pocket of his jeans, pulled out what he was searching for, and walked on jelly legs to the furthest wall in the room. It took exactly one second and a mountain of courage to do what he had come to do. Then, as the horrific cry began to build once more, he ran out of the derelict house

Photo by Andrea Oxtoby.

A deserted ruin of a farmhouse held a sinister secret.

and to his car. He didn't look back, or even take a moment to pick up the broken flashlight. He left it to keep company with the overturned lawn chairs.

The next morning, following a sleepless night, Danny's mother called him to the phone. It was Mitch calling. He wanted to know if Danny had gone back to the house.

"What happened?" he said. "Did you hear anything?"

Danny squeezed his eyes shut at the memory of what he had heard.

"Listen," he said, "will you do something for me? You and Shane?"

"Not another midnight adventure," said Mitch.

"No," said Danny. "Full light of day. This afternoon, if you guys can get away."

The two friends made an arrangement, then hung up the phone. Danny pushed a little bit of breakfast around on a plate to please his parents. But, in truth, he had no appetite and was interested only in ransacking the tool shed to see what useful things he could take away in the small trunk of his car.

It was three o'clock on the nose when Danny, Shane, and Mitch all met at the crossroads.

"You look like hell," observed Shane.

"What happened here last night?" asked Mitch.

Danny shook his head.

"Something, for sure," he said. "Something weird. And I've got a hunch. That's why I need some help. I can't do this by myself."

He then opened the trunk of the car. It held a rusty assortment of tools: a hatchet, a sledgehammer, and a couple of crowbars.

"Grab something," said Danny. Without a word, the other boys did just that.

It was easier being in the house, in the *room*, in the bright light and high heat of the afternoon. For a moment, Danny doubted himself and felt silly for having dragged his friends away from their chores. But then he saw the wall; the wall where he had drawn a huge, accusing letter "X" with chalk that now lay broken on the floor where he had dropped it. The terror came flooding back and he knew that what he had experienced had been real. He turned to the other two boys.

"I heard it again last night," he said. "Worse than the first time. And it seemed to be coming from that spot." He pointed to the chalk mark. Both Shane and Mitch looked. "Now, like I said, I've got a hunch. It could be a wrong one, but I want to check it out. So I need some help taking apart that wall."

The boys looked at each other and then, again, at the exposed, weathered lath slashed with white chalk. And they shrugged.

"Not like anyone's gonna notice if we do a little damage to this dump," said Shane. He hefted the hatchet that he held in his hands and sauntered across the room.

Mitch sighed and followed him with the hammer.

"Let's do it," he said. "Let's see about your hunch, Danny."

He positioned himself to the left of Danny's chalk mark and swung the hammer. It landed squarely where the lines intersected. Right at the crossroads.

"'X' marks the spot," Mitch said, as the dry wood splintered and caved beneath his blow.

"'X' marks the spot," agreed Shane, as he came down with the hatchet, sending up a shower of ancient debris and dust.

"Thanks, guys," said Danny, as he joined in on the job that he would never have had the nerve to tackle on his own.

Fewer than ten minutes later, the three friends stood quietly, staring down into a cramped, hollow space between the wall they had just torn into and the wall of the room behind it. It was filled with the dust of years, a few skittering insects, and evidence of rodents' nests. All that and, still, there was room for the other thing. The other thing being a dirty, scarred heap of bones that lay there; someone's skeletal remains seeing dust-filtered sunlight for the first time in perhaps one hundred years or more. The skull tipped backward at a sickening angle, its jaw unhinged and hanging. Danny leaned over for a closer look and saw a fat spider move lazily inside an eye socket. Quickly, he looked away and willed his stomach contents back down to their proper place.

"Grab the stuff," he said. "Let's go."

Shane and Mitch didn't have to be asked twice.

The dirt road seemed a million safe miles from the horror that the three friends had just unearthed in the old house. They stood gratefully in the afternoon sun as Danny opened the trunk of his car.

"What should we do?" Mitch finally said. "Call the RCMP?"

"I'll tell my dad," said Danny. "He'll know how to handle it. He's got a buddy on the force."

The other boys nodded and put the tools back into the trunk. Shane dropped in the flashlight, as well. He had rescued it from the floor of the house.

"Shouldn't have bothered with that," Danny said. "It's busted."

Shane reached down and flipped the toggle switch on the handle. A bright beam of light cut across the shade of the trunk's interior. Danny's hand was shaking a little as he reached in and shut the flashlight off.

"Guess I was wrong," he said.

But he knew that he hadn't been. The flashlight had been just one more sign; one more message from the desperate soul that cried out for discovery in the decrepit prairie farmhouse at the crossroads.

Devil at the Dance

There is a story from northern Saskatchewan that bears great similarity to an urban legend that has circulated through the years. As with all such tales, the details may change, but the moral centre of the story remains intact. Also, in keeping with the tradition of legends, the teller of this tale insisted (and likely believed) that it was true. It was said to take place in a small community near Prince Albert.

It was Lent, and the young woman from a strict Catholic home was not supposed to be dancing. But there was a lively party being hosted at a rural dance hall, and many of the girl's friends were going. She wanted desperately to attend, and timidly broached the subject with her parents.

They were unyielding.

"Absolutely out of the question," boomed her father.

"Dancing during Lent! That's what the devil *wants* you to do!" declared her mother.

And the matter was then considered to be closed.

The girl spent days trying to think of ways to change her parents' minds, but knew in her heart that she had no chance of doing that. But the thought of laughing and twirling in her pretty spring dress, and perhaps flirting with a boy or two, was irresistible. When a friend offered to stealthily meet her at the end of the lane and spirit her off to the event, she agreed in a heartbeat.

The night of the dance arrived and the girl was more thankful than ever that her parents were fond of retiring early. As soon as they were asleep in their bed, the girl slipped out from under her own covers, already wearing her finest dress. She ran a brush through her wavy hair, stole out through the back door, and ran all the way to the end of the lane, being careful in the dark to dodge the slushy spring puddles. Her friend was waiting in a car with the engine idling quietly and the headlights dimmed.

"We'd better hurry," said the friend. "The party will be heating up by now."

As they drove off into the night, the young woman's excitement by far outweighed her feelings of guilt.

There was a large clearing around the hall, where people parked their vehicles, and the spring thaw had turned the ground soft with mud. The girls picked their way daintily across the yard to the front door of the hall, trying hard not to ruin their dancing shoes. When the door opened, however, spilling out light, music, and excited voices, they didn't spend another moment worrying about their feet.

The hall was filled with young men and women — all dressed in their very best, all with shining hair and flushed faces. The laughter was boisterous and constant. The music, provided by a three-piece band on a tiny, tread-worn stage, was lively and loud. Dancers whirled about the floor in front of the stage, dizzying spirals of energy and colour. Elsewhere in the room, people gathered in clusters, trying in vain to converse above the din.

"I want some punch," shouted the young woman, straining to be heard. Her friend nodded, and began to steer her through the crowd, toward the back of the room. As they stood waiting in a line-up at the refreshment table, the young woman suddenly sensed a change in the room. Many conversations became hushed and others stopped altogether. The band ended one tune with a fumbling final chord and were silent for a minute as they tried to decide what they should play next. The young woman's friend picked up her paper cup of lemonade and turned around. She was smiling and seemed about to say something but, instead, very suddenly, opened her eyes wide and simply said, "Oh."

The girl turned and saw what had cast a spell over the room. There, at the entrance, stood a man so wickedly handsome that the very sight of him made her heart squeeze tight in her chest. His hair was black as jet, his eyes two startling blue jewels set in a flawless face. Most of the boys in the hall were wearing their Sunday pants with rumpled shirts, and some had borrowed ill-fitting jackets from their older brothers or fathers. But this spectacular new fellow wore an expensively tailored suit of fine material that flattered his trim, muscular physique. He looked across the room, seeming to scan the crowd. When his eyes alit upon the girl, he smiled. It was a perfect smile, a perfect display of straight, white teeth. The girl thought she might faint. Instead, she turned back to the refreshment table and asked for ice water to cool her flushed cheeks.

After that, the girl found herself too distracted to enjoy the party. Several boys asked her to take a turn with them on the dance floor but each time she refused. She would make excuses, saying that she was overheated, or that the song being played was too fast, or too slow. In truth, she was keeping herself available, just in case the handsome man felt inclined to ask her. She had been watching him coyly from underneath her lashes. She made a show of talking to her friend and watching other couples on the dance floor but, since his arrival, the man had held her full attention. She noticed that he wasn't dancing either but, instead, circulated about the hall, never stopping long enough to speak with anyone. Handsome as he was, he appeared quite alone. And many of the times she stole a glance at him, she saw that he was looking at her, as well.

"Should we go, do you think? It's quite late."

The girl was startled out of her dreamy state. It was her friend, looking tired and dishevelled from hours of dancing.

"Oh ... so soon?" said the girl. "The party's only started." She could not hide her disappointment.

"We've been here hours!" said her friend. "Come on, now!" The friend grasped the girl's elbow and began moving toward the door of the hall. No more than a half-dozen steps across the room, however, the girls' path was blocked.

By the handsome stranger.

"Are you really leaving already?" he asked. His voice was velvet in the harsh din of the room.

"I guess ... I mean, I have to ..." stammered the girl. She felt as though she had lost the power of speech, so distracted was she by this beautiful stranger whose features were even more exquisite up close.

"Well, I won't have it," he said, with great authority. "You must permit me at least one dance."

The girl looked helplessly at her friend, who shrugged her permission.

"Go on. I'll wait while you have one dance," she said.

The girl smiled her thanks and let the man lead her out to the centre of the dance floor. He moved gracefully, guiding her easily with a light hand upon her waist. The throng of partygoers parted so easily for them, the girl was amazed that her dance partner didn't even need to tap people's shoulders or tell them "excuse me." People just moved naturally out of their way, even ones who had their backs turned and couldn't see them approaching. Within seconds, they were at the centre of the worn dance floor, in front of the stage. The stranger looked at the band and nodded. Immediately, the musicians launched into a lively tune, sounding better than they had the entire evening.

The girl felt as though she had stepped into a fairy tale. The stranger bowed to her in a courtly fashion, then lifted her hand in his. With his other arm he encircled her waist and, before she could take a breath, she was being whirled around the floor. The music grew louder and colours and lights appeared to spin around her head. The stranger was a magnificent dancer, so skilled and light on his feet. Soon the other couples ceased to dance and the girl could see the crowd pressing back, clearing space on the floor.

They are watching us, she thought proudly. *We must look wonderful together.*

When the music slowed, however, the girl was confused to see no expressions of admiration in the crowd. Quite the contrary, people looked disturbed, even repelled. Some of the young ladies had turned their faces away. All those who stared were looking in the direction of the floor.

Immediately, the girl understood. And she was horrified.

My shoes! she thought. She had not given them a moment's thought since walking into the hall. But she knew from the disgusted looks that her dressy pumps must be smeared with dried mud. And so she looked down....

And she screamed....

But before she could do anything else, the handsome stranger had his grip on her and he whisked her across the length of the hall and out the front door. Before anyone in the crowd could even think to intervene, the stranger and the girl were gone, having vanished into the darkness.

The girl, according to legend, was never seen again.

The handsome stranger — well, no one *wanted* to see him.

For the thing that everyone was staring at so intently as the couple danced was not anything so innocent as streaks of mud on the girl's shoes. Her feet were of no interest to the crowd. *His,* however, captured their attention. It had only become apparent as he danced that the reason he was so light on his feet was perhaps because he didn't have feet at *all* but, rather, animal hooves — fiery red and split in the toe, scratching against the wooden floor.

The young woman's mother had told her that it was the devil calling her to ignore the traditions of Lent and go to the party. She was right. In the end, the disobedient girl did the Dark One's bidding, and ended up meeting the devil at the dance.

Saskatchewan's Strange Creatures

Every country and culture the world over has its own stories of magical, mysterious, and monstrous creatures. Saskatchewan is no different. This province's folklore is rich with such tales. These accounts are often categorized — and dismissed — as mythical. And some may be exactly that. But there are others that deserve more serious attention. Particularly when there are credible, first-hand experiences to take into account. One "legend" that seems worthy of such consideration, and even of scientific investigation, is that of the Sasquatch.

Saskatchewan's vast tracts of northern wilderness make it an ideal home for the legendary creature known alternately as Bigfoot or Sasquatch. This tall, hairy, humanoid being is said to thrive in forested, sparsely populated areas. No wonder there have been so many eyewitness accounts in the northern part of the province.

One of the reasons that Sasquatch stories seem more credible than the average folktale is because of the many documented sightings. Archival records date back as far as the mid-1800s, and are filled with accounts of pioneers who discovered larger-than-life footprints or witnessed swarthy giants wandering around the woods. Research groups seeking evidence of Sasquatch's existence have been consistently filing away these reports for well over a century, and continue to do so today. One of the more interesting recent accounts came from a northern Saskatchewan woman in 2006.

According to the December 15, 2006 edition of the *Saskatoon Star-Phoenix*, Shaylane Beatty was driving from Deschambault Lake to Prince Albert on a sunny Saturday afternoon. She intended to shop for a few Christmas gifts. But, instead of spending a pleasant afternoon in the shops, Beatty experienced something that she will likely never forget.

She was driving near Torch Lake when she first noticed what she believed to be an enormous animal wandering between the tree line and the road. At first, it appeared to be a bear. As she drew closer, however, Beatty saw that the huge creature was walking upright and did not resemble any animal that she had ever seen. According to the *Star-Phoenix*, it was "About 2 ½ metres tall and muscular, with long, floppy arms attached to broad shoulders and covered in dark brown hair." The beast turned to look at Beatty as she drove by. This sent the woman into such a state of shock, she nearly lost control of her vehicle.

"My heart was beating real fast," she told the *Star-Phoenix* reporter, Jeremy Warren. "I was getting dizzy and short of breath. I kept repeating, 'I can't believe I'm seeing this.'"

She knew that she had seen it, though. And so, the next day, she returned to the area with two of her uncles to look for some physical evidence. The amateur investigators were in luck. In deep snow, they found hundreds of footprints, each measuring fifty centimetres in length. They took photos of the prints and collected samples of hair that may have belonged to the Sasquatch. Then Beatty and her uncles tracked the beast until dark. As they followed the trail, they noticed that whatever creature had made the footprints had moved with apparent ease through the deep snow that they were struggling to walk through. Also, Beatty's uncles found it impossible to match the creature's stride, even when they leapt from one print to the next.

Lifelong Sasquatch-hunter Tom Biscardi, who runs *www. searchingforbigfoot.com*, calls Shaylane Beatty's experience, and the evidence that she and her uncles gathered, "the find of the century." Indeed, in the face of such compelling information, it's difficult to banish Saskatchewan's Sasquatch into the realm of myth and legend.

Equally fascinating — if less credible — are stories about the shadow people of Cypress Hills. The Cypress Hills are one of Saskatchewan's natural wonders, the highest point of elevation on the map between the Rocky Mountains and Labrador. It is a place of unique beauty that appeals to nature enthusiasts from around the world. However, it is said that those who dare to leave their campsites at night to wander around the hills may experience something more supernatural than natural: the apparitions known as "shadow people." These are murky, nondescript shapes of people that are surrounded by haloes of eerie green mist. They appear on the edges of the hiking trails, often travelling as "families," with different-sized forms that are thought to represent children, teens, and adults. These entities are non-threatening and even timid, vanishing whenever they are approached. The shadow people are not frightening; they are not even believed to be ominous. But they are considered to be a great mystery, unique to one of the province's most beautiful geographical areas.

There are those who believe that the shadow people are the restless spirits of victims who were killed in the infamous Cypress Hills Massacre (a tragedy that occurred in May of 1873, when a vigilante group of American hunters attacked a sleeping Assiniboine camp, murdering twenty innocents). Whether that is true or not, there is certainly a possibility that this story is one of Native origin. Saskatchewan's First Nations have had a tremendous impact on the province's folklore, with many Native legends finding their way outside of that culture. One powerful example of this involves the story of the terrifying creature known as the windigo.

The windigo (also known as wendigo) is a fearsome, cannibalistic being believed by the Algonquian people to roam through the northern forests of Saskatchewan. This monster is said to be a shape-shifter of the most frightening kind; it can assume either a physical or phantom form, and destroy its victim by either devouring the flesh and blood or by possessing the mind. People who are possessed by the windigo are eventually driven to cannibalism, and are particularly obsessed with eating their own family members. Conversely, it is believed that people who resort to eating human flesh in survival situations will then be overtaken, after doing so, by an evil spirit that turns them into a windigo. And — powerful though it may be — no one wants to be a windigo. This creature is described as a massive being with a demonic appearance, possessed of supernatural speed and strength. It can hide in the wind and disguise itself as part of the forest. As well as striking terror into the hearts of any who witness it, it is said to be a harbinger of doom. An appearance of the windigo is believed to be followed closely by the death of a family member.

Of course, not all creatures of Native lore are as nasty as the windigo. Some are reasonably harmless (at least in modern accounts), interesting, and even tourist-friendly. One that comes to mind in this category is the Turtle Lake Monster.

Turtle Lake is a long, narrow lake situated approximately 120 kilometres northwest of the Battlefords. It offers good fishing, sparkling waters, and sandy beaches. It would be perfect, if not for the massive, writhing creature said to lurk in its depths. Ask any of the locals — they are all familiar with the story, which predates settlement of the area. The Cree were the first to speak of it, telling cautionary tales about people who had vanished after venturing into the monster's territory. Today, the Turtle Lake Monster averages one sighting per fishing season, inspiring descriptions that place it somewhere between three and nine metres, either scaly or smooth, and with a head that resembles either a pig, a dog, or (for the more traditional) a seahorse. Inconsistency is part of this creature's charm. Most people believe that witnesses have either seen an oversized sturgeon or an overturned canoe. Or, perhaps, they've listened to too many of the stories and have fallen victim to their own fertile imaginations. But maybe, just maybe, there is something to the story. After all, it wouldn't be the first time the legend of a seemingly unbelievable underwater creature was found to have some basis in reality. Only a few years ago, marine biologists had their first look at the giant squid, a ferocious, fourteen-metre-long behemoth that is now believed to have inspired the Norse tales of a sea beast called the "Kraken."

The fact is, the vast majority of our planet is covered by water. What lies beneath is a great mystery, so it is little wonder that people have always told tales of sea serpents, merpeople, and monsters of the deep. Saskatchewan may be far from oceanfront, but it does boast more than one hundred thousand lakes. With that comes an interesting assortment of lake lore. The Turtle Lake Monster is one of the more high-profile stories, but it is not alone. According to several people in Fort Qu'Appelle, southern Saskatchewan may have its own slimy contender.

Jan Drummond, of the Calling Lakes Paranormal Investigators, has heard stories that would keep the most avid swimmer out of the waters of nearby Echo Lake. According to Jan, her sources once "saw a serpent-like creature come up from the water and go right across the bridge." There were three people who witnessed the serpent at the same time, which makes the story intriguingly credible. Jan was tempted to speculate as to where the creature might have come from.

"They say that there are underground caverns beneath Echo Lake," she said. "If there are caverns that no one's ever gone in to investigate — I suppose it's possible that something from 'way back when' could live down there. They definitely saw something come out of that water and go across that bridge. Something quite large."

Jan's daughter, Amy, also a paranormal investigator, is also convinced that something mysterious dwells in the waters of Echo Lake — but the creatures she speaks of are quite different in stature.

"There are mermaids, supposedly, in our lake," she said. "When I was a kid, my babysitter lived lakeside. She had her dock out there. We'd always try to catch minnows in our little plastic buckets." According to Amy, minnows weren't the only catch. She has a vague, childhood memory of running to show the older children a diminutive creature in her bucket that had hair, arms, and fins. "To me," said Amy, "it looked like a little, tiny mermaid." Unfortunately, the bucket was emptied back into the water before Amy had a chance to show her babysitter. Today, she has no adult perspective of that incident to rely upon. "I was really young," she admits, "so it could have been a weed, or something in the shape of a mermaid." Still, she has a very vivid memory of being amazed, watching this miniature mermaid swimming around in her plastic bucket. "It had little arms, and a tail, and hair," she says, "and I could hold it in my [cupped] hands."

Though tales of tiny mermaids are rare, tales of mermaids themselves are as old as the sea. Even Christopher Columbus made a captain's log entry on January 9, 1493, in which he described three mermaids he had observed. The description was quite routine in nature, perhaps due to the fact that Columbus claimed to have witnessed these creatures on previous occasions. And if they can exist at sea, why not in the waters of a quiet Saskatchewan lake?

Truth be told, though, Saskatchewan is more famous for its creatures of the land. And of these, one of the best-known is the rugeroo. Rugeroos are said to be ancient Native spirits that are able to take on the forms of animals. They are vicious beasts that will harm anyone who challenges them. Even those who are wise enough to leave the rugeroo alone will be followed by a pair of disembodied red eyes until well away from the creature's haunt. It is said that the rugeroo can turn itself into any animal, or even a combination of animals, but that its favoured form is that of a coyote. The abandoned Roche Percee Mines near Bienfait are well-known for being haunted by rugeroos, but they have also been witnessed in other locations around the province. A young woman named Courtney Christensen has seen a rugeroo near Fort Qu'Appelle on two separate occasions. The animal she describes is immense, frightening, and almost impossible to compare with any single known animal.

"It was like a giant wolf-bear thing," Courtney said. "It was *huge*. A little bit taller than a deer, but fat and furry." The father of a friend who also witnessed the monstrous animal has long tried to convince the girls that what they saw was a cougar. But Courtney, who still shudders at the memory of being stalked by the beast, can't believe that. "I swear to God, it was *not* a cougar," she says. She remains convinced that she saw a rugeroo.

According to Jan Drummond, rugeroos can also materialize in combined forms, mixing the features of a variety of animals. In 2008, she was told of a sighting at a reserve near Fort Qu'Appelle.

"It had the head of a deer; it had antlers," Jan recalled. "It had the legs of a man. And it was climbing on the roof of the school. A number of different people saw it. We can't find anybody who will talk about it, but a lot of different people saw it. From what I heard, they think it was a bad omen. That bad things were going to start happening on the reserve."

Every culture has its own omens of disaster and death, and Saskatchewan seems to have several. They include unusual signs of nature, the appearance of certain birds or animals, and specific supernatural phenomena. One interesting incident, interpreted as an omen, was recorded in Choiceland in the late 1970s. The small town north-east of Prince Albert endured a fifteen-minute downpour of "shiny black bugs," according to the September 29, 1977 edition of the *Saskatoon Star-Phoenix*. There was no natural explanation for the appearance of those millions of insects, which were concentrated in a two-block area, but some residents believed it to be "a sign of hard times to come."

Another, more universally known dark omen is that of the demon dog called Black Shuck. Also known as Old Shuck, Barghest, Galleytrot, Hellbeast, and Whisht Hound, this evil black beast is just as unlucky by any other name. This creature is huge, with fiery glowing eyes. His feet make no sound, and are said to leave no tracks. It is believed

Saskatchewan's pristine prairie landscape is said to be home to a variety of supernatural creatures.

Photo by Andrea Oxtoby.

that to meet this heinous hound means bad luck, even death. In some parts of the world, it is considered bad luck to even speak the beast's name. Amy Drummond was willing to take that risk when she shared the tale of her encounter with Black Shuck.

It was a mild summer evening in Fort Qu'Appelle, just before dusk. Amy had gone for a jog, her black lab by her side. She had been running for some time when she stopped for a moment to catch her breath. Before she started out again, she happened to look down the very long street ahead of her. That's when she saw a large, black dog running in her direction.

"I remember looking at it and thinking that there was something strange," said Amy, "but I couldn't figure out what it was." Amy's dog seemed to sense something unusual, as well. He stayed by her side, but his complete attention was focused on the other animal. Her dog's apparent nervousness made Amy take another hard look at the animal that approached them. As the dog drew closer and closer, she finally realized what it was that seemed so strange.

"I couldn't hear its nails hitting the pavement," said Amy. "My dog, I could hear its nails scratching when it ran. This one, I couldn't."

Suddenly, Amy was overwhelmed with a horrible feeling. She turned around and ran in the opposite direction. Though she didn't look back, she felt with dark certainty that the huge, black dog was following her. She ran until she was incapable of going any further, then took refuge in the light of a street lamp.

"It wasn't dark yet, but the street lights were starting to come on," said Amy. "And we hit this light and I stopped to catch my breath. I couldn't run anymore." Finally, Amy turned to look behind her. The black dog was still there — waiting just outside the circle of light cast by the street lamp. "This dog stopped just short of the light," said Amy. "It would not come into the light."

As soon as Amy was able to run again, she went straight home. There, the mysterious black dog left her. What would not leave was the ominous feeling that the creature had induced. She mentioned this to her mother, Jan. The two women concluded that Amy was likely only nervous about starting a new job the next morning, as a production assistant on the

CTV television series *Little Mosque on the Prairie*. As Amy went to sleep that night, she did her best to ignore the sensation that something terrible was about to happen.

The next day, Amy drove into Regina and went to work on the production set. She was busy and distracted, yet still unable to shake the dark mood of the previous day. What was more, she was bothered all day by the sense that she should call home, which was impossible.

"I was on a film set," explained Amy. "You can't have cell phones. If a phone rings and it ruins the shot, you get fired." So Amy could do nothing but wait, and work. Shooting didn't wrap up until eight o'clock that evening. As soon as Amy got back to her grandparents' home, where she stayed when she was working in the city, she tried to call her family in Fort Qu'Appelle.

There was no answer.

Initially, Amy tried to tell herself that there was nothing to worry about. She knew that her father was away at work, and thought that her younger brother might be working late hours, as well. Her mother, she reasoned, could be out for any number of reasons. But the dark feeling intensified. Five minutes after she tried calling home, her own phone rang. It was Amy's dad, asking her if her brother had been able to reach her with news about her mother. Amy said that he had not, and braced herself for what her father said next.

"She's in the hospital," he said. "She's just had a stroke."

And the words formed in Amy's mind: *black dog means death*.

Amy wasted no time. She jumped into her car and raced back to Fort Qu'Appelle to be with Jan. When she arrived at the hospital and walked into her mother's room, she noticed something instantly.

"That feeling that I'd been feeling for the [previous] two days left," said Amy. "It was completely gone. As soon as I walked into that hospital room, that was it." At that point she remembered having read somewhere that Black Shuck could be an omen for bad luck, as opposed to death, and she began to relax. And, as it happened, Jan Drummond recovered completely.

"I got lucky," says Amy, remembering that experience.

According to John Pawelko of the Calling Lakes Paranormal Investigators, Black Shuck has haunted the Qu'Appelle Valley for many years. He recalled an experience that he and a friend had back in the summer of 1962.

"We were driving home in the moonlight, and we got lost," John explained. "We ended up cutting through these [unfamiliar] roads." At one point, the two young men "made a pit stop," as John put it. As they stood outside the car, they saw a large, dark shape emerge from the field of grain. Not wanting to risk an encounter with anyone or anything at that time of the night, John and his friend jumped quickly back into the car and drove off.

"Now, this road goes for about three or four miles straight," John said. With no turns or other vehicles to worry about, he managed to get up to a good speed. He felt confident that he and his buddy had left whatever it was far behind. But then his friend spoke.

"He said to me, 'You know, there's a big dog beside you!' I looked down [at the speedometer], and we were going about eighty miles an hour. And [yet, this dog] was looking in my window!"

The size and supernatural speed of the dog was so shocking to John, all he could think of was how to escape it. He turned off the road the first chance he had.

"We came out by this little cemetery," he said. "And there was this [apparition] standing by the side of the road — dark, hooded, and about eight feet tall."

Were the dog and the apparition two separate entities? John didn't stay to investigate.

"I wasn't stopping for nothing," he said.

Interestingly, that wasn't the first time that John had been pursued by an animal that was ominous and apparently supernatural. When he was younger, he would ride several kilometres on horseback to watch television at his uncle's home. One night, on the way home, he was chased by a riderless black horse.

"It was right behind me," John recalled. "I could feel the horse's breath on my neck. Now, the horse I had was a Persian thoroughbred, a fast horse. He just opened up and he was cruising. I was hanging on for dear life. [Still], I could feel this other horse's breath. He chased me for a long time."

On another evening, as John was driving home from his uncle's farm, he encountered the same horse, standing in the road. The horse stared at John, its head lowered and its nostrils flared. But John, in the safety of the car, felt braver on this occasion.

"I said, 'Okay, this is for you!'" John stepped on the gas pedal and took aim at the horse, thinking that he would frighten the animal away. He may have done that — although the horse didn't run. He simply vanished into the darkness, before John's car could run him down.

"I never hit him," said John. "Never saw him again, either. He disappeared."

John wasn't afraid of the phantom horse after that. And, perhaps *because* he wasn't afraid, he never met the animal again.

As unsettling as these incidents were, they at least involved animals that people expect to see on the prairies. The same can't be said for some earlier reports from Saskatchewan's south-eastern corner involving none other than jungle cats. The October 30, 1936 edition of the *Regina Leader-Post* ran an article with the headline POLICE JOIN BIG GAME HUNTERS AS OXBOW LIONS AGAIN ROAM COUNTRY. It was an account of the RCMP joining hunters in an attempt to track down three lions that were witnessed by a number of local people near the town of Oxbow. The big cats had been roaming the area for a period of at least two weeks at the time the article ran, frightening children and killing livestock. Some were of the opinion that the animals were cougars — but witnesses insisted otherwise. They claimed that one of the large, tawny-coloured cats had a distinctive mane, identifying it as an African lion.

Fast-forward fourteen years and move north to Yorkton, where newspapers reported that the RCMP were once again dealing with reports of an unusually "large, cat-like animal, described as four feet high with a dark brown back and light colored [sic] undercarriage." The most interesting piece of evidence in this case was the animal's tracks. The big cat left a three-inch-deep print in ground where a man of average weight would make no impression. What's more, the tracks were four inches in diameter, indicating an immense paw.

Paranormal writer, researcher, and lecturer, W. Ritchie Benedict, keeps files of information on these and other "out-of-place" animal sightings.

"The common explanation is that they were escapees from a zoo," says Benedict, "[but] when the zoos and circuses were checked, there were no records of any animals being AWOL." This led Benedict to look for other explanations. The theory that he eventually developed is intriguing.

"All of these events may be leading us to the biggest scientific breakthrough of all time," he says. "Not exactly time travel, but dimensional travel."

If Benedict is right — if people, objects, and even animals can travel from one place to another, or even from some unknown dimension to our own — this would provide an explanation for numerous paranormal phenomena, ranging from strange animal sightings and crisis apparitions to teleportation and bilocation. But, until the scientific community knows this for a fact, the creatures, ominous apparitions, and strange animal sightings in Saskatchewan will remain a mystery.

Ghost Hunting on the Prairies: Prairie Specters

"Prairie Specters" blogger Chris Oxtoby poses by the crumbling brick entrance to his favourite Saskatchewan haunt, the Weyburn Mental Hospital.

Photo by Andrea Oxtoby.

Case File Quick Facts

Name: Prairie Specters
Date Founded: June, 2008 (but started investigating long before that)

Website: *www.prairiespecters.blogspot.com*

Mission: To create a forum for people who are interested in reading and sharing Saskatchewan ghost stories.

Blogger: Chris Oxtoby

Favourite Saskatchewan Haunt: Weyburn Mental Hospital. "Sometimes I even dream I'm there," says Chris.

Q & A with Chris Oxtoby

Chris Oxtoby recently turned his interest in the paranormal into a popular blog called "Prairie Specters." I had lunch with Chris and his wife, Andrea, an accomplished photographer who sometimes accompanies him when he visits haunted locations.

Q: How long have you been doing the blog?

A: Just a year now. It hasn't been very long, actually. I wanted to start something that was local. There are lots of other different sites out there that are from the southern states, that kind of stuff. I wanted to do something with a focus on western Canada, something where people could log on and write out their experiences … a resource where they could get information on the haunted sites in the area.

Q: Have you had this interest for a long time?

A: Oh, yeah. I've been reading the books for a long time. I remember taking ghost books out of the library in grade four. It's always been an interest.

Q: Have you had much response to the blog?

A: Yeah, a lot. [In four months] I've had almost a thousand hits. Quite a few people are interested. A lot of people email, asking me how to get access to certain sites, especially with Weyburn. (In September 2008,

Chris wrote about having taken a tour of the deserted Weyburn Hospital site.) A lot of people emailed, asking me to take them on the tour. But I'm not the person to talk to, [plus] they've started demolishing the place now, so as far as tours go, that's done. We were lucky to get in.

Q: Do you see a difference, in the last decade, in the amount of interest there is in the paranormal?

A: Oh, yeah, for sure. With all the television shows that are on right now, you can tell. *Most Haunted*, *Ghost Hunters*, that kind of stuff. People are interested in that. If you go on the net, almost every state has its own [paranormal research] group now. And, in the past two or three years, there's definitely a lot of stuff going on in Saskatchewan. But a lot of people think they can just find some old place, go in, and it all happens. Just like on TV.

Q: Do you do the kind of investigating where you're trying to capture something in photos, or recordings, or gathering some kind of measurable evidence?

A: We haven't gone that far, yet, in terms of getting equipment. Not sure whether we want to go in that direction. We just like going to the sites. We're interested in the buildings, in the history of them. I am a member of the Saskatchewan Ghost-Hunters Society (page 15), a group based out of Saskatoon. They do more on the side of investigating. But I'm just deciding if I want to go more in that direction, or if I want to stay on the side of documenting, and taking a few pictures. Both sides interest me. But investigating is just kind of a side. My main thing is getting the information out for people to read.

Q: Have you had any personal experiences that could not be explained?

A: We used to live in an apartment above a store that was over a hundred years old. We had a couple of weird things happen there. There was a picture frame that moved across the bedroom during the night, while we were sleeping. And there was an old [unused] stairway that ran directly behind our bedroom, down into the store. More than once, at three o'clock in the morning or so, we would hear footsteps going down those stairs.

I also remember one time I was with someone, and we were using a Ouija board. We were speaking to some spirit, and I remember bubbles coming up on the board. You know how there's a [laminate surface] covering the particle board? Well, I remember air bubbles coming up under that. I quit right then. I knew that was bad news. And I don't really get scared that easy!

5
Personally Paranormal

Mario's Story

Tugaske is a tiny village in south-central Saskatchewan. Though it is small in size, it is huge in stature in certain musical circles. The reason is a place called Timeless Instruments; a custom shop and guitar-building school owned and operated by a local man named Dave Freeman. Dave's intricately designed string instruments and seven-week immersion training sessions are renowned by luthiers the world over. And, in 1998, they attracted a stranger from New Jersey named Mario Garcia.

Mario came to Saskatchewan in January, narrowly escaping delays caused by the massive ice storm that devastated the eastern seaboard that month. His train pulled into the Saskatoon station on New Year's Day, just two days before he was scheduled to begin his training. Dave Freeman met him there, and together they drove to Tugaske.

Mario described himself as being on "a soul-searching mission" at that time. If he was seeking change in his life, he was about to find it. Though he could not have imagined it that night as he rode across the frozen prairie beneath a vast, glittering winter sky, he was about to encounter a new home, new friends, and an amazing supernatural adventure.

And it would all happen in what he described as "this faraway place called Saskatchewan."

†

Across the street from Timeless Instruments is a house where Dave Freeman's students live during their training. It was late, that first evening, when Mario and Dave pulled into Tugaske, so Dave did little more than unlock the house and help Mario carry in his things.

"After picking my room," said Mario, "it was off to la-la-land."

It had been a long day. Exploring the house, and discovering some of its decidedly unique features, would have to wait until after a good night's sleep.

The next day, Dave came back to the student house to show Mario around. Last stop on the "fifty-cent tour" was the laundry room, which was located in the basement. Mario found himself uncomfortable there, but tried to shake the feeling off.

"I learned how to use the machine, and tried to dispel how creepy the basement felt," he said. "I tossed in a load of laundry and waved farewell to Dave as he left."

What *didn't* leave was the distinct sense that there was another presence in the basement with him. Mario decided to deal with his feelings in a practical fashion.

"Being no stranger to ghosts, I introduced myself to a visibly empty room, then briskly walked upstairs to settle in."

Mario's straightforward approach seemed to work. After a little while, the creepy feeling left him. He was still quite aware, however, that he was not in the house alone. Fortunately, there was more human company on the way.

"Later that afternoon," said Mario, "a second student arrived — a real nice guy from Manitoba. That night, [he], Dave, and I shared a pleasant dinner and conversation. I turned in early, eager to begin school the next morning."

As Mario lay down in bed, he experienced the strangest sensation: a cool wind that brushed past his face and then swept out of his room, beneath the closed door. It was an odd thing, but one that he would soon become accustomed to.

"Every night [after that]," said Mario, "no matter what time I lay down to sleep … that same breeze would move past me."

After a week or two, Mario felt comfortable enough with the house and the other resident that he chose to leave his bedroom door open one night. On that evening, as he felt the familiar breeze caress his face, he followed its trail with his eyes. Just outside his door, the air current took on a form.

"[There was] an elderly woman in Victorian dress," Mario said. "I saw her stop at the top of the stairs, smile at me, then float down the stairs to the first floor." The name "Grandma" popped into Mario's mind. "Now," he said, "I had a better idea of what entity I was sharing the house with."

Mario was happy to have met "Grandma," but he made no mention of his spectral encounter to either Dave or the other student in the house. Having experienced many such things in his lifetime, Mario had learned early on that it was best to keep quiet about them. So he said nothing and considered his growing relationship with the spirit to be a private matter.

"Days passed," said Mario, "and every night Grandma would pass by me in my room (I figured she was tucking me in). Then she would stand there on the staircase and descend after I wished her a good night."

The spirit limited her appearances to this bedtime routine until, one night, when she visited Mario as he slept.

"One night, I had a disturbing dream," he said. "I was standing at the bottom of the staircase looking up, and what I saw made no sense. Grandma and an elderly man (Grandpa, I suppose) floated down the stairs with one of my best friends, Tom Kelley (a police officer in my home town of Elizabeth, New Jersey), between them. [Grandma and Grandpa] each had a hand on one of Tom's shoulders.

"They came to a stop right in front of me. Grandma smiled and spoke to me. She said 'Don't worry, we'll take good care of him.'" Mario saw then that Tom's eyes were closed, but noted that he seemed asleep, not dead.

And then the dream was over. Mario awoke to a cold, clear January morning, in a place that was far removed from New Jersey and his friend Tom Kelley.

The dream stayed on Mario's mind as he performed his usual morning routine. Hours passed at the shop, but working on his guitar didn't serve to distract him from his sombre mood. Mario obsessively re-ran the dream in his mind, trying to make sense of it. He grew increasingly pensive and worried. Finally, during his lunch break, he decided to call his girlfriend back in New Jersey.

The first thing she said to him was, "Did you see the news?"

When Mario said that he had not, she told him that he should call Tom's house. Mario hung up the phone, redialed, and braced himself for what he knew had to be bad news. Within moments, he was talking to his friend's mother. In between sobs, she told him what had happened.

"Tommy had been on duty," said Mario, "and had pulled over on a busy road to help a stranded motorist. As he stood there ... he was struck by a speeding car and was hit so hard that his body landed some forty feet from the point of impact. So massive were his head injuries and so thick and large was the pool of blood he lay in, that the detective on scene called for a body bag. [But] as the paramedics began to bag him, Tommy took a breath. They went to work on him. [They saved his life, but] he lay broken and in a coma."

Mario sunk to the floor during the phone conversation. As he listened to Tom's mother tell the story, his mind kept drifting back to the dream. Grandma's words played over and over in his head. *Don't worry; we'll take good care of him.* Mario hoped that she would.

With as much confidence as he could muster, Mario told Mrs. Kelley that he was sure that Tom would be all right. He promised to pray for his friend before he hung up the phone.

Suddenly, all that he knew and all that he had experienced since arriving in Tugaske became too much to bear alone. Mario needed to talk to someone. He felt that he had a genuine friend in Dave, so he sought him out.

"Dave listened to me," said Mario. "He heard me out. Then a knowing look came over his face. He told me that a previous student had an experience similar to mine. She had slept in the room that I now occupied, and I was now using the same work station that she had. As if that was not enough of a coincidence, we also built the same types of guitars."

So Dave knew about the grandmotherly figure that watched over his students. And Mario knew that when strange things happened in the house, he had someone in whom he could confide.

The days and weeks passed. Mario patiently finished building his first guitar, started working on a second instrument, and awaited news of any change in Tom Kelley's condition. In the meantime, a new crop of students arrived to share the school and the house. One, in particular, complained about the atmosphere.

"One day, while we worked away in the shop, one of the students, Marcus, mentioned how creepy the basement was. Dave and I smiled."

The man went on at length about how he always felt that he was being watched in the basement. Finally, Mario shared his Grandma stories with Marcus and all the other students in the room. At first, everyone thought that Mario was making it up. But when Dave backed him up, most of them were convinced.

Most of them — but not Marcus.

Marcus was certain that he was being taken for a fool, and became very vocal about his disbelief in ghosts. He often told Mario that Grandma was either a figment of his imagination or a total fabrication. Marcus was always looking for an opportunity to re-engage in the same argument, whether it was at school or in the student house. On one occasion, as all the students crowded into the kitchen of the house, engaged in various stages of cooking and eating, Mario teasingly warned Marcus not to make Grandma angry. Marcus exploded at the suggestion.

"F*** Grandma!" he said. "There's no such thing!"

At that exact moment, a collection of newspapers that lay on top of the fridge lifted up, flew through the air, and landed on top of Marcus's head. All the other students stared at him in stunned silence. Mario never forgot the sight.

"Marcus stood there motionless as the papers wafted down around him, looking like a deer caught in headlights. [We all looked] around the room. No doors were open, no breeze had blown in, every window was closed. Yet we all agreed on what we had seen."

When the shock wore off, the laughter began. Marcus was teased mercilessly for the rest of the day about his foolish decision to bad-mouth Grandma.

Dave enjoyed the story when he heard it later that day. And, as everyone sat around the shop sharing ghostly tales, he might have wished that he had one of his own. If that was the case, before the day was over, Grandma was happy to oblige.

Dave used the student house to store some lutherie supplies that he had no room for at the shop. Later that day, he went over to pick up some materials. He walked into the back porch, and reached to open the kitchen door. But the knob turned before he could touch it, and the door swung open. Dave moved aside, expecting one of his students to step out in a rush to get back to work. But no one was there. Dave walked into the empty house, remembering that every single person was accounted for across the street at the shop.

Everyone agreed that it was another encounter with Grandma. The students were all convinced that she truly existed, and regarded her with respect.

"Needless to say," said Mario, "no one ever bad-mouthed Grandma again. (At least, not out loud!) And if Marcus still reserved doubts about Grandma, he kept those thoughts to himself."

As for Mario's injured friend, Tom, Grandma was good to her word. She must have taken care of him because, one month after his horrific accident, he opened his eyes and asked a nurse to bring him a frozen margarita. Mario was relieved to hear the good news, and was then able to focus more fully on his own life. As he turned his attention inward, he realized that, over the course of a frigid Saskatchewan winter, he had made some lifelong friends and fallen in love with the little village of Tugaske. In the end, Mario bought a house right next door to Dave Freeman's shop. Though he still lives in New Jersey, he plans to one day obtain dual citizenship and make Tugaske his permanent home. Until then, he satisfies himself with occasional visits. It gives him a chance to catch up with all his friends … in this world, and the next.

"Whenever I'm home in Tugaske," says Mario, "I walk around town at night to get my cardio workout. And as I walk past the student house, I always look up to the window of my old room and wave hello to Grandma. [I'll never forget] how a ghost in Saskatchewan kept an eye on my best friend … almost two thousand miles away."

A Personal Haunting

Most known hauntings involve a place — a particular building or location that has spiritual activity or residual energy attached to it. But it seems possible that people might also be haunted, and in this story shared by a Prince Albert man that appears to be the case. His name is John McDonald and, for a number of years, no matter where he lived, he was relentlessly pursued by ghosts.

His experience began in the winter of 1994, when he was a young teenager returning to Prince Albert to live with his mother. By his own admission, John had been drawn into a risky lifestyle that involved alcohol and drugs. So, when strange things began to happen, he initially thought that he was experiencing some unusual symptom of withdrawal. While there's no doubt that substance abuse can create some curious side-effects, they tend to stop short of telekinesis, so it wasn't long before John was wondering what was really going on.

"It began with the light switches," he said. "I would often be sitting in bed reading, when the light switch would click, breaking my concentration and enveloping me in darkness." According to John, this happened with other lights throughout the house, as well. He often found himself left in the dark — whether he was in his bedroom, the bathroom, or the basement. Even the light inside the oven was unpredictable for John. But lights weren't the only issue.

"Objects would go missing, too, and would sometimes turn up weeks later, in places where they couldn't be missed. For example, my house keys would disappear, only to be found sitting on the pillow of my bed a few days later," said John. He added, dryly, "I think I would have known if I was sleeping with my head resting on a set of keys."

After a short time, John moved out of his upstairs bedroom and into the basement which was, essentially, a large, unfinished space. Once he was downstairs, the bizarre activity increased in both frequency and scope. Whatever paranormal force had been toying with light switches and keys now had the power to move furniture.

"I would find my bed pushed into the far corner of the room," said

John, "and my blankets piled into a heap on the concrete floor. I would find clothing that hung from a makeshift clothesline scattered across the room. Posters and pictures that I had tacked and taped to the wall would be lying on the floor, several feet from where they had been, and my alarm clock would always be flashing at 12:00, as if it had been unplugged and then plugged back in again."

John was still searching for a rational explanation. He decided that someone was playing a prank on him, and took to padlocking his door whenever he left the house.

"No one," he said, "not even my mother, had access to my room."

Yet he routinely arrived home to find his living space in a shambles. John began to believe that something paranormal was happening. This became increasingly obvious as he spent more time in the house by himself.

"I often spent nights alone," John said, "watching television in the upstairs living room. [One particular night], I was sitting alone, watching TV. The house was empty, save for myself. Suddenly, I could hear the door to my basement bedroom close, and I could hear footsteps climbing the stairs. I could clearly see the landing and, of course, there was no one there. The steps continued until they reached the living room, then ceased. This went on for several weeks."

Around that time, the owners of the house decided to renovate the basement. Workmen came in to install a half bathroom, two bedrooms, and a rumpus room. Despite the mess and chaos that any renovation entails, John enjoyed a period of relative calm. The ghostly phenomena came to an abrupt halt during construction. Unfortunately, once the project was complete and John moved back into the basement, it came back with renewed intensity. Now, no longer content to destroy John's surroundings, the entity began to attack him physically.

"I would wake up in the middle of the night feeling sharp, stinging pains," he said. "I would turn on the light and see tiny scratches running up and down my legs." John would always check the bedding, looking for a lost thumbtack or some other sharp object. He never found anything to explain the scratches.

The spirit was particularly active in the newly constructed basement bathroom. The toilet — which was newly installed and should have been glitch-free — would flush repeatedly on its own. John reported an odd smell, which he likened to "flaked fish food." And, in May of 1999, that bathroom was where John eventually met the ghost that had been tormenting him. John had just finished showering and was about to shave in the sink. When he wiped the steam from the mirror, he saw his own reflection — and that of a woman standing behind his right shoulder. It was an image he would never forget.

"She looked to be in her twenties," said John, "and she was soaking wet, with her hair dripping water. She was very pale, almost green, and she had the most menacing look on her face. She was staring deeply into my eyes through the mirror."

In an instant, the terrifying image of the woman vanished. Almost as quickly, John made up his mind to move out of his mother's house.

John's mother and sister may have questioned his decision, particularly as they had never experienced any of the unexplainable phenomena themselves. Still, John knew what he had seen, and he was determined to leave. Moving was the only way to escape the ghost.

At least, that's what he thought at the time.

John's new home was a one-bedroom, furnished suite on 6th Avenue East.

"It was a cool little pad," said John. "I spent nearly three years there."

From the beginning, however, it was apparent that John was not alone in his new apartment. When he looked at the suite prior to moving in, it was clean and tidy. The day he arrived there to stay, however, he was met with an entirely different sight.

"The place was absolutely upside-down," said John. "The fridge and stove were pulled away from the wall and swung around to face the sink. The couch was also pulled away from the wall and stood on end in a corner. All of the kitchen drawers were pulled out and stacked one on top of another on the counter. The mattress for the bed was lying on the bedroom floor, and the coffee table was placed inside the closet."

Welcome home, John, it seemed to say. *Did you think I wouldn't come with you?*

But John was still thinking that he had left the ghost behind. He told himself that the landlords had come to do some last minute cleaning and had neglected to put everything back in its proper place. He settled into his new home and enjoyed the first few weeks of relative peace.

Eventually, however, the activity started again.

At first, it was the disappearance of small objects — so easy to dismiss. Then, the sound of disembodied footsteps — possibly explained away as belonging to neighbours on the other side of the wall. But, as it had before, the activity increased steadily until it reached a point where it could no longer be explained.

One evening, John turned off the television and went to bed. A few hours later, he awoke to see flickering white light streaming through his bedroom door.

"I got up to investigate," said John, "and was shocked to see my TV on, with snow filling the screen. This was a really old TV, predating "on" timers and requiring rabbit ears, and [I had to use] a pair of needle-nosed pliers to turn it off and on. I had turned it off before I had gone to sleep and here it was, defiantly blazing in the night. I turned it off, and went back to sleep.

"The next morning, I awoke to find my TV sitting on my couch."

Something was letting John know, in no uncertain terms, that it was *present*. John thought he knew why.

"I am a First Nations person," he said. "At that time, I was regaining my traditional teachings. I was given many sacred objects from Elders, and I began to bless my home. It was the introduction of these objects into my home that brought on more manifestations."

If there was a supernatural battle being waged, the ghost in John's apartment was a strong contender. It seemed to welcome any opportunity to manifest a show of strength. And the bigger the audience, the better.

"I had a few friends over for coffee," said John, recalling one such occasion. "We were gathered in the living room. I was talking to one girl, when I saw her sister's eyes begin to bulge out of her head. Her mouth dropped open. When I asked what was wrong, she pointed to the kitchen.

"The kitchen chairs, which usually sat pushed in under the table, had rolled out and pushed towards the back door. The kitchen drawers and cupboard doors began to open on their own accord, and a tea towel that had sat folded on the counter was now wrapped around one leg of the table.

"Needless to say, my apartment emptied quite quickly."

John was left alone in his haunted apartment — and he was angry. He began to scream and swear at the presence in his home, demanding that it leave him alone. The apartment and everything in it remained still, but the temperature dipped dramatically. John began to shiver. He understood that this was a message from the ghost. It was summer, and Prince Albert was in the midst of a heat wave. Only moments before John's tirade, the apartment had been sweltering hot.

Later that night, there came another message. And a messenger whom John thought he recognized.

"That night as I slept," he said, "I felt the presence of someone standing at the foot of my bed. I awoke to see the image of a little old lady, angrily pointing at me and shaking her finger. Her image was like an older version of the lady who [I had seen in the mirror] so many years ago."

This time, however, John reacted differently. He wasn't afraid — but he *was* angry.

"I slowly sat up in bed," he said, "rose to my feet, and stood defiantly, looking down at her. She suddenly disappeared, and I went back to sleep."

Shortly after that night, John took in a roommate. He didn't know if it was the presence of an extra person, or the result of his showdown with the ghost, but his remaining time in that apartment was quiet.

But there was one more apartment to come....

"I moved into another basement suite with my girlfriend, on Halloween of 2001," said John. "It wasn't too long before things started acting up again. Things would go missing, turning up weeks later or not turning up at all. The toilet paper in the bathroom would unroll itself entirely onto the floor, and little objects were moved around constantly. For which I got blamed," he added.

The energy associated with the activity seemed entirely different this time. After so many years of experience, John knew that he was dealing with a ghost — but he felt sure that it was a *different* ghost. He no longer felt the presence of the evil woman who had followed him for so long. This time, the spirit seemed to be that of a mischievous little boy. John's girlfriend saw the child on two occasions, and John had seen shadowy glimpses of a small form ducking into doorways. He felt that the little boy's ghost was simply seeking attention. While his antics were often annoying, they were nothing compared to the malevolent activity of the other spirit. She seemed to be permanently gone, however, and John was glad to be rid of her.

Several years have passed now, and John's life has dramatically changed. He is married, and the father of four young children, including triplets. He and his family live just north of Prince Albert, in a farmhouse old enough that any creaks and groans are easily explained away. However, something in him must be drawn to the paranormal, for he still works in Prince Albert, with Ruth Gillingham, program supervisor of the famously haunted Prince Albert Arts Centre. In the course of his work, John has a weekly meeting in the Arts Centre. Just recently, he shared a strange experience there with a colleague.

"The meeting was in the studio upstairs, across from the gallery," said John. "The double doors were propped open, as the room was quite stuffy.

"In the middle of our meeting, the audible sound of a single boot step could be heard just outside the doors. Immediately following that, the double doors swung shut. This occurred at nine-thirty at night. The building was locked up … we were the only ones in the building, and neither of us were wearing boots. My friend and I looked at each other and, at the exact same time, we both said, 'I knew that was going to happen!'"

John also knew that the ghost "lived" at the Arts Centre and was unlikely to follow him home. Given his history of being personally haunted, *that* must have been a relief.

The Scream

Imagine a scene that could be taken from any number of horror movies:
An isolated, rural setting….
A teenager, completely on his own, except for the family dog….
A warm summer evening that draws him outdoors….
And then a shocking—
But wait. We're getting ahead of ourselves.

First, you should meet Trent. And know that it is the summer of 1990, when he was approximately fifteen years old. And you must witness the lay of the land at his family's home, an acreage just a few kilometres north of Prince Albert.

"It was right in the middle of the bush," said Trent, as he described the property. "And there's an Indian burial ground there. Now it's a healing lodge. [But] we lived right along the edge of where that burial ground would be. Where this happened was behind the house. I was on the deck, and we had somewhat of a clearing in the backyard. Just grass, and then there was a treeline."

According to Trent, the deck at the back of the house faced the treeline and the burial ground. A powerful yard light in the front served to illuminate the clearing in the back, but nothing beyond the trees. Trent was at home alone, sitting on that deck having a cigarette, when he experienced something that remains crystal clear — yet unexplainable — in his mind today.

"It was late at night," Trent said. "Pitch dark out. I was out on the deck with the dog, and there was nobody else home but me. And it was quiet. You know what it's like in the bush — just super quiet."

Trent was leaning against the railing, enjoying the peace and solitude, when …

"[Right across from me, from] just inside that tree line, there was the loudest, most bone-chilling scream that I've ever heard in my life," said Trent. "I didn't know what it was, but it sounded human. It didn't sound like an animal; it sounded like a woman screaming in a horror movie."

Trent felt his body go cold with shock. His dog jumped to its feet, with its tail standing straight up and the hair bristling along its spine. Trent stared across the clearing into the dense, black bush. He could see nothing.

"I was really freaked out, because I thought there was somebody in the bush," he said. "I thought there was a person in there, so I yelled, 'Hello?'"

The instant that Trent called out, he received another shocking fright. It was a second scream. Again, it seemed to originate from just beyond the treeline, but this time, instead of being in front of him, it was directly to his right. Whoever — or whatever — was screaming had moved ninety degrees through the brush in a matter of seconds, without so much as snapping a twig.

"That was pretty thick bush," said Trent. "You would hear something moving around in there. You could hear rabbits. But I didn't hear anything until it screamed again."

With the second scream, Trent's dog began to growl. It was a low, guttural sound and still the only sound that Trent could hear, aside from his own ragged breath. He could hear nothing moving in the bush. He could *see* nothing moving in the clearing. And, yet ...

"There was another scream, directly on the left of me."

Trent was frozen with fear. He barely had time to register the shriek from the left, when ...

"It happened in the front, again."

Another piercing scream — the fourth — from the original position, front and centre of the deck. Something was either circling the deck, or had surrounded it. Trent was terrified, and he was not alone.

"Our dog was a full-grown German shepherd," said Trent. "I'd never seen that dog scared of anything in my entire life. But that dog started barking, and there was another scream."

This time — most terrifying of all — the banshee-like cry came from directly beneath the deck.

The dog began whimpering, and started circling the door. Trent was jolted out of his shocked state and took the dog's suggestion to heart. He bolted into the house, slamming and locking the back door behind him. Once inside, he grabbed a loaded rifle for protection. As he armed himself, he heard another noise — the sound of the garage door opening. Trent's mother and brother had arrived home, and Trent ran to meet them.

"I told them to get in the house," said Trent. "I said there was something in the bush, but I didn't know what was going on. I was really, really freaked out."

Trent's mother called their closest neighbour, and had him come over to the house. The man looked around the property, but didn't hear or see anything out of the ordinary. Trent was insistent, however, so the RCMP were called next. They explored the area and found no sign of anything untoward. It was as if nothing had happened — but Trent knew what he had heard. For years after, he would review the details in his mind.

"I remember very distinctly," he said. "It was a human scream. It wasn't an animal. I've heard rabbits — rabbits can scream. But it wasn't that sound. It was human. I didn't actually see anything but, I swear to God, whatever it was, it was nothing that I had ever experienced before. And I've never heard it since."

Trent's father frequently teased him about the incident, insisting that he was spooked by a coyote, or a cat, or something of that nature. But Trent didn't see how that could have been possible.

"Nothing was moving across the clearing," he said, "because, with the yard light, I would have seen it in the grass. This was in the bush, outside the tree line — and I didn't hear any movement in the bush at all.

"I tell you," he continued, "this scream was not an animal. And it couldn't have been a human, because no human could move that fast. And it couldn't have been multiple people, because [each scream] was the same tone, same pitch, same identical sound."

Trent even made a point of checking beneath the deck the morning after it happened, to see what evidence he might find there.

"Underneath the deck," he explained, "it was sand. And there were no tracks in the sand. No tracks of any kind."

So, if it was not human, and not animal, what creature made those heart-stopping screams on that quiet summer night? Trent has no answers and no proof — but he has a theory.

"The reason I brought up the burial ground issue is because it could have something to do with it," Trent said. "You know, a lot of the Natives would go out there and put tobacco in the trees ... and they'd leave cigarettes on the rocks, you know, as offerings to the spirits." Though Trent was basically a good kid, he does admit to not being as respectful of this cultural tradition as he should have been. "I would take those cigarettes, and I'd smoke them," he admitted. "I was fifteen, I was just a kid, and I didn't have any money."

Is it possible that the spirits didn't consider that to be an acceptable excuse? Was the screaming wraith meant to impart a moral lesson, as Trent tried to enjoy one of those cigarettes on his back deck? It's impossible to say. But, today, Trent sees no harm in covering his bases.

"It's private land now, because of the healing lodge," he says. But, every summer, when I go back [to Prince Albert] to visit, I go back to that area. And I leave cigarettes out there."

This ongoing apology must have been accepted, because Trent hasn't had a supernatural experience since.

John's Stories

John Pawelko is a member of the Calling Lakes Paranormal Investigators (page 57). Though he's been ghost hunting professionally for only a few years, John has experienced the paranormal throughout his life. He shared many of his stories during the course of a conversation one evening. Here are three of the most thought-provoking:

The Wedding

"I went to a wedding on a Friday night, and never left the farm," laughed John, quickly adding that there were no illicit substances involved in this particular "trip." What did take place was something that might be explained as inter-dimensional travel, or a dream that was so incredibly realistic, it produced physical souvenirs. It happened when John was a young man, still working on his parents' farm.

"It was in the fall, about harvest time," John said, "and I was tired. So when Friday night came around, I didn't go anywhere. Just went to bed."

The day in the fields had been long and exhausting, and John was looking forward to a good night's rest. He fell asleep almost the moment his head hit the pillow, and immediately entered into a state of vivid dreaming that seemed to last throughout the night.

"I dreamt I was at a wedding," John remembered. "I was the best man. But I didn't have a clue who the bride and groom were. Didn't recognize anybody."

John Pawelko spent years searching small Saskatchewan towns for the church he once visited in his dreams.

He didn't know any of the people and he wasn't familiar with the location. Everything was new to John, and he remembered it all in exact detail.

"It was a yellow brick church," he said. "Corner lot, with a sidewalk. And the sun was going down, so I knew it was an afternoon service." John went on to describe the style of the front doors on the church, and even the type of hinges on those doors. "It's funny how you remember little details," he said. "I remember the

Photo by Andrea Oxtoby.

vestibule; the porch. And the bride. She was tall and dark-haired. She had short hair and glasses and the white dress. Her dad was tall, too. He had a moustache and looked like Clark Gable. Distinguished-looking fellow, in a black suit and white shirt. But I never did see the groom." John only knew that he was standing behind the man who was about to be married, and that he was standing one riser above him, on the front steps of the church.

John's dream continued past the church service. He remembered being at a hall, dancing and celebrating. The party seemed so real, John woke up feeling as though he was suffering from a hangover.

"When I woke up in the morning, I had a terrible headache, and I was just drained," he said. Still, he viewed this as nothing more than coincidence until his mother came out of his bedroom, after making his bed.

"She said to me, 'Did you go someplace last night?'" John recalled. "I said, 'No, I never left.' And she said, 'Well, there's confetti in your bed. And your shirt is dirty, and so is your suit.'" John was stunned, and went to look for himself. Sure enough, in his bedroom, there was solid evidence of the wedding he had attended — in his dreams.

Unlike most dreams, which seem to evaporate quickly upon waking, all the details of the mysterious wedding stayed with John. In fact, the location seemed so real to him that he was determined to one day find it.

"I drove around for ten years, looking for that church," he said. "Every town I went through, I looked around to find that church. I remember the yellow brick, the doors, the trees along the street. It was facing west, because we watched the sun go down. I never did find it."

Chances are he never will … at least, not in this dimension.

Lost Time

In the early 1960s, when John was a teenager, he went to a drive-in movie with some friends one Sunday night. On their way to the movie, the group travelled on the main roads. But driving home required a slightly different plan.

"It was a bit of a 'booze cruise,'" explained John. "Everybody was supposed to be twenty-one, but we were only sixteen, so we didn't go by the main roads." When the movie ended at midnight, John and his buddies made their way home using a network of little-known back roads that cut through the Qu'Appelle Valley, just south of Abernethy. It was a short journey but by the time John arrived at home his parents were frantic. They demanded to know where he had been. John said he had been at the drive-in.

Their response was, "For two *days*?"

"It turned out," said John, "it wasn't Monday morning, it was *Tuesday* morning." Though he had no sense of extra time passing, John had lost a full twenty-four hours as he had driven home.

That exact road no longer exists, but decades later John remains cautious of the area in general. At least, that is, around the witching hour.

"I never drive through the valley at midnight," he says.

The Melville Hitchhiker

Another story from John's teen years began with him taking a drive into Melville one warm July day. When he arrived in town, he noticed a girl walking along the side of the road. She was young and pretty so, naturally, John stopped and asked her if she would like a ride. The girl said that she would, and climbed into the passenger seat.

"She was carrying school books," John said. "She told me, 'I missed the bus.' Now, it was July but, at the time, I never thought anything about school being out. I just asked her where she lived."

The girl gave John directions to her family's farm, which was north of Melville, on the number ten highway. John chatted with the girl as he drove, trying to make a good impression. She listened quietly, gesturing occasionally to give directions. Finally, they arrived at her home. As John pulled up into the farmyard, he asked the girl what she was doing on the weekend. She told him that she had no plans.

"Well, then," said John, "do you want to go to the drive-in Friday night?"

The girl said that she would, then turned and walked into the house. John was happy as could be, and began to eagerly count off the days until the weekend. When Friday finally arrived, however, nothing was as he expected.

"When Friday came, I drove in the yard, and it didn't look right," said John. "The house was all decrepit. Abandoned. There was grass all over the yard; it looked like nobody drove in there. I thought it must be a mistake, so I went back to the road and looked around. It was the right place."

The right place — but everything about it was wrong. John had an uneasy feeling in the pit of his stomach. He knew that he wasn't going to find his date in the abandoned farmhouse, so he drove back into Melville. He found a group of friends there, and started asking questions.

"I said, 'You know, I had this strange thing happen. I picked up this girl.' And they wouldn't say nothing." John was persistent, though, and finally someone told him what had happened. "They said, 'You picked up so-and-so,'" he said. "Now, I can't even remember what her name was. But they said she got killed, either getting off the school bus or getting on the school bus. She got run over and she got killed. Later on, those guys were always like, 'Hey, picked up any dead girls lately?'"

John never did pick the girl up — or see her — again. And despite his friends' teasing, he might have been just a little disappointed about that.

"She was good-looking," he said, in conclusion.

Pictures of the Past

Prince Albert is a community with a colourful past that dates back, unofficially, to 1776. That's when Peter Pond built the area's first fur-trading post where the Sturgeon River meets the North Saskatchewan, just west of where the city sits today. By 1866, a Presbyterian missionary named James Nisbet chose a nearby site to establish a mission that would be named in honour of Queen Victoria's late consort. Within eight years, about three hundred English-speaking settlers were living there. Development continued at a steady pace, and the rest, as they say, is history. History that can occasionally, as one Prince Albert woman discovered, show itself in the present.

In 1998, a woman named Deborah was working as a photographer's assistant in an old-house-turned-studio on 13th Street East. She was working at her desk one day, alone in the building, with no one to keep her company except her little dog, who lay sleeping at her feet. And — perhaps — a visitor that she was not yet aware of.

As Deborah sat working quietly, the dog jumped up, suddenly alert, and darted across the room. He was normally a quiet little pet, easy to have in the office, but he had become uncharacteristically agitated. He was barking and snarling with all the ferocity he could manage, his attention focused on the doorway that led to the studio's back room. Deborah put down her work and tried to hush the dog, but he was not about to be calmed. Nervously, Deborah eyed the door to the back room. Her dog was extraordinarily upset, so she knew that something was amiss. Though she didn't relish the thought of perhaps facing down an intruder, Deborah knew that she had to check the back room. She left her desk and walked quietly toward the doorway. Once she reached it, she could see why her dog was so upset.

There, in the room filled with photographic equipment, was an image that Deborah had never before seen. It was a woman in a long, blue-and-white Victorian-era dress with a matching bonnet. Over and above her unusual costume, the woman seemed particularly strange. There was such an unnatural quality to her appearance and her movement that Deborah knew instantly that she was looking at a ghost. With an awkward gliding motion, the woman in the bonnet began moving across the room. As she moved, so did the dog, rushing in to attack.

It is a commonly held theory that hauntings fall into different categories, with one of the more rare being what is sometimes called an "intelligent haunting." In these cases, the ghost is as aware of its surroundings and the percipient as that person is of it. As the dog launched itself toward the spirit with its lips curled back and its teeth viciously bared, Deborah's ghost displayed that unusual awareness. As Deborah would later write, "She suddenly froze in fear."

Deborah reacted instinctively, and gave the dog a sharp command. He reluctantly obeyed it, stopping before he reached the woman. The dog turned and began moving slowly away from the apparition. The woman, seemingly relieved, continued on her way across the room. Her relief was short-lived, however. The movement of the strange image upset the dog again and he once more jumped in her direction, snarling and with his hackles raised. Again the ghost stopped, apparently terrified by the animal. Once more, Deborah was able to call her dog off before he reached his target. This stop-and-go pattern repeated no fewer than three times before the bonneted lady successfully reached the other side of the room and moved smoothly through the wall, vanishing before Deborah's eyes.

"I went and checked the other room," Deborah wrote, "but no one was there. She was gone."

The spirit had vanished, perhaps going back to her own era or, perhaps, back to the grave. The strange experience certainly stayed on

Deborah's mind but, for a time, life went back to normal. For a rather *short* time, that is.

No more than a week or two later, Deborah had another unexplainable experience at work. Again, she was alone in the studio, working quietly at her desk. This time, the dog was not there to alert her, but her "sixth sense" was. For, as she worked, she was suddenly compelled to turn and look in the direction of the small stairway that led out of the office. She later wrote about what she saw.

"Plain as day, there was a man dressed in a dark blue soldier's uniform looking at me." Showing the same sort of awareness that the other spirit had exhibited, the man smiled at Deborah. He then turned and walked into the same back room where the first ghost had both appeared and disappeared. Deborah quickly left her desk and followed him, but when she reached the back room, it was absolutely empty.

Deborah never saw either of the apparitions again, and finds it difficult to imagine where they came from or why they chose to show themselves to her in that brief period of time. Her guess is that the house was as old as the city itself and had likely seen many interesting times and people. The experience left her curious about the building's history and about the nature of ghosts, in general. Her little dog had a much more straightforward reaction. He refused to go in, or even near, the back room of the photo studio ever again.

A Father's Help

In the November 1994 edition of the short-lived magazine *Haunted Houses and Strange Events*, there is an incredible account of family love and support reaching between this world and the next. The author of the tale, Vilee Johnson, told the story of how her father — a healer, clairvoyant, and Native leader — continued to care for his family in the days and years following his death.

The events took place in November of 1972. Vilee's father, Louis Caplan, had just passed away in his Alberta home. The family was devastated and, also, in a quandary. Vilee's mother, who was very ill, was scheduled for long-awaited hip surgery at the Victoria Hospital in Winnipeg just two days later. No one was sure whether they should keep the appointment, or postpone it until after the funeral. In the end, the especially wintry weather conditions made the decision for them.

"We couldn't bury my father right away, because the ground was frozen and no plot could be dug for him," wrote Vilee. With her father's remains in the mortuary, Vilee and her husband set out to drive her mother from Sylvan Lake, Alberta, to the hospital in Winnipeg. They no doubt felt torn about leaving Louis behind — but they would soon discover that was not the case at all.

Louis Caplan had once told his daughter, "When I die, the snowflakes are going to be so big, the wipers won't be able to move on the windshield." At the time, the prediction might have seemed odd but, as Vilee and her husband took turns battling the wicked winter driving conditions, those words made sense. The snow fell heavily and steadily and began to drift on the roads. As the family approached Regina, police were flagging motorists down and warning them not to go any further. Vilee explained how important it was that her mother be in Winnipeg on time for her surgery. Though the highway wasn't closed, the police cautioned that it was unlikely they would make it all the way to Manitoba. Finally, they let the family go ... with one final warning. "You're going at your own risk," the police officer said.

Not long after, Vilee and her husband were likely questioning the wisdom of their decision to carry on. The ditches were littered with vehicles while others sat stalled on the shoulder of the road. As Louis Caplan had said in his prophesy, the falling snow was so thick that the wipers could not effectively clear the windshield. It was impossible to see the road ahead and Vilee was growing desperately worried. Not knowing what else to do, she cried out to her dead father.

"Dad," she said, "you haven't been dead very long. Please help. We've got to get Mom to Winnipeg."

Within a minute, the snow had stopped, the windshield was dry, and there was a clear path to follow on the road ahead. If Vilee had any doubt that her request had been supernaturally granted, she needed only to look out the car's back window — where the blinding blizzard continued as it had all day long. Vilee thanked her father for the miracle, and the family drove on.

Hours passed. The sky grew darker as night approached, and Vilee and her husband were exhausted from driving. They saw a roadside motel in the distance and decided that they would stop and rest for a few hours. If they left early enough in the morning, they would still have Vilee's mother to the hospital on time. Everyone was looking forward to some much-needed sleep but, as they pulled into the parking lot of the motel, their hearts sank. A neon sign in the office window read NO VACANCY. They decided to park the car for a few minutes while they considered all of their options. As they sat discussing the situation, Vilee could only think of one thing.

"I had the urge to go in and at least give it a try, to see if something couldn't be arranged," she wrote. "I got out of the car and went in to the front desk to ask if, by chance, they still had any rooms available."

At first, the desk clerk confirmed that everything had already been booked. But when Vilee told the woman where they were from, and why the trip was so important to them, the clerk's expression changed. She asked for Vilee's name. When Vilee told her, the woman apologized immediately. She said that a room had been booked for them, and paid for. The reservation had been made a few hours earlier, by a Native man with a moustache who had told the clerk all about his wife's journey to Winnipeg for a hip operation. The description of the man was an exact match for Vilee's father.

Louis Caplan had cleared the roads for his family. He had seen to it that they had a place to rest. But he was not done assisting them. Early the next morning, when Vilee went out into the bitter cold to warm the car for the journey ahead, she was met with another pleasant surprise. Despite the fact that every other vehicle in the parking lot was buried in fresh snow and ice, her car was clear and dry. Louis was obviously continuing to help, and the last leg of the journey, from the motel to the hospital in Winnipeg, went smoothly in every way.

With the stress of the trip behind her, and her mother safely in surgery, Vilee looked for a quiet space in the hospital where she could reflect on all that had happened and prepare for what might be coming next. She was very worried about her mother. But, as she focused on her concerns, the image of her father suddenly appeared before her.

"It was as if I was in a trance," Vilee wrote. "I knew this was not a dream [because] I could still see some people walking by."

Vilee took the opportunity to offer her father heartfelt thanks for all that he had done to help them. He wasn't seeking her gratitude, however. He had come with a message of his own. The elderly man stared deeply into his daughter's eyes and spoke two words:

"Mama fine," was all he said.

And then, as suddenly as Louis had appeared, he was gone. But he had left Vilee with the understanding that her mother's surgery would be successful, and that they would all make it home safely. This knowledge, and the comfort it provided, may have been his greatest gift of all.

The spirit of Louis Caplan continued to watch over his wife, in particular, long after his death and that trip to the Winnipeg hospital. Twenty years later, Vilee wrote that anytime her mother wasn't feeling well, she would wake to see her father standing in her bedroom doorway.

"He doesn't talk," wrote Vilee, "but he points to Mom's room and I know right away that Mom is ill."

On one such occasion, Louis alerted Vilee to the fact that her mother had suffered a heart attack. Another time, it was a stroke. There is little question that the elderly woman's years would have been cut much shorter, had it not been for the watchful spirit of her dead husband. A spirit that Vilee knows was helping them all, on a snow-drifted Saskatchewan highway, the very day after his own death.

A Veteran's Final Wish

In one sense, Josephine Phillip's father died a very quick death.

"He was teasing my brother while watching a hockey game," Josephine said. "All of a sudden he didn't feel well. He vomited, and collapsed by the front door. Shortly after that, he fell into a coma and never awoke. It turned out that he had a massive heart attack."

At the time, it must have seemed to Josephine that she lost her father very suddenly. One moment he was there, full of life, having fun with his family, and the next, he was gone. But that was just the passing of his physical body. In another sense, it would be years before Josephine's father left her life.

Although she didn't realize it for quite some time, the signs were there almost from the beginning.

"There was many a night when I was in my bedroom reading that I would smell cigarette smoke," Josephine said. "Occasionally I would also smell men's cologne. These scents played with my memory, but I couldn't quite place where they were from."

The memory finally rose to the surface one day when Josephine was visiting her mother. The two women were sitting at the kitchen table, talking, when Josephine's mother lit a certain brand of cigarette. Josephine was immediately reminded of the scent that so often filled her bedroom at night — and of her father. It had been his brand of cigarettes. Soon after, she also realized that the cologne she thought she smelled was actually aftershave — the exact type that her father used to wear. Suddenly, these scents were no longer a mystery. Josephine was certain that she was being visited by the spirit of her father.

Having come to this conclusion, it made perfect sense to Josephine when her children, a five-year-old daughter and two-year-old son, began to tell her that they had seen an elderly man in their bedrooms. Josephine's daughter told her that the man had stood just inside of the door to her room, and had been looking at her. When she moved in order to get a better look at him, he had walked right through her closed door. At the same time, her son began to speak of a man who would sit at the edge of his bed and watch him. The man always smiled, and seemed friendly. Neither of the children was afraid of this visitor.

"I had never told them about what I had experienced," said Josephine. "I know that it would have been very hard for a two- and five-year-old to fabricate [such a story]."

So Josephine knew that there was a spirit present in her home, but that didn't concern her. For one thing, she was no stranger to living in a haunted house (see The Holbein Horror, page 73). For another, she felt certain that there was no threat to her family.

"For a couple of years I didn't think [about it], because he was a part of our house and he was benevolent," Josephine said. However, as time progressed, the spirit grew needier and more persistent.

"The smell of smoke and cologne became more frequent, until, basically, it was a daily occurrence," said Josephine. "My husband, who didn't believe in spirits, changed his views when he also started to feel the presence. [He would be] sitting downstairs, playing on the computer, and he would feel something brush against his legs. He would reach down to pet the cat but ... nothing was there. He also started smelling the cigarette smoke, and he would feel someone touch him as he was getting ready [to go to] sleep."

In the meantime, Josephine had taken it upon herself to have her father properly recognized as a Canadian veteran. At the time of his death, officials had been unable to find the man's veteran number, so all that had been possible was a civilian burial. Though it was too late to change that, the family felt that it was important to at least have a military headstone placed on his grave. The grave remained unmarked for many years, as Josephine worked toward this goal.

"I spent many hours on the phone and writing letters trying to get that elusive headstone," Josephine said.

It was a lengthy process and, as the months and years went by, other members of the family were distracted from the issue by the daily events of their own busy lives. Quite the opposite, however, Josephine found her anxiety over the subject steadily increasing.

"It was always in the back of my mind," she said. "Almost an obsession."

Finally, she received the good news that her father would receive his official military headstone. It was dampened by the bad news that the family would be entering into another waiting process, as it would take an unspecified amount of time for all the paperwork and financing to be issued. During this period, Josephine's anxiety continued to build.

"I had to wonder if, in fact, the headstone was truly going to be sent," she said.

Then, one night, Josephine had a dream that she described as seeming "more than a dream." In it, the familiar scents of cigarette smoke and aftershave came to her, and she felt fully aware of the presence of her father. She was even able to see him.

"My father was looking at me over his shoulder," she said. "The scenery behind him was dark grey. The only illumination was a pinpoint of light, far off in the distance. His face was streaked with tears and he said that he was going to be all right. [He said] that he could move on, and that he was leaving now. There was a figure further in the distance [and] I was given the strong impression that it was my grandfather."

When Josephine understood that her father was finally, truly leaving her side, she experienced a moment of panic. Though she was grateful that he was at last able to move on to the place where he was meant to be, she understood for the first time how much comfort she had drawn from his presence over the years. She was still emotional when she awoke, but chose to simply tell her husband about the dream and then let the matter rest. It was, after all, just a dream.

Or was it?

"It was two days later that I received a letter from Veteran Affairs," said Josephine, "stating that the headstone was being made and would be in place as soon as weather permitted."

Was this official recognition truly the only thing that this military man needed in order to leave the physical plane? Ask Josephine, who still lives in the same Prince Albert house.

"There has never again been the smell of cigarette smoke, nor have the children seen the elderly man since," she says.

It would seem that Josephine's father has moved on.

A House-Warming Bouquet

It was March of 1995, and Diana Woytiuk was sitting vigil in a sterile hospital room with her oldest sister, Marianne. Marianne was only thirty-seven years old, but she had been battling breast cancer for three years and was now dying of the disease. It was a sad time, but not without its moments of joy and comfort.

"We were lucky enough as a family to have spent a great deal of time with her during her treatments," said Diana. "And when the call came that she had gone into the hospital for the last time, we were all there."

Marianne lingered for three days, slipping in and out of a coma, with her family gathered around her. Frequently, as Diana watched her sister drift back and forth between this world and the next, she felt that they were visited by spirits.

"I could detect the smell of roses in her hospital room," Diana recalled. This was a comfort to her, as she had grown up believing that this meant they were being watched over. "I was told as a child that when there are no roses present, but you still smell the scent, it means that a loved one who has passed on is visiting you." Soon Marianne passed on, as well. The vigil was over, but it would not be the last time that Diana experienced that lovely, otherworldly scent.

Later that same year, Diana met her husband, Keith, while both were in the Emergency Medical Technician program at the Saskatchewan Institute of Applied Science and Technology (SIAST). Keith came from a strong tradition of emergency medical service. Several family members worked as EMTs, and Keith's grandfather, Michael Dutchak, was described by Diana as "somewhat of a legendary figure in Saskatchewan EMS." He founded Blaine Lake Ambulance, then went on to develop Spiritwood Ambulance, Parkland Ambulance in Prince Albert, and then MD Ambulance in Saskatoon. The name of the Saskatoon ambulance service gave birth to a common misconception, but Diana asserts that "the *MD* in MD Ambulance stands for Michael Dutchak — not medical doctor!"

Diana and Keith were married in 1997, and settled in the small community of Blaine Lake, an hour's drive north of Saskatoon. In December of the following year, they purchased Blaine Lake Ambulance Care from Keith's grandfather and moved into the base that had been built nearly thirty years earlier. It was a two-storey white concrete building. The first floor contained office space and a garage where Keith and Diana parked the ambulances. Upstairs were the living quarters, which had a bit of a sad history.

"Grandpa's first wife, Ida, suffered a massive stroke in the living quarters and died later in a Saskatoon hospital," said Diana. "My husband never got to know his grandmother, as he was only a year old at the time."

There remains the possibility, however, that Ida knew *him*, and was pleased to see her grandson moving into what was once her home....

Diana and Keith's move into the base at Blaine Lake included tackling what she described as "some long-overdue renovations." One of their priorities was to update the kitchen by painting the dated dark cabinets a lighter, fresher colour. It was one of those jobs that sounds easier than it is. In fact, it was a long, laborious process that included sanding off every square inch of the existing stain, then applying a stain blocker before putting on paint. The application of stain blocker was the worst part of the process — it had a reeking, chemical smell that filled the house and took a long time to dissipate.

"If you've ever worked with stain blocker," said Diana, "you know that the only thing you smell is the stain blocker — sometimes for hours on end."

Diana was working with the doors, one by one, and had resigned herself to breathing in the horrible smell all day long. Then, suddenly, incredibly, she realized ...

"I could smell roses."

It wasn't a subtle whiff, nor was it a fleeting one. The scent was as powerful as it was lovely, and it lingered in the air for at least twenty seconds. Perhaps being reminded of the comfort she felt years earlier at her sister's bedside, Diana was not alarmed. She felt certain that she was being given a sign by some loving, if unseen, spirit. And she acknowledged the sign when she spoke.

She said, "I don't know who you are or what you want, but you are welcome to stay for as long as you want." Later, she wasn't sure why she spoke those exact words, but her message seemed to be appreciated. The scent of roses drifted away then, and Diana was left with a wonderful feeling of peace and calm. "Not the 'hair standing on end' thing you would expect after a psychic encounter," she later said.

Diana has now had ten years to reflect on her strange experience, and feels certain of a few things.

"Whatever 'it' was, meant no harm," she says. "It was a welcoming presence, a motherly figure that had come to bestow upon us her blessing for the business venture Keith and I had undertaken. Was it my sister, or Keith's Grandma Ida? I'll never know."

The one thing she does know?

"I haven't smelled those roses since."

Grandma's House

It was Moose Jaw, the early 1990s, and a couple named Donna and Vic Stewart (pseudonyms) had a friend visiting in their home. The children were tucked in bed where they couldn't hear the adults' conversation, so their parents felt free to talk about things that they tried to shield them from during the day. They were telling their friend that they were certain — absolutely certain — that their house was haunted.

"Things such as our TV, VCR, and stereo all had minds of their own." Donna recalled that she and Vic had just finished telling their friend about the electronics phenomena, in particular, when the VCR switched on by itself. A tape had been left in the machine, and it began to play, then fast-forward and rewind. No one had touched the machine or its remote control. It was like a performance, taking place on cue, to prove the veracity of Donna and Vic's story. It was more than enough proof for their friend.

"The guy immediately left," said Donna. "He said he would never come into our house again." The man was true to his word. He never returned. The Stewarts, however, had no such option. They had to live with the ghost.

They had purchased the home in 1987 from the estate of Vic's grandmother, who had passed away a few months earlier. In 1988, the young couple moved in, full of plans to renovate the home. They knew that living amidst renovations would be chaotic, but felt that it would be worth it. But they had no idea that the physical clutter of a construction zone was only a small portion of the challenge they would face.

"During the time that we were renovating, we had some strange activity in the house," said Donna. At first, it might have been dismissed as confusion or disorganization. The Stewarts seemed to frequently misplace their keys or their mail, and important notes or documents would sometimes go missing. No matter how careful they were to keep track of their things, it never worked. The couple grew increasingly frustrated.

"Many times, I would leave keys or bills on our kitchen table," said Donna. "When I would go to get them, they would be gone. We would search and search, but never could find them." Often, Donna and Vic would simply give up and leave the house without their bills, or whatever else they needed. When they returned home later, "the items would be back on the table, right where they were left to begin with." The couple was plagued by these annoying disappearances. They never actually found any of the missing things — the items would simply "show up" on their own.

Autonomous electronics equipment and hide-and-seek possessions would be enough for any haunted homeowners to cope with, but the Stewarts lived with much more. Most frightening to Donna was the fact that things in the house would move about right before her eyes. The blinds would open and close on their own. Things would constantly fall off counters, shelves, and vanities. The Stewarts would hear doors opening and closing all over the house. And frequently, when the phone rang, there would be nobody on the line. Witnessing this type of activity occasionally would be disconcerting. But Donna and Vic lived with it daily.

"There were times," said Donna, "when things would happen every day, several *times* a day. It became almost overwhelming. You never knew what was going to happen next, [because] the activity in the house would be absolutely crazy."

There were several other people who witnessed the phenomena, as well. One evening, the Stewarts had a number of friends gathered at their kitchen table. Donna was about to sit down and join them, when her chair suddenly tipped over. No one had touched it; there was no natural force that could have moved it. Later that same evening, a large bag that was propped against the wall began to slowly tip over. One of the guests, who was aware of the many ghost stories, simply looked at the bag and said, "Stop it, Grandma." The bag stopped moving immediately.

It was reasonable to think that at least some of the paranormal activity in the Stewart house was caused by the spirit of Vic's grandmother, who had lived in the home for many years. Donna became more convinced of the ghost's identity after her children were born. She and Vic had a son in 1990 and a daughter two years later. One night, soon after their baby girl was born, Vic and Donna's son came into their bedroom in the middle of the night. He told them that the lady in his room wanted to sew, and she told him to go sleep with his daddy. The little boy's room had once been Vic's grandmother's sewing room — a fact that the two-year-old child could not have known or understood.

"He often talked about the people who lived in his room," said Donna. "We always thought it was imaginary friends. When that incident happened, it told us that those friends probably weren't imaginary."

There were other reasons to believe that the spirit, or spirits, haunting the Stewart home were relatives, for Donna and Vic had seen a disturbing pattern emerge.

"When the activity really heated up, a member of my husband's family, on his mom's side, would pass away," said Donna. "Once they passed away, everything would stop. It was almost like flipping a switch. Nothing out of the ordinary would happen for months." Eventually, however, the strange phenomena would begin again, and the Stewarts would begin the countdown to another funeral.

The stress of this grim harbinger, as well as the daily toll of living with constant ghostly harassment, finally became too much for the family to bear. The Stewarts sold their house and moved to another in 1995. They kept a curious eye on the place though, and watched it sell another four times within the following dozen years.

Was this just real estate roulette, or did the haunting play a role in the home changing hands so frequently? It's impossible to say. Donna actually wonders if the ghost is even there now. She fears that it may have followed her family to their new home. Today, her sixteen-year-old daughter often speaks of an eerie shadow-figure that dwells in the basement of the family home. Donna's son, now eighteen, claims that he has also seen the shadow, and that it has been there for a number of years. There is another form — a glowing woman in white — that has only been seen by the Stewarts' daughter. Though Donna has never seen these apparitions, her children's reports are enough to make her shudder.

"I will never forget the strange things we experienced in that [other] house," she says. "I know one thing; I never want to go through that again."

With a bit of luck — and "Grandma's" cooperation — perhaps she never will.

Ghost Hunting on the Prairies:
Paranormal Saskatchewan

The Paranormal Saskatchewan investigation team. Founder and lead investigator Colin Tranborg stands front and centre.

Case File Quick Facts

Name: Paranormal Saskatchewan

Date Founded: June, 2005

Website: *www.paranormalsask.com*

Mission: To pursue an interest in the paranormal, and share information about local ghost stories.

Founder and Lead Investigator: Colin Tranborg

Favourite Saskatchewan Haunt: A Saskatoon hotel that prefers to remain anonymous. (Visit the Paranormal Saskatchewan website for some unbelievable EVP from this location!)

Q & A with Colin Tranborg

Paranormal Saskatchewan is a small ghost-hunting group based out of Saskatoon, headed by founder and lead investigator Colin Tranborg. Colin works with co-investigators Travis, Trevor, Dwayne, Stefanie, Paul, Larissa, and Candice. I met Colin for coffee one afternoon to learn more about the Paranormal Saskatchewan team.

Q: How did the group get started?

A: What really got our interest going is that we used to work security around the city. We worked at some of the hotels — a lot of night shifts — and we all sort of had experiences there. Ever since then, we started getting together, and started going to these places. We take pictures, get recordings, write things down.

Q: How are you different from other paranormal research groups?

A: We're a younger group, just getting our base started. And we're basically doing this just because we have a big interest in it. It's not profit-based or anything like that. We've had some people approach us about doing investigations for them, but we're not quite comfortable with that, yet. And some groups get into investigating other phenomena, like UFOs. That's all interesting, but our main focus is ghosts.

Q: What type of equipment do you use?

A: We use cameras and recorders — digital recorders. We're trying to get an EMF meter, as well. There are some of the guys that want them. But I've got a little bit of a background in electronics, and what EMF really is, it's just checking electromagnetism. And pretty much anything with current can give it off. Your cell phone can give it off; the wiring inside the walls can give it off. So it's hard to eliminate all the possible environmental causes.

Q: Do you try to set scientific standards of evidence?

A: Yes. When we do things, we try to remain very skeptical. Skeptical-minded. You can get into a zone where, if it's dark out — especially if you're in a cemetery at night — your senses are heightened and you feel that natural fear. It can affect your judgment. A gopher can run across the field, and you'll think it's something [supernatural]. You have to bring yourself down to reality and rule out as much natural phenomena as you can.

  When you take a picture, you can get an orb, but you have to make sure that orb isn't dust, or pollen, or a bug. We take lots of photos, and there's maybe only a handful where we can say, "Oh, this is something different." You take enough pictures, you get an idea of what [natural phenomena] looks like, how it behaves. For example, dust has a very unique look to it. It's very faded through, and you can sort of see what you would call a nucleus in the centre. It's kind of self-evident. And dust moves very fast. We take sequences of pictures, and if there's something in one photo that's gone in the next, that's dust. Little things you can try to rule out.

Q: Any interesting investigations recently?

A: Two nights in a row, we went walking through one of the biggest cemeteries in Saskatoon — Woodlawn. We've been there before. And we get this huge chill when we get to this one area. It's like a military section. Every time we go there, I don't know, you just get the hair standing up. So we started taking pictures. And one [of our investigators], Trevor, he said he felt like someone was following him. Like there was someone right behind him.

So we started taking pictures. And in one picture that we got, there was a tombstone here, and then a ball of white light with a tail of movement right behind it. And we saw it right away, so we took another picture ... and it was still there, just a little bit higher. And, as we were walking away, Trevor said, "There's still something behind me." So we took a picture on the path. And there was the same white ball of light in the middle of the path. It had a [movement] tail, like it was following us.

Q: What were some of the experiences that you had while working security?

A: At the (name omitted) hotel, about three o'clock one morning, I was downstairs by the ice machine. I got this chill, and felt like I was being watched. I looked up at the door, and there was a female standing there, right by the door. [She was] about twenty years old. She just sort of looked out of place. She was wearing a grey dress ... a casual dress. And she just looked at me and disappeared. And I've seen more than just the one girl there. I've seen a man standing by the pool. At night, when you're doing your rounds, you're supposed to check the pool room, because it's supposed to be locked. [There are several locked doors you have to pass through.] When you look through the glass, you can see the whole pool. It was dark, but I could see the shape of a man standing there. But by the time I got in there, he was gone. In the same hotel there's a separate little bar. I walked in at one point, doing rounds. There's this old piano there, with a seat. And there was this little girl sitting there. She had blondish hair. She looked at me and said, "hello." When I turned back, she was gone.

Then there's the (name omitted). It's a fairly new hotel, but haunted. Again, it was a night shift, about three o'clock in the morning. I'd heard rumours that there was a lady that would walk around there at night, just disappear. The main front desk area is very open ... it opens up to a balcony area upstairs and, this night, I was up on the top looking down. I saw this lady wearing a white dress walking through. She had sort of longish grey hair. She looked up at me, and

I was looking down at her. Then — the weirdest thing — she turned and she sort of imploded into a little ball and vanished. After that, I told one of the other guards and he said, "You've seen the woman."

Q: What do you hope to accomplish?

A: Just to share information. If you go online, and search for *paranormal,* you'll find things from all over the world — but not directly from Saskatchewan. But there's a lot here. We'd like to show the rest of the world, "Hey, Saskatchewan has ghosts, too!"

Bibliography

Books

Gee, Joshua. *Encyclopedia Horrifica*. New York: Scholastic, 2007.

Guiley, Rosemary Ellen. *The Encyclopedia of Ghosts and Spirits*. New York: Facts on File, 1992.

Guiley, Rosemary Ellen. *Harper's Encyclopedia of Mystical and Paranormal Experience*. New York: HarperCollins, 1991.

Hryniuk, Margaret and Frank Korvemaker. *Legacy of Stone: Saskatchewan's Stone Buildings*. Regina, Saskatchewan: Coteau Books, 2008.

McLennan, David. *Our Towns: Saskatchewan Communities from Abbey to Zenon Park*. Regina, Saskatchewan: Canadian Plains Research Center, 2008.

Riess, Kelly-Anne. *Saskatchewan Book of Everything*. Lunenburg, Nova Scotia: MacIntyre Purcell Publishing Inc., 2007.

Waiser, Bill. *Saskatchewan: A New History*. Calgary, Alberta: Fifth House, 2005.

Willet, Edward. *Historic Walks of Regina and Moose Jaw*. Calgary, Alberta: Red Deer Press, 2008.

Wilson, Garrett. "The Assiniboia Club." In *Regina's Secret Spaces: Love and Lore of Local Geography*, edited by Lorne Beug, Anne Campbell, and Jeannie Mah, 56–57. Regina, Saskatchewan: Canadian Plains Research Center, 2006.

Periodicals

Burt, Mrs. Harry. "The Unexplained ..." *News of the North*, August 28, 1963.

J.A.D. "Unexplained." *News of the North*, July 6, 1962.

Johnstone, Bruce. "Regina's Assiniboia Club to Close Next Week." *Saskatoon Star Phoenix,* December 27, 2007.

Martin, Ashley. "Regina's Most Famous Haunts." *The Carillon*, October 30, 2003.

Ridley, Brett. "Ghosts Like Going for Coffee, Too." *The Carillon*, October 31, 1998.

Unknown. "A Fiendish Sacrifice." *Regina Morning Leader*, March 10, 1891.

Unknown. "'Human Wireless' Able To Lift Veil of the Future." *Regina Morning Leader*, June 28, 1924.

Unknown. "Ituna's 'Ghost' Proves Most Unusual: It Appears at Un-ghostly Hour Noon." *Regina Morning Leader*, September 13, 1924.

Unknown. "Skeleton Find Stirs Old Cemetery Mystery." *Yorkton Enterprise*, January 29, 1953.

About the Author

Jo-Anne Christensen is the author of several bestselling regional ghost story books and short-story collections, including *Ghost Stories of Saskatchewan*, *More Ghost Stories of Saskatchewan*, *Ghost Stories of British Columbia*, *Campfire Ghost Stories*, and *Haunted Hotels*. She lives in Edmonton.

Photo by Patrick Hawley.

Also by Jo-Anne Christensen

Ghost Stories of Saskatchewan
978-0-88882-177-5 / $16.99

This eerie collection showcases Saskatchewan's most intriguing ghost stories: accounts of misty apparitions, unexplained noises, violent poltergeists, and startling premonitions. You needn't look far to find a ghost in the haunted province of Saskatchewan!

Ghost Stories of British Columbia
978-0-88882-191-1 / $17.99

It has been called Canada's most haunted province. While such a claim is impossible to prove, British Columbia does abound with tales of the supernatural. *Ghost Stories of British Columbia* is a comprehensive collection of these tales, drawing from the province's history, its archives, and its people. They are the mysterious, the unexplained, the eerie and amazing stories meant to be told by campfire or candlelight. They are the true ghost stories of British Columbia, and they wait for you in these pages.

Of Related Interest

**Ghosts: An Investigation into
a True Canadian Haunting**
Richard Palmisano
978-1-55488-435-3 $22.99

This amazing true story is a frightening account of a three year investigation into the multiple haunting of a once grand Mississauga mansion on the shores of Lake Ontario. In this chilling tale, spirits interact with each other, trying to protect themselves from the intruders. Find out how far they are willing to go to get the investigators to leave and never come back.

The Big Book of Canadian Hauntings
John Robert Colombo
978-1-55488-449-0 $29.99

Another mammoth book that has been assembled by John Robert Colombo to send shivers up and down your spine. This new Big Book will bring excitement and delight to even more readers across the country who find the unknown to be fascinating, baffling, and frightening!

Available at your favourite bookseller.

DUNDURN PRESS
www.dundurn.com

Tell us your story! What did you think of this book? Join the conversation at
www.definingcanada.ca/tell-your-story by telling us what you think